Saltwater and Secrets

Amanda Knipp

Contents

Prologue

Surfing isn't just a sport.

To me, it's much more than that. It's a way of life. It's the sand behind your ears, the saltwater on your skin, and the sea breeze in your hair. It's the way the sunlight dances on the water and glints off whitecaps. It's the way a surfer trails his hand across the glassy surface of a wave, conveying a beautiful feeling of connection—a connection that runs deeper with its surrounding environment unlike any other sport.

Just think about all the different types of waves in the universe—light waves, seismic waves, sound waves—yet ocean waves are the only kind humans can ride. They happen to move at just the right speed, with the right amount of force and height, so that surfers have no problem catching and riding them.

Gliding across the face of a shimmering wave expresses a feeling like no other. You can feel the cool spray when the lip curls over, sometimes encasing you in a roaring turquoise barrel before spitting you out onto the shoulder. You can dig your hand into the water and make a strong bottom turn. You can make beautiful lines across the surface of the ocean as you carve up and down a wave. Surfing gives you a rush of adrenaline and exhilaration like no other sport.

And once you start surfing, you're hooked. You might as well kiss your old life goodbye, because now you have a new one—one that revolves around the ocean. Dedicated surfing requires checking all the surf cams, memorizing the long-term swell forecasts, and verifying which beaches have the best conditions—not to mention waking up for dawn patrol. The waves wait for no one. If a swell hits, you drop everything and head to your home break. That's just the way it is.

Why else do surfers get up at the crack of dawn? Why else do we stay and ride waves long after sunset, when we can hardly see the water? Why else do we endure reef cuts, sunburns, sore muscles, and wipeouts so brutal that our boards get snapped in two?

It's not just to surf, I can tell you that much. It's to ride a wave. It's to enjoy that beautiful, inexpressible feeling that comes from gliding across the glassy water with nothing between your bare feet and the crashing wave except a piece of fiberglass.

So why has surfing become my way of life? There isn't really one answer that can satisfy. I guess I'd have to say this: I can't get enough of it.

Chapter 1

The sound of crashing waves roused Alana from her sleep. With her eyes still closed, she smiled and let the monotonous swoosh of the tide soothe her awake. She held her breath and counted the seconds between each breaking wave—one, two, three, four, crash! Her eyes quickly shot open when she realized the swell was much bigger than she had previously thought.

Suddenly feeling wide awake, Alana tossed her covers off and swung her legs over the side of the bed. She strode over to the window and pulled the curtains aside, allowing a gracious view of the ocean. As the hazy morning light trickled into her bedroom, she leaned forward and pushed one of the panes open for an even better view.

She rested her elbows on the sill and swept her gaze over the surroundings. The ocean glittered like a million crystals in the sunlight. It stretched as far as the eye could see, from the short palm tree-studded outcropping of land on the right all the way to the barnacle-encrusted pilings of Ventura Pier on the left. Alana breathed deeply and took a long whiff of the salty sea breeze drifting past her window.

Her attention was diverted from the open ocean to the thundering whitewater closer to shore. Every minute or so, a new set would appear on the horizon as an oncoming bump of water. As soon as the seafloor became too shallow for the waves' height, the peaks would snap over and break all the way down the beach in a flurry of whitewater.

The surf forecast had predicted the swell would peak overnight, but it never guaranteed the waves to be this good. They were easily four foot, with glassy conditions and lots of open shoulders. Alana knew then and there it was going to be an awesome day.

Quickly closing her window, she dashed over to her dresser and began rifling through a stash of bikinis. After shimmying out of her pajamas and pulling on a swimsuit, she brushed out her long, sun-bleached hair. She then pulled a cover-up dress over her head and rushed out the door.

Alana suddenly paused at the top of the stairs. She cocked her head to one side and heard Tammy, her little sister, snoring from her bedroom only a few yards away. After a moment's deliberation, Alana retraced her steps and quietly pushed Tammy's bedroom door open.

Tammy's petite figure could be seen sprawled on top of her covers, her face turned to one side while her long blonde hair lay in a tangled knot on top of her head. Alana stifled a giggle and rapped loudly on the door. "Hey!" she whispered. When Tammy didn't stir, Alana knocked louder and flipped on the light for good measure.

The snoring abruptly stopped. Tammy grunted and raised her head, her eyes blinking uncertainly in the blinding light. "Alana," she groaned, her voice thick with exhaustion. "What time is it?"

"It's time to wake up, Sleeping Beauty."

Tammy frowned and rubbed her eyes. "I'm serious."

"Six thirty."

"Then I'm going back to bed," she huffed, turning over and flopping back into a sleeping position.

Alana obediently turned out the light, but not before whispering one last sentence into the dark: "You know, the surf looks pretty good today..."

Tammy didn't move a muscle. She did, however, murmur a curious reply: "Mm...how good?"

"Four foot, glassy, clean conditions." Alana grinned, knowing Tammy definitely wasn't going back to sleep anytime soon now that the thought of surfing was fixed in her mind.

"I'll be there in half an hour," she mumbled into her pillow.

"Great. See you in the water." Alana quietly closed her sister's door before heading downstairs. She knew she had done the right thing by waking Tammy. The latter was just as passionate about surfing as Alana. Even though she could be a nuisance at times, the one place the sisters got along one hundred percent of the time was in the water.

With the image of crashing waves in her mind's eye, Alana gobbled a granola bar and guzzled a glass of orange juice before walking into the storage room. Flipping on the light switch, she let her eyes roam over a haphazard collection of skateboards and multiple surfing posters nailed to the wooden walls before her gaze landed on their quiver of surfboards.

Alana walked over to the far corner of the room and trailed her hand along the smooth rails of each board. Most were decked out in color, while a few remained stark white. She smiled when she spotted her favorite 5'8" shortboard squeezed between two longboards. It had neon pink highlights down the rails to match the three fins on the bottom. Alana carefully pulled it out and tucked it securely under her arm, making sure to wrap the leash around the tail so it wouldn't get snagged.

On her way out the door, her gaze lingered a little longer on the faded longboard sitting in the corner. It was decades old and dinged in multiple places, but to Alana it was the most treasured one out of the whole quiver. It had been her dad's surfboard back in the '60s before he passed it to her older brother, Dylan. On a rare occasion, Dylan would let Alana and Tammy use the magic board, but those times were few and far between. Ever since the accident, Dylan had stopped competing. He was on his way to becoming a pro when he was only sixteen, but dropped all his contests two years later when the tragedy struck. He hadn't just dropped from competing, though—he had dropped from surfing in general.

The accident had occurred five years ago. Alana had been twelve at the time, and Tammy had only been six. But they hadn't taken it as hard as Dylan. It was like a knife to his heart, crushing all his dreams of making the World Tour. Alana had asked him a few times what it was like to be a pro, but he was reluctant to reminisce.

Yet the accident hadn't stopped Alana and Tammy from surfing. The love of the ocean was in their blood. They were soul surfers at heart, along with Alana's group of best friends from junior high—Maya, Koa, Jake, and the Anderson twins, Blaine and Cole. Since none of Tammy's friends were passionate about surfing, Alana occasionally let her tag along with the gang.

After flipping off the light, Alana strode out of the storage room and headed to the front door. She didn't bother leaving a note for Dylan, who was still sleeping upstairs. He knew if Alana wasn't in the house, she was out surfing—especially during dawn patrol. It was an unspoken agreement between the siblings.

Alana grabbed a towel and the house key before slipping out the door. The cold immediately bit her skin and peppered her bare arms with goosebumps. She shivered as she locked the front door behind her and made her way down the sidewalk. Her surfboard felt ice cold against her thin arms, but she wasn't about to let the weather keep her from having a good time. Besides, the water was always a few degrees warmer than the chill morning air. It would feel great once she was in the ocean.

The beach was only a few minutes away. Thanks to Dylan's job as an auto mechanic, the Walker siblings could afford to live in one of the cozy apartments lining the shore. Their living space was small, but the location made up for it big time, that was for sure.

Alana grinned as she rounded the corner and paused on a strip of grass, letting the salty sea breeze tousle her hair. She breathed in the scent like it was her first breath of fresh air. As a wave of warmth washed over her, she knew she was officially stoked. Today was going to be amazing.

"Thank you, Lord," she whispered, her words lingering in the crisp air. Before she could murmur another prayer, she suddenly felt a hand on her arm. She shrieked in surprise and jumped away.

"Whoa!" a familiar voice laughed. "It's just me, Alana."

She immediately relaxed. "Koa. What were you thinking?"

"Sorry," Koa said sheepishly. "I didn't know you were so lost in thought. What were you doing, anyway?"

Alana shrugged. "Nothing. Where's the rest of the gang?"

"Oh, I'm sure they're coming." His slight Hawaiian accent pierced the quiet air as he strained to see the ocean over Alana's shoulder. He let out a yelp when he spotted an outside set rapidly approaching. "Check out those waves!" he cried. "Let's hit the water."

Alana followed him across the street and down a flight of stairs. As soon as they reached the sand, she tossed her towel down and wrapped it safely around her house key. Then she pulled her cover-up over her head and flung it onto the sand as well. As she strapped her leash around her right ankle, she glanced up and studied the waves carefully. They were peeling around the Point in near-perfect A-frames, and already a decent-sized crowd had formed. The lineup was going to be packed today.

"Ready?" Koa asked, bouncing up and down on the balls of his feet.

"You bet I am!" she called back, grabbing the rails of her board and jumping over a small whitewater wave. She landed stomach-down and immediately started paddling. With each powerful stroke, she shot forward across the surface of the water—yet nowhere near as fast as Koa. Since he had a much longer, thicker board, he was able to paddle more quickly.

Before long, they reached the impact zone, and Alana knew she would soon pass Koa. While he gripped his rails and flipped upside down in a turtle roll, she performed a flawless duck-dive.

"See ya in the lineup!" she called over her shoulder after resurfacing. Koa floundered in the whitewater behind her, his longboard difficult to control in the breaking waves.

That was the beauty of shortboarding—being able to dive underneath the swells and watch as they rolled overhead. Alana smiled as she placed one foot on the tail of her board, quickly pushing the nose down just as a wave broke over her head. As soon as she was far enough underwater, she angled the nose back up. She watched the tinted blue clouds of whitewater billowing overhead with awe.

Letting out a stream of air bubbles through her nose, she broke through the surface and continued paddling. Now the lineup was only a short paddle away.

"Took you long enough," she joked when Koa finally paddled up next to her. They sat down on their boards in unison.

"Just wait until I spray you on my next wave," he said playfully.

"Not unless I spray you first."

Koa raised an eyebrow. "Do I sense a challenge?"

Alana grinned. She had full confidence in her surfing. If Koa wanted a challenge, then she would give him one. "Alright," she said, "whoever makes the biggest turn and sprays their opponent wins. Deal?"

"Deal." They shook hands in mock professionalism.

"Hey, Koa!" a voice called. "Alana!"

They turned and smiled at the brown-haired surfer stroking towards them. He was paddling on his knees, his ankles conspicuously without a leash—the sign of a talented longboarder.

"'Morning, Jake," Alana greeted him. "Where's your little tagalong?" She was referring to Maya, his closest friend and the only girl he had eyes for.

"Oh, she's coming," he replied, glancing back toward the beach. Sure enough, a few moments later Maya paddled into view, her brown hair swept up into a messy bun.

"I'm glad you could make it today," Alana told her. "The waves are awesome!"

"Speaking of waves," Koa said, "I think there's a set coming."

"Outside!" Jake hollered, causing the foursome to burst into action. All the other surfers in the lineup began paddling frantically toward the oncoming bump. Koa was the first to get in position, and he effortlessly stroked into the wave before it even broke. His friends watched as he cross-stepped to the nose, placing his left foot over his right, before reaching out to hang five.

Meanwhile, Alana's sights were set on getting her own wave. A few surfers were already paddling into a peak, so she dug her hands deeper into the water and stroked over the swell. She grinned when she saw the third wave stacking up in front of her.

"You got this one, Alana!" Maya cheered.

Alana quickly spun her board around so she was facing the beach. Just as the lip began to curl over, she stroked into the wave and popped up to her feet. She threw out her arms and rushed forward to gain speed. After racing around the first section of whitewater, she bent her knees and made a strong bottom turn. This set her up beautifully for a smooth off-the-lip maneuver: she rocketed up the face of the wave, pointing the nose of her board straight up in the air, and whipped her torso around to snap her board back into position. Arcs of water droplets were sent flying through the air.

The subsequent drop gave her a rush of excitement. With adrenaline pumping through her veins, Alana made another bottom turn and banked it off the whitewater a second time. She raced across the water as fast as she could, but the section in front of her was close to breaking. She geared herself up for one last maneuver to complete the ride.

The lip began curling over, and Alana felt the spray of whitewater as the wave went from a midnight blue to a seaweed green. She knew she had to time this trick perfectly, or she would never be able to pull off a frontside grab. She had the speed. She had the ramp. Now all she needed was a little boost...

Alana hit the whitewater just as the lip snapped over, sending her rocketing into the air. She quickly grabbed her rails as a familiar feeling of weightlessness set in. She soared above the foaming whitewash for a good three seconds before crashing back into the wave, bending her knees to absorb the impact.

"Yes!" she exclaimed, sticking the landing.

With a goofy smile plastered on her face, she dove off her board into the surf and let the wave roll over her. After resurfacing, she climbed back on and started paddling towards the lineup, ready to catch another one.

"Yo, Alana!"

She narrowed her eyes through the piercing glare of the sun and saw two shortboarders emerge from the glittering sheen of water. They had the same bleached-blonde hair and twinkling green eyes: Blaine and Cole, the Anderson twins.

"Hey guys," Alana said, reaching over to gave Blaine a high-five. As usual, his brother Cole gave her a quick nod and glanced away.

"You got a sick air," Blaine raved. "I can't believe you pulled it off with that junk wave."

"Yeah, it was a little on the small side, but at least the section gave me enough boost."

Their conversation was temporarily suspended as another wave bore down on them. They pushed their boards underneath the foaming water and resurfaced on the other side.

"So how's business going?" Alana asked, referring to Mr. Anderson's surfboard shaping company. Cole and Blaine were talented artists when it came to shaping, designing, and painting boards. Their craft was a masterpiece like no other.

"It's good," Blaine said nonchalantly. "Same as usual, I guess."

"Really? I thought it would pick up more in the summer. It's already mid-July and kooks are everywhere." She gestured to the dozens of surfers around them, a good percentage of them beginners on giant foamboards.

"My dad likes to do business with more experienced surfers," Cole butted in.

"Oh, like you?" she teased.

"You better believe it."

"I don't know...last time I checked, I was a better surfer than you."

Blaine chuckled. "She's got a point, bro. Nobody at C Street surfs better than Alana."

"Oh really?" Cole asked coolly. "Then how about a little contest? Right here, right now. What do you say, Alana?"

She narrowed her eyes. "What sort of contest?"

"Whoever can pull off a frontside air reverse wins."

Blaine raised his eyebrows. "A frontside air reverse? Good luck, guys." He shook his head and resumed paddling towards the lineup, leaving Cole and Alana bobbing up and down on their surfboards.

"Okay," Alana said slowly. "But I wouldn't count on winning if I were you."

"It's a competition," Cole shot back. "Anything can happen."

"Oh, I'll give you competition, alright." She smiled wickedly. "Let's do this."

"May the best surfer win."

They leaned forward and started paddling in unison. Alana dug her hands deeper into the water with every stroke, psyching herself up to win. A frontside air reverse? That was nothing. She could do it in her sleep.

Time to kick some Anderson butt, she thought eagerly.

Chapter 2

It was on. Cole knew he had to bring his game if he wanted to beat Alana. There was no "going easy" on her—when it came to surfing, she was undeniably the best. Cole loathed her for it. It wasn't easy being second best to a girl, especially if that girl happened to be Alana Walker.

Suddenly, movement in the corner of Cole's eye brought him back to the present. He noticed a bump rapidly approaching from the horizon. Bringing one hand up to shield his eyes from the glaring sun, he realized a set was coming. He glanced over his shoulder and began paddling. Dang it. Alana was farther outside than he was, in perfect position to catch a set wave. Meanwhile, Cole was stuck with one of the inside waves, which had irrefutably less power and force to launch him into an aerial maneuver. And if he wanted to pull off, say, a frontside air reverse, then a junk wave obviously wasn't going to cut it. He needed to go big and he needed to go powerful.

So it came as a bit of a surprise when the wave in front of him suddenly stacked up. No one else had even tried to paddle for it, except for one beginner who ended up falling off his board in the process. Cole was caught off guard when the wave suddenly hit a bump of backwash and began to curl over.

He had a split-second decision. Though he knew he was too much on the shoulder, after a hasty deliberation he decided to just go for it. He kicked and paddled as hard as he could until he felt the wave launch him forward.

He popped up to his feet in one smooth motion. He heard the foaming whitewater as it churned behind him, splashing over his heels and the tail of his board. He made a quick S-turn before twisting his hips and carving a long, drawn-out cutback. This brought him back to the pocket, the power source of the wave, just in front of the roaring whitewater. Using the little speed he had, Cole drove down to the trough of the wave and dug his hand into the water. He spotted a small backwash wave heading straight towards him, and that's when he knew he had a shot at beating Alana. Sure, he had a small wave, but it would stack up when it hit the backwash like it did before. This would set him up beautifully for an aerial.

Cole shot across the glassy blue-green surface of the water and raced back up the wave towards the lip. Just after the backwash slammed into his wave, he bent his knees and jumped into the air, grabbing the rails of his board in the process. The force of the backwash colliding with his wave created a sort of choppy launch pad, sending him hurtling into the air. But he had misjudged the takeoff, and Cole knew he had to make a fast rotation or he wouldn't land it. He had gone too far out and not far enough up.

The maneuver was over in a matter of seconds. Though he twisted his upper torso as he soared through the air, he had achieved much less lift than desired. The result was an awkward, fumbled landing: he strained to keep his balance as the nose of his board slammed into the wave, sending him hurtling backwards. His arms pinwheeled while his knees buckled.

It was a complete failure. Cole hadn't even done as much as a 180, but he was trying his hardest not to wipe out anyway. He ended up doing an awkward backflop into the water, and milliseconds later the rest of the wave slammed into him. He was sent tumbling through a murky, foaming whirlpool.

When he finally ruptured the surface, spluttering, Cole yanked on his leash to pull his surfboard towards him. He climbed on with a scowl etched on his face, hoping against hope that no one had seen his epic fail—especially not Alana.

But he didn't have to worry about her—she was currently stroking into a large set wave. It was a beauty: nothing but six feet of pure, sea-green water stacking up like the Red Sea. Alana dropped into the wave like an angel of the sea, gliding along the wall of water without the slightest fear. She raced up and teased the lip before cruising back down, her gaze never once leaving the blue-green shoulder in front of her. She bent her knees and pumped her legs for speed until she was a good distance from the pocket. Then she twisted her hips and made a long, slow cutback towards the whitewater. She continued to carve beautiful lines across the surface of the wave until her ride began to close out. Her final maneuver, the attempted frontside air reverse, was done in what seemed like slow motion.

Cole watched critically as she set up her aerial with a strong bottom turn. She hit the lip just as the wave broke, sending her flying into the air. She casually bent her knees and grabbed her front rail, as if she had done this a million times already, and made a near-complete rotation before landing back in the whitewater.

Her board glided smoothly into position, and she straightened up with a knowing smile on her face.

"I think we know who won!" Alana hollered as she raced past Cole, who was still paddling. He shot her a dirty look before duck diving under her wave, letting the churning whitewater roll over him. He tried in vain to ignore the burning embarrassment flooding his cheeks. Yeah, we know who won, his thoughts simmered. Big deal.

He was greeted with two smirks from Blaine and Jake, who were waiting for him in the lineup. "I don't want to talk about it," Cole said automatically.

"What? You're too macho to admit you were beaten by a girl?" Jake teased.

"Well," Blaine said, "at least we know you need to work on your frontside air reverse."

"Yeah, whatever." Cole folded his arms and fixed his eyes on the horizon. He hoped another set would come, because then he wouldn't have to talk face-to-face with Alana herself. Now that was one conversation he really wanted to avoid.

Unfortunately, as luck would have it, an inconvenient lull soon followed. Cole found himself bobbing up and down with no waves in sight. The sun was beating down through his sticky rashguard, making him uncomfortably hot. He rolled off his board and took a dip in the water before climbing back on.

As soon as he resurfaced, Cole glanced up to see Alana peering down at him, an impish expression on her face. "How's it going, loser?"

"Fine, until you showed up," he retorted.

By the look on her face, Cole could tell Alana knew he was more pissed off than he let on. It was a bit of a known fact that Cole had a temper on him.

Alana merely shrugged her shoulders at his insult. "It was just for fun, you know."

"Right. Like you don't take contests seriously."

Cole had her there, and she knew it. Alana took everything seriously when it came to surfing. "Okay, so maybe I really wanted to win," she admitted. "So what? Isn't that what competing is all about? Liven up a bit, Cole."

Liven up? Easier said than done, he thought sourly. He refolded his arms across his chest and continued to stare her down. But it was hard to stay mad at someone so...so...

His thoughts were interrupted by the arrival of a new set. As he started paddling toward the oncoming waves, he thanked whichever omnipotent Being in the heavens had awarded him the timely disruption.

"How was the surf?" Mr. Anderson asked as the twins entered the kitchen, still dripping wet.

"Great," Blaine said automatically. "The waves were peeling nicely around the Point. There were easily some head-high waves out there."

"Sounds like fun." Mr. Anderson smiled warmly at them before taking a sip of his coffee and turning his attention back to his newspaper. That left the twins to ransack the kitchen by themselves. They rummaged through all the cupboards and scanned the contents in the fridge to see what they could eat for brunch. They had surfed for a solid four hours, and it was already eleven in the morning. Cole's stomach was growling.

When he finally sat down with a huge bowl of cereal and four slices of toast, Cole felt faint with hunger. Just as he raised a spoonful of Cocoa Puffs to his lips, his dad suddenly interrupted him.

"Oh, before I forget," he said, folding up his newspaper. "There's one last board I want you to work on today. Can you get it done before lunch?"

Cole shrugged. "Sure."

"Atta boy." Mr. Anderson tossed his paper into the trash bin before heading out the door, whistling a tune. As soon as Cole finished scarfing down his food, he stuck his bowl and spoon in the dishwasher and headed into the garage.

Boards upon boards lined the walls, taking up every spare inch of the room with the exception of the work area. Mr. Anderson spent the majority of his time in his "workshop," as he liked to call it. The surfboards he shaped were of the best quality and design. They were hands-down the most remarkable boards produced by a local shaper. Surfers came from miles around to check out his quiver at his humble surf shop, Anderson Boards.

Cole quietly stepped up to the shortboard lying in the middle of the garage. It was propped up on a rack, its smooth white surface gleaming under the overhead light. He trailed his fingers down its flawless rails, slowly awakening his inner artist. Dozens of images emerged in his mind as he took in the shape and size of the surfboard. It looked to be about 5'6", with three fins on the bottom and a shimmering gold stringer down the middle. Except for Mr. Anderson's logo and the stringer, the entire board was a spotless white.

Cole quickly grabbed a double action airbrush from his dad's workbench. After preparing his paint and attaching the airbrush to its air source, he studied the surfboard like an artist would observe a blank canvas. He had plenty of ideas to decorate the board, but he preferred to just start airbrushing without a clear goal in mind. He let the ideas flow as he moved his arm up and down, spraying intricate details here before using another color and spraying sweeping curves there.

He didn't even know what he was doing until he took a break to observe his work. Cole grinned when he took in the turquoise lines of waves on the right side of the board, framed by two tall palm trees and a stretch of yellow-orange sand. But when his gaze swept over to the surfer he had sprayed on the left side of the board, he began to grow anxious.

"Oh crap," he muttered. "Oh crap oh crap oh crap."

The surfer, who was calmly observing the turquoise waves, had flowing blonde hair and piercing blue eyes. Though only half her face was visible, it was clear who she was. The real question, though, was why he had airbrushed her onto this fresh surfboard.

Cole shuddered. He needed to get out. He needed a break. He needed to clear his head from all thoughts—especially those of Alana.

Something was definitely wrong with him.

Chapter 3

Maya finished rinsing the shampoo out of her hair and gave it one last squeeze. She then turned the water off and stepped out of the shower, shivering in the sudden cold. After drying and dressing, she wrapped her damp hair in a towel and walked out of the bathroom.

From the living room came her mother's loud chattering. Mrs. Mallory had her phone in one hand and her purse in the other. As soon as she saw Maya, she said, "Just a second," into the phone before turning to her daughter. "Honey, do you mind picking up a few things at the store for me?"

"Um—"

Maya barely had a second to put her two cents' in, as Mrs. Mallory immediately began scribbling items down on a Post-It. "I need milk, crackers, another vegetable tray, and two pounds of ground beef. Check the percentage of fat before you decide which one to get. Oh, and don't forget the lemonade—we ran out this morning."

Maya sighed, but forced herself to smile nonetheless. "Sure thing, Mom." She stuffed the Post-It into her pocket and headed back to the bathroom, where she squeezed out her hair one last time and quickly ran a brush through her brown locks. On her way out the front door, she stuffed her feet into some flip-flops and grabbed the keys hanging on the chain near the door.

"Thanks, hon!" Mrs. Mallory called, flashing her daughter a smile before turning back to her phone conversation.

This time, Maya frowned and sulked into her mother's car. She knew exactly who her mom was talking to, and she didn't like it. Tonight was church, and Mrs. Mallory had promised—after much begging on Maya's part—to join her at the five o'clock service. It looked like one phone call was going to ruin the entire evening.

Maya grumbled to herself as she carefully backed out of the driveway, making sure to steer clear of the large campervan parked by the garage. It was the same camper her dad had used when they went road tripping together years ago—many years ago. That was before her dad got a promotion and started working more. That was before her parents began fighting.

She quickly turned up the radio to drown out her sullen thoughts. The drive to the grocery store only took a few minutes, but with all the stoplights and intersections, it seemed to take much longer. Maya was in a sour mood when she entered the grocery store and methodically collected the items on her mother's list. When she turned down the dairy isle, she suddenly paused upon seeing a familiar brown-haired boy standing in front of the milk.

A small smile crept up on Maya's face. After her leaving her noisy cart at the end of the aisle, she quietly stepped up behind him. She mentally counted to three before saying, "Boo."

He jumped. "Hey!" he screeched, whirling around to face Maya, who doubled over in laughter. "Oh," he sighed, "it's you."

"Sorry Jake," she chuckled. "I just couldn't help myself."

Jake shook his head, a smile lighting up his features. "So what are you doing here?"

Maya pointed to her cart. "Getting groceries, same as you."

"Then why is your hair wet? Did you go for another surf?"

"You ask too many questions," she laughed. "Actually, I just got out of the shower. My mom told me to pick up a few things at the grocery store."

"Oh, cool. Is she...?" Jake smiled hopefully.

"Coming to church tonight?" Maya shook her head sadly. "Probably not. She's on the phone with my dad right now."

"I'm sorry to hear that."

"It's okay."

"Are you used to them fighting all the time?"

"I don't think I'll ever get used to it. But they don't really fight; it's more like they—and I quote—debate." She rolled her eyes. "With really loud voices."

Jake laughed and squeezed her hand. "Do you need a ride tonight?"

"I got it. But thanks." Maya glanced down at their intertwined hands. "Save me a seat, though, okay?"

"Will do." Jake winked and turned back to the milk. "See you tonight, Maya."

"See ya." She reluctantly let go of his hand and headed to her shopping cart. Ten minutes later, she left the store in much better spirits than when she had entered. Though her mother wasn't going to church, she could at least look forward to Jake and the rest of the gang being there.

Cole slumped down in his seat and folded his arms stubbornly across his chest. The darkening sky was tinged with bold colors of the sunset, but it did nothing to lighten his spirits.

Blaine sighed from where he sat next to his brother. He pulled the keys out of the ignition and stuffed them in his back pocket. "Are you gonna sit there and sulk all evening, or are you going to join me?" he asked tiredly.

"Just give me a minute," Cole said, locking his jaw and continuing to stare straight ahead.

"Whatever." Blaine rolled his eyes and slid out of the car, letting the door slam closed behind him. Cole could see the annoyance written on Blaine's face as he began pacing in front of the car, his gaze fixed on the double doors that marked the entrance to the church. Sunday was church day in the Anderson family, so if the twins' dad was too busy with his work—like he was tonight—that meant Blaine and Cole were responsible for attending the nightly service by themselves.

The twins had been raised as Christians since the moment they were born, but church had always been boring in Cole's opinion. Blaine, on the other hand, had always looked forward to the service, complete with worship, prayer, and a message from Pastor Browne. He always found the willpower to stay focused throughout the entire church service, whereas Cole been caught snoozing one too many times in the pew.

From the other side of the windshield, Blaine shot his twin a glare and tapped his wristwatch impatiently. Cole sighed and shoved open the door, making sure to grab his Bible on the way out. He slammed the door behind him and meandered towards the entrance, never once making eye contact with Blaine.

As soon as they stepped across the threshold and into the brightly lit sanctuary, a gust of cool AC hit them smack in the face, followed by a loud chorus of How Great is Our God by the church choir. Cole grumbled to myself as he slid into a near-empty pew near the back of the room. Blaine plopped down next to him, clearly upset by his brother's behavior.

From a few rows up, the twins saw Koa sitting with his family, and across the aisle Jake was busy trying to quiet his younger siblings.

Cole's gaze flickered back to the stage, where the choir was wrapping up their song and Pastor Browne was climbing the stairs to his podium. Cole noticed Alana sitting with her younger sister just a few rows from the front. Her white-blonde hair was unmistakable as it caught a flicker of light and shimmered like a spray of jewels.

His attention was suddenly jerked away when Blaine elbowed him in the side. "Hey!" Cole protested. "What gives?"

Blaine merely put a finger to his lips and jerked a thumb towards the stage. Cole realized Pastor Browne had bowed his head and was leading the entire congregation in prayer. Cole obediently lowered his head as well, but his eyes continued to dart around the room. Blaine was murmuring words to himself, his hands clasped and his attention clearly focused on praying. The elderly couple on the other side of Cole were both nodding, eyes closed, as they, too, focused on the pastor's prayer.

"...and please guide us through Your Spirit, allowing this hour be a moment of awakening for everyone here tonight. In Your begotten Son's name, Jesus, Amen."

An echo of amen's rippled throughout the sanctuary as hundreds of heads jerked back up, their attention now focused on Pastor Browne. He smiled and grabbed his leathery brown Bible in one hand. "Let's start where we left off last week, in John chapter 13. As many of you know, we have been reading through the gospel of John..."

Cole felt himself zoning out as the pastor continued to make various announcements. Only when he heard the rustle of pages next to him did Cole snap back to the present. He realized Blaine had grabbed the Bible right out of Cole's lap and flipped to John 13. He handed it back to Cole with a look that said, Pay attention.

Cole scowled at him. When he glanced down at the open Bible in his lap, he saw that the pages were crisp and brand new. Nearly half of the chapter was written in red, indicating Jesus' words. Though he had received the Bible as a birthday present when he turned thirteen, he rarely used it. The only time he ever opened it was at church, and even then he rarely bothered to read the passage.

"Now, many of you know this is the chapter where a famous scene takes place—Jesus washes His disciples' feet," Pastor Browne continued. "It's easy to just skim over this passage because it's rather well known. The disciples have returned from a walk and their feet are dirty, so Jesus takes off his robe, gets a towel, and starts washing. Just a simple but powerful act of kindness, right?"

Cole glanced around the room. All eyes were focused on the pastor. Cole yawned and stretched out in his seat.

"But what many people miss is the underlying message beneath Jesus' act of kindness. As we begin reading in chapter 13, verse

1, we find that much more is going on than merely washing the disciples' feet.

"'It was just before the Passover Festival. Jesus knew that the hour had come for him to leave this world and go to the Father.' Now here is the key sentence: 'Having loved his own who were in the world, he loved them to the end.'

"Now you may be thinking, well, of course Jesus loved them. God is love. Jesus is love. It's a principal of the Christian faith. But listen to what verse 3 says: 'Jesus knew that the Father had put all things under his power, and that he had come from God and was returning to God; so.'"

Pastor Browne paused and glanced up from his Bible. He stepped away from the podium and surveyed his audience scattered throughout the room. "That 'so' is more important than you think," he continued. "If you understand what we've just read, then you know that God has just given his Son unbelievable power. Jesus is ruler over everything, he has come from God, and he is going to return to God. Now that's powerful."

For the first time that night, Cole actually reread verse 3 in his Bible. Something in the pastor's tone had struck him, and he couldn't help but pay a little more attention to the sermon.

"With this amazing, unfathomable power in mind, guess what Jesus does? Reveal his glory to the disciples? Perform another miracle?" Pastor Browne smiled. "Actually, what he does next is greater than all of those combined. Verse 4 goes on to say, 'So he got up from the meal, took off his outer clothing, and wrapped a towel around his waist.' Keep in mind that this is God we're talking about—God in human flesh. Our Savior, who in the next few days will be crucified for the sins of the world.

"'After that, he poured water into a basin and began to wash his disciples' feet, drying them with the towel that was wrapped around him.'"

Cole had to admit that those words painted a staggering picture. It was humbling, and it actually made him think—something he normally didn't do in church. He had been raised knowing that Jesus was his Savior, Jesus died on the cross for his sins, Jesus loved him, so on and so forth. But Cole had never realized the extent of Jesus' love. If he truly was so powerful as Pastor Browne described, what could have possibly provoked him to perform such a lowly act—a task that a servant was supposed to do? If anything, his disciples should have been eager to wash his feet—he was going to sacrifice himself for them a few days later.

Cole's interest was piqued. "In verse 12," Pastor Browne conclud-ed, "we read, 'When he had finished washing their feet, he put on his clothes and returned to his place. "Do you understand what I have done for you?" he asked them. "You call me 'Teacher' and 'Lord,' and rightly so, for that is what I am. Now that I, your Lord and Teacher, have washed your feet, you also should wash one another's feet. I have set you an example that you should do as I have done for you. Very truly I tell you, no servant is greater than his master, nor is a messenger greater than the one who sent him. Now that you know these things, you will be blessed if you do them.'"

The sanctuary was clothed in expectant silence. Pastor Browne paused and glanced around the room, a warm but thoughtful smile on his face. "So the question is, brothers and sisters, do you understand what Jesus has done for you?"

The choir began filtering back onto the stage and the orchestra returned to their instruments. Pastor Browne silently closed his Bible and concluded, "Let us hold in our hearts Jesus' last words in that passage: 'Now that you know these things, you will be blessed if you do them.' Amen, brothers and sisters!"

"Amen!" a hundred voice echoed in reply.

As Cole stood with the rest of the congregation, he felt his heart swell with an indescribable feeling. It was like he had just taken a long, refreshing draught of water. Something was stirring within him.

The choir soon broke into a new song, and voices of all tones and volumes immediately joined in, singing these heartfelt words: "Amazing love, how can it be? / That you, my King, would die for me?"

Chapter 4

"Tammy, pass the orange juice."

Alana sighed when her little sister blatantly ignored her and continued raving about their surf session yesterday. Tammy was kneeling on the edge of her chair, waving her fork wildly between two fingers. Her eyes glowed with delight. "You should have seen it!" she gushed to Dylan, who was busy buttering his toast. "The wave was way over my head!"

"Tammy," Alana tried again.

"When I took the drop, I thought I wasn't going to make it because it was so steep!"

Alana spoke through gritted teeth. "Tammy."

"You should have been there, Dylan," Tammy exclaimed. Dylan merely grunted and took a bite of toast, causing a thin stream of crumbs to fall into his lap.

"Fine," Alana muttered, abruptly pushing back her chair and standing up. She leaned across the table and grabbed the orange juice, nearly knocking Tammy's plate of eggs off the table. Then she plopped back down and poured herself a tall glass.

Tammy caught her plate just in time. "Watch it, Alana—you almost ruined my breakfast!"

"Did not," Alana retorted. "Besides, you were the one who kept ignoring me."

"I was telling a story to Dylan!"

"About that stupid wave you caught yesterday? It wasn't nearly overhead."

"It was too."

"You have a long way to go before you're ready to surf bigger waves," Alana said with a roll of her eyes. "Even Dylan knows that." She glanced across the table at their older brother, who was busy scarfing down the last of his toast.

"Hey," he said in between mouthfuls, "leave me out of this. I'm not getting in one of your lame sister fights."

Tammy didn't heed his warning. She launched right into an objection, pointing her fork at her sister accusingly. "Alana thinks I can't surf."

"Hey, I never said that!"

Tammy gave her a disapproving look and continued ranting to Dylan. He finally dropped his fork onto his plate and held his hands up, exasperated. "Girls! Is this really worth arguing over?"

Alana stared at her orange juice. Tammy started it, she thought.

Dylan closed his eyes and took a deep breath. "Sorry," he said, in a much quieter volume. "Tammy, I'm sure Alana didn't mean anything she said. Why don't you go upstairs and get changed? Alana will take you surfing in a few minutes."

"I what?" Alana shook her head. "Dylan—"

He glanced up and gave Alana a look that said, Don't argue. Then he gave Tammy a reassuring smile. "Does that sound good?" he asked her.

"Yeah," Tammy said quietly. She ate one last forkful of eggs before scooting her chair back and sprinting up to her bedroom, leaving the two older siblings alone in the kitchen.

"Gee, thanks for that," Alana muttered, crossing her arms over her chest. "Next time, can you not volunteer me to babysit?"

"You're not babysitting," Dylan corrected. "You're taking your sister surfing."

"It's practically the same thing."

"Come on, Alana." Dylan rolled his eyes. "You should hear yourself right now. You're complaining about going surfing. Is this really coming from a girl who lives and breathes the sport?"

"Yeah, once you throw Tammy into the equation." Dylan gave her a look of disbelief, so Alana added, "She's a nuisance! You saw how she treated me during breakfast. She was outright ignoring me."

"Yes, but I saw how you were treating her as well. You really crushed her, Alana."

She glanced away. Part of her knew Dylan was right, but she was too steamed up to admit it. She wasn't really looking forward to dragging Tammy along to the beach.

"She's your sister. Give her some grace."

"Grace?" Alana raised an eyebrow. "So now you're preaching to me?"

"Alana—"

"You don't even go to church anymore. What gives you the right to—"

"Alana." Dylan's commanding tone immediately silenced her. "You know exactly why. But just because I don't go to church doesn't mean I can't instruct you. I'm your older brother, and I've been walking with God longer than you have."

He had a point. But Alana merely shrugged.

"You should be thankful that Tammy actually enjoys surfing," Dylan continued in a softer tone. "What if you had a sister who didn't want anything to do with surfing, or the beach, or even the outdoors in general? Think about that one for a while."

"It doesn't change the fact that she's annoying."

Dylan smiled. "It may not, but don't let that stop you from being a good example. You're the older sister, so you need to show her what a role model looks like. You never know—you and Tammy could grow up to be best friends."

Alana snorted. "That'll be the day."

"Well, it's up to you. Rather now than later, right?"

She sighed. "Right," she mumbled, grabbing her dishes and quickly rinsing them off in the sink. After heading upstairs to her bedroom, she closed the door behind her and slipped on a bathing suit underneath her T-shirt and boardshorts.

Before heading back downstairs, Alana glanced out her bedroom window while sweeping up her hair into a messy ponytail. She frowned when she saw some meager three-foot waves trickling in. They were nowhere near as big as yesterday. The swell that had peaked two nights ago was already beginning to fade, leaving small-scale surf and less-than-ideal conditions in its wake. Alana didn't wake up early that morning because the waves hadn't looked worth it.

But apparently Dylan thought otherwise. After tying her ponytail, Alana turned away from the window and pushed open her door. She strode into the hallway and rapped a few times on Tammy's closed door. "Ready?" Alana called.

"Yes." Tammy's voice sounded a bit muffled through the thick wooden door. A few moments later, it opened to reveal Tammy dressed in her favorite teal swimsuit and black rashguard. "Let's go!" she exclaimed, her eyes bright with excitement.

Alana followed her downstairs and into the garage. They grabbed their shortboards and headed out into the bright sunlight. A soft breeze was blowing in from the sea. Alana could smell the faint scent of salt in the air as they jogged towards the beach, their bare arms peppered with goosebumps.

As soon as they rounded the corner, the ocean came into view. It was just as vast and beautiful as yesterday, but when Alana's gaze swept over to the few waves trickling into shore, she sighed in disappointment.

"What's wrong?" Tammy asked, quickening her pace. "Hurry up!"

Alana didn't say anything as she followed Tammy down a flight of steps to the shore. She shoved the nose of her surfboard into the sand, then untangled its leash and strapped it securely around her ankle. Her gaze never once left the waves. She noticed they were breaking closer to shore and not as much around the Point. The majority of the surfers in the lineup were longboarders, and she immediately wished she had opted to take a bigger board out today.

"Oh well," she murmured, yanking her shortboard out of the sand and tucking it underneath her arm. She smiled faintly when she saw Tammy copying her movements, shoving the nose of her board into the sand as well before strapping on her leash.

Maybe Dylan was right, Alana thought as she watched her younger sister. I should be glad that Tammy loves to surf. It's the one thing I can teach her, after all.

"Almost done?" Alana asked.

Tammy straightened back up and grabbed her surfboard in both hands. "Yeah, let's hit the water."

She charged straight towards a whitewater wave, leaped over it, and landed belly-first on her board. Alana did the same, and the two began stroking towards the lineup in unison. When the waves became too big to paddle through, they pushed the noses of their shortboards under and performed duck dives. Alana noticed Tammy was having trouble forcing her surfboard under the waves.

"Hey," Alana said, pushing a strand of wet hair out of her eyes, "next time you duck dive, trying grabbing the rails a bit higher up. That might give you the leverage you need to sink your board."

Tammy glanced over, surprised at the words of encouragement. "Okay." Alana watched as she tried her suggestion and slipped easily underneath an oncoming wave. Upon resurfacing, the sisters shared a knowing smile.

As soon as they reached the lineup, they sat down on their boards at the same time. They bobbed up and down over a few swells before a set appeared on the horizon. "Go for this one," Alana urged. She pointed to a small wave fast approaching. "It's got your name written all over it."

Tammy grinned and spun her board around. Being on the shoulder, she barely scratched into the wave, but since she was so light the crest of the lip easily picked her up. Just as it began to curl over, she popped up to her feet and took the drop.

Alana hooted when she saw Tammy's head disappear behind a cloud of whitewater. She watched her sister glide up to the lip, sending arcs of spray flying through the air.

A loud crash of whitewater suddenly jerked her attention back to the horizon. Her eyes widened when she realized a wave was breaking right in front of her. She scrambled to duck dive under the surface, barely making it underneath the foam before it could sweep her towards shore.

As soon as she resurfaced, Alana saw a second wave stacking up. She quickly paddled into position and popped up to her feet just as it began to break. She grinned as she dropped down to the bottom of the wave and raced around a section of whitewater. She peered over her left shoulder at the blue-green wall of water behind her. It was time to carve this backside wave.

Alana twisted her hips and made a long, drawn-out bottom turn. Using her speed to race back up the wave, she threw her arms and pulled a nice snap off the lip. She made a few more turns, mostly cutbacks to bring her back into the pocket, before attempting one last maneuver. Just as the section in front of her collapsed, she threw out her back foot and pulled a beautiful floater. She sailed over the billowing whitewash before gliding back down to the trough of the wave.

Tammy hooted and gave Alana a shaka from where she was paddling inside. Alana smiled and gave her a thumbs-up just before Tammy duck dived under her sister's wave. Alana dove off her board into the cool water, still smiling. As soon as she resurfaced, she climbed back on to wring out her soaked hair.

"Nice floater, Alana!" a voice called.

Alana turned around and saw a familiar surfer paddling towards her. "Koa! I didn't expect to see you in the water today," she greeted him. "How's it going?"

"Good." Koa grinned and sat down on his longboard. "I really wasn't going to surf today, but I was out for a wave check when I saw you and Tammy."

"You just can't stay away from me, can you?" Alana teased.

"Apparently not." He smiled, showing off his two dimples on his tanned skin.

They chatted on and off as they made their way to the lineup, waiting for the next set to show. Koa ended up stroking into a small, gutless wave and popped up to his feet before it even broke. Alana watched as he cross-stepped up to the nose, hung ten, and then lost his balance and tumbled right off the front of his board.

"Is that Koa?" Tammy asked, paddling up next to her sister.

Alana nodded. "It looks like he's practicing his wipeouts."

Tammy giggled. "At least I didn't wipeout. Did you see my wave?"

"I sure did. You were ripping."

The compliment made Tammy's eyes light up with excitement.

"You know, you're on your way to passing me up as the best surfer at C Street," Alana added.

"What's this about the best surfer at C Street?"

The sisters both turned to see Koa sitting on his longboard, a goofy grin on his face.

"Oh, I was just telling Tammy how good she's getting," Alana explained.

"Totally. It looks like you have some competition." Koa winked at Tammy.

"We'll see." Alana gave both of them a mischievous grin before turning her attention back to the horizon. She closed her eyes as a gentle sea breeze tousled her hair, spraying a thin veil of mist over her face. A Bible verse from her quiet time with God that morning came to mind: This is the day the Lord has made; let us rejoice and be glad in it.

"Thank you, Lord," Alana whispered. "Thank you for giving me such a beautiful day, even if the waves are small. Thank you for a great friend like Koa." She heard Tammy laughing as she chatted with their Hawaiian friend, so Alana added, "And thank you for giving me a little sister who loves to surf."

Alana imagined the warm sunrays baking her arms as evidence that God was smiling down on her. At least, that's what it felt like—true joy, the kind that warms one from the inside out.

She grinned.

Chapter 5

The trio surfed for a few more hours before calling it a day. Koa's final ride was a crumbly, powerless two-footer that barely gave enough room for him to do a quick cross-step. He ended up banking it off the whitewater and nearly lost his balance in the process, so he rode the rest of the way in on his stomach.

As soon as he stepped off his longboard, his toes sank into the cool sand. He trudged onto shore with his board tucked underneath his arm. When he glanced down the beach, he saw Alana and Tammy emerge from the water.

"Hey, I'm gonna go rinse off in the showers," he called. "I guess I'll see you guys later."

"Oh, wait—I'll go with you," Alana called back, quickly unstrapping her leash and wrapping it around the tail of her board. Tammy followed them up a flight of stairs, where the trio took turns rinsing themselves and their surfboards in the outdoor showers. Koa was almost done getting the last smatter of sand off one his fins when he saw something out of the corner of his eye. He glanced up and immediately wished he hadn't looked.

"It seems we have company," he muttered, narrowing his eyes.

"What?" Alana gave him a confused look, and Koa pointed over her shoulder. Her gaze immediately fell. "Oh. Just ignore them, Koa."

"Ignore who?" Tammy asked.

"Nobody," Alana said quickly. "Hey, why don't you go home and get dried off? I'll meet you there in a few minutes."

Tammy frowned, but after a few moments' deliberation conceded. "Okay," she said. "But only if you take me to get a smoothie later."

Alana sighed. "Tammy..." But after seeing a certain someone approaching in her peripheral vision, she caved. "Fine. I'll see you in a bit."

Tammy smiled and ambled away, leaving Koa and Alana in an awkward silence. Both of them were unsure of what to do next, so Alana quickly turned off her side of the shower and flicked a strand of wet hair out of her eyes. The reason she didn't want Tammy hanging around was because of her.

Taylor Rosalind sauntered past, pushing her straightened hair out of her face with long, slender fingers. She wrapped a hand around Cole's bicep, subtly pulling him closer. Alana frowned.

Taylor and Cole had a rocky, on-and-off relationship. One minute they would be inseparable at school, and the next they would treat each other as mere acquaintances. Alana liked to think they considered themselves 'friends with benefits.'

"Hi Koa," Taylor said in her sugary voice, giving a brisk wave. Koa raised his head, smiled faintly, and then pretended to be busy studying a ding on the rail of his board. It was hard not to miss the scowl on Alana's face as Taylor and Cole blatantly ignored her. Alana glared at Taylor's retreating back.

Koa thought he caught a glimpse of bitterness in Alana's eyes, but he remained silent. Taylor had always put Alana down and made fun of her group of friends every chance she got. Moreover, she was a bad influence for Cole, and had him wrapped around her little finger.

Koa immediately felt guilty. It was obvious that Cole was flaky and immature, and it was true that he and Taylor had a weird history together, but it simply wasn't Koa's place to judge his friend.

For a few moments, the only sound to be heard was the crashing of waves and the whir of skateboard wheels over cement as a kid raced by. Then Alana broke the silence by muttering, "She ticks me off."

"I think she ticks everybody off," Koa said with a dry laugh.

"Except for Cole."

"Yeah, well, he doesn't count. I don't know what he sees in her, but they always get back together. How many breakups have they gone through already? Seven?"

Alana shrugged. "Don't know, don't care." She waited until said couple was a good distance away before heading over to the railing. She set her surfboard down and gazed at the glittering ocean.

"Hey," Koa said, coming up behind her. They bumped shoulders and laughed softly as they continued to watch the waves, content with studying the scene in front of them. Something about the way the tide caressed the shore, the pelicans swooped over glassy waves, and the sun made the surface sparkle like crystals, calmed their racing hearts.

Alana interrupted the quiet again by saying, "You know, I wish the waves weren't so small today."

"Yeah."

"And I wish the swell never faded away."

"So there would be great waves all the time?"

"Exactly."

"I'm with you there."

They lapsed into another silence. Then Alana suddenly gasped. "Oh my gosh! Koa!" She turned and grabbed his shoulders, shaking them fiercely. "That's it! You're a genius!"

"Well, duh, I thought that was already established." Koa laughed, causing Alana to roll her eyes. "No, but seriously," he said, "what's got you so excited?"

"Great waves all the time—if the swell never goes away, there would be great waves all the time!"

Koa gave her a look. "So...?"

"So what if there was a way to chase the swell?"

"What do you mean?"

"Remember the movie The Endless Summer?"

"Of course. It's a classic."

"Well, instead of going around the world and surfing in an 'endless summer,' we can travel down the coast and surf an endless swell!"

Koa was quiet for a few seconds, his eyebrows scrunched in contemplation. "Yeah, but the fact is, there's no such thing as an endless swell. Swells are generated by storms, and storms—"

Alana sighed. "I know, I know. Swells can be unpredictable. But we know that different beaches fire during different swells, right?"

He nodded.

"So..."She grinned. "What if we went on a surfing safari down the coast and chased each swell? Depending on the swell direction, it would be possible to surf great waves all the time by hitting different-facing beaches. It would be like The Endless Summer, except it would be an endless swell. Get it?"

The idea was actually pretty great. No—it was insanely, amazingly great. Koa threw up his hands. "You're a genius, Alana."

"It's totally possible," she said excitedly. "We still have two months before school starts. That leaves us with a huge window for our surfing safari."

"Wait—are you saying we're actually going to attempt to do this?" Koa gave her a funny look. "You have no idea how much gas, money, and food we'll need. Not to mention transportation."

"I know, but there is a way to fit everyone in our surf gang in just one vehicle—maybe two."

Koa crossed his arms over his chest. "How?"

"Well...here's where it gets a little tricky." Alana forced a laugh.

"Surprise me."

"Okay." She took a deep breath. "We need a van—a surf van."

"Like a Volkswagen?"

"Exactly." She gave Koa a hopeful smile, but both of them were thinking the same thing—the only person in the gang who owned a VW surf van rarely took it out of the garage.

Koa snorted. Here he was, enjoying a conversation with Alana, and Cole Anderson had to come into the equation. "Great," he muttered. "We have to deal with Cole, don't we?"

"Come on, Koa! It'll be worth it. I'm talking about great waves for as long as we want. Wouldn't that be amazing?"

He smiled. "Yeah, it really would." After taking in her animated expression and the way her hands gripped the rail with excitement, he caved. "Alright. Let's do this."

"Coke or Dr. Pepper?" Taylor asked, holding out two ice-cold cans of soda.

"Dr. Pepper," Cole said automatically, taking the beverage. He leaned back against the Rosalinds' plush leather couch.

Taylor sat down on his lap and pulled out her phone. She spent a few minutes texting, but the faster her fingers flew across the screen, the more her flirtatious smile dissolved into a frown.

"Something wrong?" Cole asked.

"It's my parents," she muttered. "I can't believe it. They told me they wouldn't get back from their business trip until tonight, but now they're coming home in two hours." She groaned and rested her head against Cole's chest. "They're so annoying."

"At least you don't have a dad who works from home," Cole said.

"Oh, is that why I hardly ever come to your place?" she teased.

"Maybe." He wrapped his arms around her waist.

A fleeting image suddenly came to his mind—one of Alana and Koa standing at the railing, watching waves together. That was the last he had seen of them, and it gave him a weird feeling. He knew Taylor could be a prick when she wanted to be. He felt a little sorry for his friends, but there was nothing he could do about it, right?

Taylor kissed him, her lips tasting like cherry Cola. But in his mind's eye, Cole could clearly see the look of disappointment on Alana's face. Deep down, he knew Taylor was in the wrong, not his friends. And he had gone along with her.

"What's wrong?" Taylor asked, propping herself up on one elbow.

"Nothing," Cole said automatically. "I guess I'm just not in the mood." Not anymore.

Taylor rolled her eyes and sat up. "Then what do you want to do?"

Cole glanced through the window at the spotless blue sky overhead.

"Cole," she snapped. "Hello, anybody home?"

"Sorry—I'm out of it today."

"I noticed."

He ignored her and took a swig of his Dr. Pepper. After placing it back on the table, he returned to Taylor's side and pulled her close. He needed to stay focused and not think about Alana anymore. He was being silly, letting his conscience get the best of him. Here was the perfect distraction right in front of him, so why not make the most of it?

"Sorry, baby," he said. "Now where were we?"

Chapter 6

C ole sighed as he tossed his basketball into the air. It landed back in the palm of his hand before he tossed it up again. A Green Day song was blasting through his headphones, so he didn't hear anyone knock until Mr. Anderson suddenly pushed open the door to Cole's room.

Cole was caught off guard for a second. Instead of catching the basketball as It flipped through the air, he turned, causing the ball to descend directly onto his face. "Ow!" he exclaimed, sitting up and tenderly touching his nose. "What do you want?" he snapped at his dad.

Mr. Anderson sighed and shook his head. "You're this close to being grounded again, Cole. Remember what I told you about talking back?"

"Yes," Cole muttered, yanking the headphones out of his ears.

"Good. Well, now that we're on the same page, can I show you something in the garage?"

Cole shrugged and followed his dad out of the room. They walked into the garage, where Mr. Anderson flipped on the light switch, bathing the workshop in a soft yellow glow.

Cole's heart immediately dropped to the bottom of his stomach. He could not believe this was happening right now. His gaze flickered from his dad, to the airbrushed surfboard lying in the middle of the garage, and back to his dad again.

Mr. Anderson suppressed a laugh by coughing loudly into his fist. "So tell me, Cole," he said, obviously trying to conceal his amusement, "what is this?"

He gestured to the board, and Cole's heart started racing. "Um..."

Footsteps could be heard coming from the hallway. Blaine suddenly appeared in the doorway, his curious eyes darting from Cole, to their dad, to the fresh surfboard. He smiled widely. "Nice design, bro."

"Blaine," Mr. Anderson said sternly, "this is between Cole and I."

"Okay," he said, but his shoulders were shaking with silent laugther.

"Blaine. Out." Though Mr. Anderson crossed his arms over his chest, his eyes were twinkling in amusement.

As soon as his brother left, Cole sighed and buried his head in his hands. "Can I leave now?" he groaned.

"Oh, you're not off the hook yet. You still have to explain what this is." Mr. Anderson pointed to the surfboard.

Cole sighed, realizing his dad wasn't going to budge. "I just—I don't know—I thought it looked cool," he stammered.

"You've never done something like this before."

"Dad, I've been designing boards for almost six years."

"I'm talking about her." Mr. Anderson gestured to the surfer girl, her blonde hair swishing around her shoulders, airbrushed onto the left side of the stringer. She was gazing intently at the turquoise waves, a slight smile on her face. "What's up with the girl?"

The way Dad asked the question made Cole think he knew something Cole didn't. "Why? What's so bad about it?" he asked testily.

"Nothing. I was just curious. What prompted you to draw a girl?"

"I dunno."

Mr. Anderson gave his son an expression that showed he clearly wasn't buying it. "Cole," he said quietly, "if there's a certain someone on your mind, don't be afraid to tell me. I like that you're taking out your feelings on your work, but you don't—"

"Dad," Cole groaned. "Really? Is this what you dragged me in here for?" He threw his arms in the air. "I do not have a special someone and I do not take out my feelings on my work!"

Mr. Anderson smiled mischievously. "So this girl doesn't resemble anyone in real life whatsoever?"

"Of course not!" Lies, all lies.

Mr. Anderson could tell this conversation was exasperating his son, so he put a hand on Cole's shoulder. "Okay, okay. You just gave me a little surprise with this design, that's all."

Cole frowned. His racing heart had slowed now that he was sure his dad didn't suspect anything, but the next words out of his mouth were even worse.

"However, since this board was supposed to go to a buddy of mine, I don't know if I can ship it to him."

"Huh?"

Mr. Anderson's smile faded. "Look, Cole, your artwork is amazing—it always has been—but I wasn't expecting you to airbrush a girl. I just can't give this to my friend. He won't take it."

"So what are you saying?" Cole asked, starting to become panicked.

His dad sighed. "I can try to sell this to some of my regular costumers, but if it doesn't sell within the next few months, I lose my profit."

Cole narrowed my eyes. "What are you getting at?" he demanded.

"I'm not getting at anything. All I'm saying is, if this board doesn't sell, then we're short a few hundred dollars."

"So you want me to pay you," Cole deadpanned.

"You never know, some of my regular costumers might be willing to buy it."

"How much?" Cole asked with a sigh.

Mr. Anderson shifted from one foot to the other. "I'm just giving you a warning, son. It's not for sure."

"How much?" Cole repeated.

"Five hundred."

Cole couldn't believe it. "You're kidding me, right? What a joke."

"I'm sorry, but..." Mr. Anderson held his hands out, palms facing up.

"If no one buys the board, then I owe you five hundred. Yeah, I get it." Cole scowled at his father before turning around and storming out of the garage. "Thanks for all the support with my artwork, Dad."

"Cole!" Mr. Anderson called after him. "I wasn't finished!"

"Just leave me alone!" Cole hollered, stomping back to his room and slamming the door behind him. He knew he had been a jerk, and he also knew he was sure to be punished later for his rude behavior, but his mind was a jumble of emotions. He was embarrassed and a little horrified that he had airbrushed Alana, of all people, onto a surfboard.

Suddenly, his bedroom door flung open. "Haven't you ever heard of privacy?" he snapped.

"Sorry, bro," Blaine said in a voice that didn't sound sorry in the least. "I just wanted to let you know that we should leave in a couple minutes. It's already 11:15."

"What are you talking about?"

"You don't remember?" Blaine rolled his eyes. "Alana texted everyone last night saying she had something important to discuss. We're all meeting at The Habit today."

"When?"

"11:30."

Cole sighed and sprawled out on the mattress. "Tell the gang to go ahead and meet without me."

"Yeah, I don't think so." Blaine grabbed a pillow and whacked Cole's bare stomach. "Get up."

"No way." He flopped over in bed.

"You're going to miss out on a pineapple teriyaki charburger."

"So what?"

Blaine sighed. "So...it's on me."

Cole suddenly became more interested in what his brother was saying. "You mean...free food?"

"If that's what it takes."

It only took a few seconds for Cole to decide. "Okay...let's go."

By the time the twins coasted up to the entrance of The Habit on their bikes, it was already sweltering hot. The sky was a vibrant, cloudless blue, and the sun beat down mercilessly on everything in sight. They quickly chained their bikes to a nearby rack and stepped inside the cool, air-conditioned restaurant.

"Phew," Blaine sighed, using the sleeve of his T-shirt to wipe off the beads of sweat on his forehead. "How hot is it out there? Ninety?"

"Ninety-two," someone called from a booth on the far side of the restaurant. The twins grinned when they spotted the gang already crammed into one booth.

"Hey, man!" Blaine said, walking over and high-fiving the guys.

"Glad you could make it," Jake replied. "It's already 11:40. Alana here thought you two were gonna be no-shows."

Cole glanced over at Alana, who was currently trying to balance a plastic spoon on her nose. She epically failed, and the spoon landed with a plink on the table. "Oh! Hi, guys."

"Hi dorkface," Cole countered. He slid into the booth next to Jake.

"Hey, it takes mad skill to do what I can do." Alana snatched the spoon and tried to balance it on her nose once again, but she ended up poking herself in the eye instead.

Cole rolled his eyes. "Oh, right. Mad skill. How could I have missed it?"

"You're just jealous of my awesome talents."

He snorted. "Clearly."

"Okay, well, if you two are going to keep bickering like an old couple, then I'll go ahead and order," Blaine interrupted.

After an awkward silence, during which Cole faked a coughing fit, he asked, "So...how are things going between you and your girlfriend, Lover Boy?"

Jake reddened. "You're toeing a fine line, Cole," he replied.

"What? I'm only stating the truth."

"She's not my girlfriend."

"Not yet," Cole laughed.

"It's none of your business, Anderson," Maya said.

Cole held up his hands in surrender. "Whoa, babe, there's no need to get so defensive. I'm just trying to make some conversation here."

"Cole." Alana gave him an exasperated look. "Can't we all just get along here?"

He rolled his eyes.

She sighed. "Look, you don't have to put up a front with us. We're your friends. Why do you act like such a jerk all the time?"

The booth fell into another awkward silence. Her words had been like a slap in the face—a much-deserved slap. Cole realized that the truth did hurt. He acted nonchalant by whipping out his phone and pretending to text. But in reality, his mind was spinning with what Alana had just said. Was he really such a self-centered jerk? And when did he suddenly start caring about what some girl said about him, anyway?

Suddenly, two large trays filled with food were dropped onto the table, shattering Cole out of his thoughts. Blaine grinned before sliding into his seat next to Koa. "Lunch is served!" he announced. "Dig in, everyone!"

Cole quickly slipped his phone back into his pocket and reached for the nearest burger. Everyone fought over the charburgers and grilled sandwiches until Maya suddenly remembered why they were there in the first place. "Hey, Alana," she asked, "what was it you wanted to talk to us about?"

"Oh. Right." Alana quickly wiped her mouth with a napkin. "Okay, so Koa and I had been talking about this plan of ours."

"Nothing's set in stone yet, but we were thinking of doing something along the lines of The Endless Summer," Koa added.

"What do you mean?" Maya asked.

"Okay." Alana smiled and smoothed out her tank top. "So you know how, in the movie, Mike Hynson and Robert August traveled around the world chasing the summer? Well, Koa and I got to thinking, what if we could chase the swell? What if there was a way to travel down the coast and surf great waves for an entire month—maybe even longer?"

"Like a surfing safari," Jake mused.

"Exactly." Alana grinned. "Last night I was up late Googling some popular surf spots like Malibu and Trestles."

"Wait—are you saying we would go all the way to Trestles?" Blaine's eyes were as round as saucers.

"I know, it's pretty far," Alana admitted. "But we could make a mini-vacation out of it. I was thinking we could all pack a small suitcase and a few boards. Then we could split the gas money and take turns driving down the coast. We all have our licenses, right?"

Cole glanced around the table, realizing that everyone was nodding. "So, wait a second," Jake said. "Just to clear things up—you're talking about a strictly surfing trip, right?"

"Exactly."

"And we can hit any spots we want to?"

"Of course. We can go as far down the coast as we want."

"So...we could stop by Huntington?"

"Oh, man!" Blaine gushed. "Surf City! That's awesome!"

"How about County Line?" Maya asked excitedly. "I know it's not that far of a drive from here, but that's where I first learned how to surf."

"We can go wherever we want," Alana said with a smile. "The only problem is, we need some sort of transportation."

The table immediately grew quiet. The only sound was the loud rustling of paper as Cole unwrapped his second burger. "What?" he asked sharply, realizing everyone was staring at him.

Alana had a strange smile on her face. "This is where you come in, Cole."

"Uh..." He glanced around the table, totally lost. "Why is everyone looking at me? Is there something on my face?"

"Only your stupidity," Jake said.

"No, Cole," Alana sighed. "I'm talking about your van. Your surf van."

Cole dropped his burger as if it were a bomb. "You mean, my Volkswagen?"

"Uh-oh. Here we go," Blaine muttered.

"Hang on a sec." Cole ran a hand through his hair and closed his eyes. "Are you saying that you want me to loan you my Volkswagen? Just for this stupid trip of yours?"

Alana frowned. "Okay, first of all, I'm only asking you to drive your own Volkswagen. No one else will even sit in the driver's seat if you don't want them to. And secondly, this isn't just some stupid trip. It's a surfing safari, and that means sick waves for a whole month straight."

Cole jutted out his bottom lip in frustration. He knew she was right, but he was still pissed off that she would even consider taking his Volkswagen. He had bought the vintage van when it was in terrible shape, and spent over a year buying spare parts to fix it up. Now it practically looked brand-new, but the farthest he had ever driven it was forty miles out of town. Yet Alana wanted him to take it on a freaking vacation?

"Dude, we're not asking for much," Koa said calmly. It was obvious he was trying to calm Cole down before his temper flared.

Cole sighed and ran a hand through his hair again. "I don't know. I mean, is this 'surfing safari' even finalized yet? Are we all seriously going?"

"Well, that's up to you guys," Alana said. "But Koa and I already talked it over with our families, and both of us are cleared to go."

Cole glanced at Blaine. He had a hopeful smile on his face, as if urging his brother to agree with their plan and volunteer his Volkswagen. Cole snorted in disbelief. "Can we at least have a few days to think this over?" he finally asked.

"Of course," Alana said quickly.

"How long do you think the trip would take—if we all went, that is?" Jake asked.

"I don't know. It depends how many surf spots we hit," Alana explained. "I'm guessing a month, max. That's if we hit ten spots and surf at each one for more than a day."

Koa quietly elbowed her in the side. "Why don't you show them the chart?"

Cole narrowed his eyes. So not only had they been planning this trip, but they had made some fancy chart together as well? What the heck?

Alana stood up and pulled a piece of paper out of her back pocket. She unfolded it and cleared her throat. "Okay. So after researching some of the top surf spots, I came up with this list." She passed it to Maya, and the paper slowly started circling the table.

When the list was finally passed to Cole, he took one glance it and freaked out. The last spot on the list, after Trestles and

San Onofre, was Oceanside. "Are you serious?" he asked, his jaw dropping open in shock. "Oceanside is at least five hours away!"

"Well, that's why we would drive in increments, stupid." Blaine gave his twin a "duh" look.

"It's not that far," Alana protested. "I mean, we could even go as far as Sunset Cliffs."

"Sunset Cliffs?" These were only surf spots Cole had heard about, but they were too far to drive without having to stay overnight in a hotel. That immediately brought another question to mind. "Wait, have you guys even thought of where we're going to sleep?" he asked.

Alana and Koa exchanged a glance. It seemed like they had been doing that a lot lately, and it was starting to make Cole uncomfortable.

"Well, I know Maya's family owns a camper..." Alana said.

Now it was Maya's turn to freak out. "Wait, are you saying I would have to drive that beast?"

"I don't mind driving it," Blaine said, shrugging.

"I guess it's fine, but I'm going to have to ask my mom," Maya said hesitatingly.

"Of course. I think we should all think this through before making a final decision," Alana affirmed. "How about we give each other three days?"

Cole glanced around the table. Everyone except him was nodding. By the looks on his friends' faces, it was clear no thinking would have to be done—only convincing. Everyone was psyched to go on this surfing safari, and the only thing holding them back were their parents. Cole secretly hoped his dad would keep him and Blaine from going. The trip sounded like a load of crap.

Okay, so maybe the part about chasing the swell and surfing epic waves was tempting. Cole just wasn't thrilled about driving his precious Volkswagen—especially not for a whole month straight.

The table had grown uncomfortably quiet. Jake finished off his second sandwich before tossing a five dollar bill onto the table.

"Thanks, man." Blaine grabbed the money, but not before Maya, Koa, and Alana donated their share of the cost too. Cole rolled his eyes, fished around in his front pocket, and gave his brother a handful of loose change.

"Gee, thanks, Cole," Blaine said dryly. "How can I ever express my gratitude?"

"Whatever. You said you would cover me, anyway." Cole stood up and made it halfway across the restaurant before he heard Alana call his name.

"Wait, Cole—don't forget to think about the surfari," she urged. "I know your van means a lot to you, but this would be the trip of a lifetime."

Cole set his jaw and continued walking. "Sure," he muttered, "but no promises." He flung open the door and stepped out into the parking lot, the temperature hitting him like heat from a brick oven. He wiped his brow before unchaining his bike and sliding on.

Cole knew his brother was probably trying to convince the gang that, yes, Cole would cave and go on the trip eventually. Well, I don't think that's going to happen, Cole thought stubbornly, even though common sense told him they were definitely going on that surfari. If Blaine went, Dad would definitely force Cole to go, too.

Yay life.

Chapter 7

C ole pedaled until his calves were burning and his forehead dripped with sweat. He decided to coast the remaining few blocks home as a cool-down. But something caught his attention out of the corner of his eye, and he turned to see a familiar cherry-red sports car parked at the gas station across the street. He lifted a hand to shield his eyes from the sun. Sure enough, it was her—Taylor Rosalind.

Cole quietly crossed the street and coasted to a stop in front of her car. Resting his elbows on the handlebars of his bike, he gave her a half-smile and said, "Hey."

Taylor glanced up, her eyes widening in realization when she saw him. "Hey yourself," she said, a smile creeping up on her face. After returning her gas pump to the machine, she walked over and gave Cole a light peck on the cheek. "So what's new?"

"Nothing, really."

"Mm-hmm. I can see that look on your face."

"What are you talking about?"

Taylor planted her hands on her hips and gave him a look.

"No, really," Cole said, feigning innocence. "What's wrong?"

Realizing she wasn't going to get anything out of him, Taylor stepped closer and wrapped her arms around Cole's waist. "I can tell when something's on your mind," she said.

Cole's insides began to stir. He reminded himself that he carried no obligation towards her.

"Tell me, what's really going on?"

"Nothing." Cole resisted the urge to kiss her, but it was becoming increasingly harder by the second.

"You know, my annual party is coming up soon."

"Which one?"

"The end of summer bash."

"Yeah...about that." He had to force the words out. "I might not be able to make it."

"What?" Taylor pulled away, slightly offended.

"Tay, listen, I know this is your biggest party of the year—"

"Of course it is!"

"I just don't think I'll be able to make it."

The news hit her like a slap in the face. She looked horrified for a second before quickly getting her act back together. "Oh," she said softly, resting her hands on Cole's shoulders.

"I'm sorry."

"It's fine." There was an awkward silence, and she almost pulled her hands away. "Why can't you come?"

"It's a long story," Cole admitted. Even though his handlebars were separating them from touching completely, he wrapped his arms around her and pulled her close. "Trust me."

"That's the problem, Cole. How can I trust you if you never tell me what's going on?"

"Tay..."

"You're going somewhere, aren't you?" she murmured.

"Maybe."

"Where?"

Cole paused, but he figured it would make no difference to tell her the truth. "The gang and I are going down the coast. It's just a quick surf trip."

Taylor mulled his words over in her mind for a few moments. "Are you sure you're going?" she asked.

"It's not set in stone, but there's a good chance I am."

She sighed and folded her arms over her chest. "You're going with that Alana girl, aren't you?"

"Well, duh, she's part of the gang."

"She's a joke. I don't know why you even hang out with her."

Cole smirked. "What's it to you?"

Taylor didn't reply, but let out an angry huff.

"I knew it—you are jealous."

"Because I see the way you look at her, Cole! It's like you're obsessed or something."

"Why would I be obsessed with Alana?" The question was phrased perfectly, but it tasted foul in his mouth.

"Whatever. I'll talk to you later, Anderson."

Cole raised an eyebrow. "So now we're on a last-name basis?"

"Only with you, babe." She returned the nozzle to its pump before slipping inside her car. Cole watched as she slipped a pair of sunglasses over her eyes, put the car into reverse, and backed away. He couldn't get over the feeling that every time Taylor walked away, she left him wanting more.

Blaine pushed open the front door and automatically made a beeline for the fridge. "I'm home!" he called.

Mr. Anderson appeared in the doorway a few moments later. "You're eating chicken?" he asked as Blaine dug into the leftovers.

"Yeah," he said with his mouth full.

His dad laughed and shook his head. "I thought you just ate lunch."

Blaine merely shrugged.

"So how did it go? You said it was a meeting?" Mr. Anderson asked, genuinely curious. He rested his elbows on the countertop.

"Cole hasn't told you about it?"

"Cole isn't home yet."

"Oh." Blaine paused for a moment, then resumed eating his chicken. He crossed his ankles as he leaned up against the refrigerator. "Well, apparently Alana and Koa have been thinking about taking a surf trip down the coast. It would be just the six of us, and we would be gone for about two weeks, maybe more."

"Really."

"Yeah, really."

"It sounds great, but what about food? Gas? Transportation? And you would need a whole lot of money."

"That's what we've been talking about." Blaine licked his fingers and stuck the remaining chicken back inside the fridge. "Cole stormed out of the restaurant after Alana suggested he should use the Volkswagen."

Mr. Anderson raised his eyebrows. "I'll admit that van is pretty old, and it does mean a lot to your brother—"

"Maya would bring her family's campervan too. That's where we would sleep."

"And I'm guessing you would all chip in for gas?"

Blaine nodded. His father stroked his chin for a few seconds, deep in thought. "I don't know when you guys plan to leave, but you and Cole are free to go. It sounds like a fun surf trip."

Blaine grinned, but only for a moment. "Sweet! But...?"

"But what?"

"I can tell you're hesitating."

"You're right; I am." His dad sighed and pushed off the counter-top. "Don't get me wrong, Blaine, I trust you completely. It's your brother I'm worried about."

"He doesn't even want to go."

"Really? Is this all because of his van?"

It might have something to do with Alana, too. The words were on the tip of Blaine's tongue, but he only said, "I don't know."

"You know him better than me."

"But it'll take both of us to convince him to go."

Mr. Anderson frowned. "I'm your father. I'm not sure if I should be convincing him to go on this surf trip. It is a little risky, you know."

"I get that. But you also have authority. Cole blows me off every time I try to talk to him."

Mr. Anderson smiled sadly. "True..." He thought for a moment. "All right. I'll see what I can do."

Blaine let out a relieved sigh. "Great."

With a fresh smoothie in one hand and her phone in the other, Taylor headed upstairs in her bikini to do some tanning on her parent's roof patio. That, and she needed some time to think. After plugging in her phone to its speakers, she turned the volume up and settled back into a pool lounger. She slipped on a pair of sunglasses and closed her eyes, allowing the warm sunrays to hit her already tan skin.

Though she appeared as cool and collected as could be, in reality Taylor was anxious. She ran her conversation with Cole over and over again in her mind, trying to come up with some way to prevent him from going on that dumb surf trip. Who would want to cram into a car with five other smelly teenagers anyway? Surfing had never appealed to Taylor, and she couldn't understand why Cole was so hooked on the sport.

She knew she had that boy wrapped around her finger, and she wanted it to stay that way. A surf trip with Alana was exactly the thing to pull Cole away. Taylor frowned. She knew that girl meant something to Cole, but he wasn't the type to have feelings for someone. And Alana was such a tomboy. Taylor gave a little huff. Besides, there was Alana's hair—always stringy, always salty. Taylor shuddered just thinking about it. Alana couldn't possibly be a threat.

Taylor crossed her legs and settled back against the lounger. She knew there were other girls besides Alana—girls who Cole had dated in the past. But she didn't mind if Cole dated other girls, because in the end he would always come back to her.

Yet there was a possibility that all that could change. What if Cole did really move on one day? The thought had never occurred to Taylor. She realized, with a sudden pang, that Cole meant more to her than she'd originally thought.

Reaching for her phone, she immediately began tapping out a list of things to pack. Money, tank tops, shorts, food...

Jake whooped as Blaine executed a perfect railslide, skated a few feet over to the bowl, and dropped down in one fluid motion.

"Sick!" he exclaimed. "I should've brought my camera. We would have such awesome footage."

Blaine used his momentum to skate back up to ground level. He laughed and wiped the sweat off his brow. "Yeah, we definitely would."

"You look tired, man."

"Tired is an understatement."

They both laughed and took a seat on the bench to watch a new group of skaters enter the park. "It's a bummer the waves are flat," Jake sighed.

"Hey, look on the bright side—you got to skate with me."

"That's the bright side?"

Blaine rolled his eyes. "So what's your take on the surfing safari?"

"I asked my parents last night. They said I could go, but my mom was kinda reluctant. She doesn't want my kid brothers to burn down the house while I'm gone."

Blaine laughed. "Doesn't she stay at home to watch them?"

"Well, technically she works from home, so it's more like I'm the babysitter while she's in her office."

"Oh." The guys fell quiet as a couple girls, skateboards underneath their arms, walked past the park. "Hey, she's kind of cute," Blaine said.

"The blonde or the brunette?"

"Both, I guess."

"They're such fakes."

Blaine laughed again. "You don't even think they're mildly cute?"

"You can totally tell they're not skaters. Why are they carrying their boards when they can ride them? And who even skates in flip flops?"

"Dude, I'm asking about you their looks, not their skating ability."

Jake shrugged. "Doesn't matter."

"Because there's someone else on your mind?"

Jake turned to face his friend. "What are you getting at?"

"You didn't answer the question." Blaine smiled triumphantly.

After a pregnant silence, Jake's face fell. "Is it that obvious?"

"It's really obvious."

He sighed.

"So...ask her out," Blaine suggested.

"It's not that simple. Promise you won't tell anyone?"

"Of course I won't. But I can't stop my brother from teasing you about it," Blaine warned. "Cole's a loose cannon."

"I noticed," Jake said, rather dryly. "The real question is, do you think those girls are cute?"

Blaine grinned. "Let me put it this way—if I had to choose between a cute girl or the bowl in front of me, I'd choose the bowl." He jumped onto his skateboard and dropped into the in-ground pool, wasting no time in carving across the smooth surface.

"Hey, I would say I'm with you, bro, but then I'd be lying."

"That's okay," Blaine called out as he skated around the bowl. "I don't think Maya would want to hear you say that anyway."

The muffled giggles of Jake's younger brothers could be heard through his closed door, so he turned to face his window and strummed another chord on his guitar. He hummed to himself as he strummed the opening to Banana Pancakes. The words to the first verse soon came to mind, and Jake sang softly as he began to play.

Suddenly, from the opposite end of his bed, his phone screen lit up. Jake paused midway through the song and glanced at the screen. He smiled when he saw that it was a text from Maya. Setting down his guitar, he picked up his phone and dialed her number.

She answered on the second ring. "Hey Jake. Sorry if I'm bothering you."

"No, not at all. What's up?"

"What's your take on this surfing safari Alana has planned?"

"I think it's great! My parents said I can go."

"Sweet, me too. Are you excited?"

"Totally."

Maya laughed. Her voice sounded angelic to Jake's ears. "Do you have any plans tonight?" she asked.

"Nope. I just finished dinner, so..."

"Do you, uh, want to go for a walk?"

Jake paused. He could distinctly hear Maya's breathing on the other end of the line. The sound of his brothers fighting reached his ears, but he ignored them and said, "A walk sounds nice. Where do you want to go?"

"How about we head from your house to the Promenade?"

Jake grinned. "That sounds great."

He imagined Maya's infectious smile when she said, "Perfect! See you in a bit."

"See you." Jake felt his fingers tingling as he set down his phone. Instead of returning to his guitar, he slipped on a pair of shoes and pulled on a light jacket. He waited impatiently by the front door until Maya knocked ten minutes later.

"Is it chilly out?" he asked as he stepped outside.

"It's not too bad. The wind makes it a little cold." Maya smiled up at him as he closed the door. They headed in the direction of the beach, winding their way through Jake's neighborhood until they came within sight of the ocean. It looked completely different at night. They could barely make out its dark, shifting surface under the glare of flickering lights on Ventura Pier.

They reached the Promenade a few minutes later. People milled about the different shops and various stands set up in the square. "That food smells so good," Maya said when she got a whiff of a barbecue grill.

"Do you want something to eat?" Jake asked automatically.

"Nah, I'm good. I shouldn't eat anything at this hour anyway."

"Tell that to all the people waiting in line."

Maya laughed, once again sending a thrill down Jake's spine, where it settled in the pit of his stomach. He edged nearer to her. They had been close friends since elementary school, and Jake couldn't deny there were some sparks between them. He just wondered when the right moment would appear.

"The sun should be setting in a half hour or so," he said casually. "Why don't we head to the beach?"

"Sure." Maya slipped off her shoes when they reached the sand, and before long they were laughing and running to the water's edge. Jake rolled up his jeans and let the tide pool around his ankles. As they kept up their light conversation and slowly worked their way up the beach, Maya intertwined her hand in his, and Jake couldn't keep a smile off his face. The blazing sunset in front of them only added to the amazing evening.

The pair took a seat on the cool sand to watch the last rays of the sun disappear behind the horizon. Jake rested his hand on Maya's and felt another jolt of excitement rush through him when she leaned her head against his shoulder. He smiled and rested his chin on top of her brown hair.

"I really needed this," Maya confessed.

Surprised, Jake shifted just slightly to better hear her. "What do you mean?"

"My parents...it's been hard."

"Oh." Jake knew that her parents had divorced a number of years ago, but divorce was a foreign concept to him. His mom and dad would never separate.

"My mom has been calling him more often," she continued. "My dad, I mean."

"Is that bad?"

She sighed. "I don't know. But it just doesn't feel right to me. He left us, and it caused my mom to lose some of her faith. And now she's back in contact with him."

Jake mulled her words over in his mind. How could he comfort her? What was he supposed to say?

"I'm sorry, Maya," he finally replied. "Maybe bringing your parents back together again is God's way of bringing your mom back to him. His ways are higher than our ways. And while we don't always understand what's going on, we can trust that God does."

Maya nodded.

"I'll be praying for your family," Jake said. "If you need anything, let me know. My parents would love to have you and your mom over for dinner."

She smiled. "That would be cool."

Jake's heart was at peace. What could be better than sitting on the sand, watching the last rays of the sun spread their light over the water, next to the girl of his dreams?

"I'm glad you texted me," he said quietly.

"I'm glad you called," Maya replied.

They sat on the shore until the sun vanished completely and an inky blackness took over the sky. Neither one said a word, and Jake listened to Maya's deep, rhythmic breathing contentedly.

Finally, Maya said, "We should probably head back."

Jake nodded and stood up, brushing the sand off his pants. They didn't hold hands on the way back to his house, but Jake was sure Maya felt the same way he did.

"I'll walk you to your house," he said when Maya turned to go down his street.

"Are you sure?" She smiled at him when he nodded. "Thanks."

"It's only a short walk away. I don't mind. And plus, it's kind of dark out here." He laughed, hoping to relieve some of the tension that had suddenly come between them.

When they reached Maya's doorstep, she paused with one hand on the knob and turned to face Jake. "Thanks for tonight," she said quietly. "It was great."

"We'll have to do this more often," he joked.

A fleeting look crossed Maya's face, and for a second Jake thought she had taken him seriously. So he was surprised when she suddenly stood on her tiptoes and planted a quick peck on his cheek.

"'Night, Jake," she said before slipping inside.

Jake stared dumbly at her closed door. He reached up and lightly brushed his fingers against the spot where she had kissed him. Then a broad smile stretched across his face, and he whispered, "Goodnight."

Chapter 8

A lana lazily scrolled down the YouTube channel. Nothing of interest had caught her eye for the past ten minutes. She sighed and typed something else into the search box: surfing lower trestles. Immediately, a new batch of videos popped up on the screen.

Her eyes were starting to grow tired from staring at her computer for so long, but what else could she do? Dylan was at work, Tammy was at a friend's house, and the waves were flat. It was a warm summer day, and Alana was beginning to get stir-crazy from doing nothing all morning.

She sighed and glanced over at her digital clock. "Only 10:15?" she muttered. "Great."

She was running out of ideas to kill time. Her gaze landed on a YouTube video that looked promising, so she clicked on the link. The film showed a group of professional surfers carving up some perfect rights. Now that's my kind of video, Alana thought with a smile.

And it definitely didn't disappoint. Alana watched, transfixed, as the surfers carved wave after perfect wave. "Wow," she breathed. "I wish I was at Lowers right now..." The water was glassy, the waves were peeling, and the conditions were epic—what more could a surfer wish for?

Alana sighed wistfully as the video came to a close. Quietly shutting her laptop, she swung her legs over the side of her bed and walked over to the window. It was a nice summer day, and it would have been perfect except for one thing.

No waves.

She chewed on her bottom lip thoughtfully. Pulling out her phone, she checked to see if she had any new texts or calls, but there was nothing. It had been two days since the meeting at The Habit, and everyone was able to go except the twins. They still hadn't gotten back to Alana. She knew Blaine was eager to go on the surf trip, but as for Cole...she could only pray that Blaine would convince him to come.

The ocean shimmered in the bright sunlight, and Alana's attention was pulled to a few small waves breaking close to shore. It was nearing low tide, and hardly any waves were trickling in.

It was something, though. After a few seconds' deliberation, she replaced her tank top with a rashguard and slipped out of her jean shorts. She dashed into the garage and pulled out the biggest longboard she had—a wide, single-fin, ten-footer with a couple dings on the rails.

She knew it was crazy, but she just couldn't resist. Even though the waves were small, it was a beautiful day outside, and it would help get her mind off the surfing safari she'd been so frantically planning.

Alana tucked the longboard underneath her arm and strode out of the garage, making sure to close it behind her. As the warm sunrays hit her tan skin, she smiled and headed towards the water's edge. The only surfers in the water were two beginners on foamboards—not exactly a suitable lineup. But Alana wasn't there to be professional; she was there to relax. The ocean was her place of rejuvenation, only outmatched by her time with God.

Humming a tune, Alana jogged down a flight of steps and ran past two teenage boys throwing a football. Upon jumping in the water, she began paddling on her knees until she heard one of them give a shout.

Alana turned and realized they were talking to her. "Hey, what are you doing?" the taller of the two asked.

"Surfing, can't you tell?" she laughed.

"Surfing what?"

Alana glanced at the ocean. Good point, she thought. "I don't know. I'm just hanging out," she called over her shoulder.

The guy nodded. "Cool," he said, before catching his buddy's football and throwing it back in a perfect spiral.

With the conversation clearly over, Alana resumed paddling. The water felt refreshingly cool as she dug her hands in, letting it lap against the rails of her longboard. She waited until she paddled a bit farther out before flipping off her board and taking a dip.

When she resurfaced, Alana was surprised to see someone paddling towards her. She raised a hand to shield her eyes from the sun. When she realized it was the same guy who had talked to her earlier, she smiled in amusement.

"Hey," she greeted him. "Aren't you ditching your friend?"

"My cousin," he corrected her. "And nah, he won't mind." The guy smiled and reached out a hand. "I'm Trevor, by the way."

"Alana," she said, shaking his hand dutifully.

"Cool name."

"Thanks."

They sat in silence for a few moments, neither one moving until a small set appeared on the horizon. Though the approaching waves were only about knee-high—if even that—Trevor and Alana both paddled for one. They popped up to their feet at the same time, and that was when Alana knew Trevor could surf. Just by the way he carried himself in the water, she could tell he knew what he was doing.

As the wave began to crumble around them, yet not actually breaking, Alana started to play around with cross-stepping. She placed her right foot over her left and walked the nose, pausing only when it dipped dangerously close to purling.

"Nice," Trevor said, flashing her a grin. He bent his back knee and did a bottom turn before their boards could collide. Both of them pulled out of the wave at the same time.

"You're not too bad yourself," Alana replied. "Are you from around here?"

"San Clemente, actually."

"Oh, wow. Do you surf Trestles?"

"Dude," he laughed, "it's my home break."

"No way!" Alana exclaimed, ignoring the fact that he had just called her a dude. The gang had a habit of calling each other that anyway. "That's insane!"

Trevor chuckled as they paddled towards the horizon. "Yeah, it's pretty rad. I learned at San O, but I've surfed Trestles most of my life."

"You're so lucky. I've never surfed anything besides Ventura County."

"Really?" Trevor seemed surprised by the news. "You seem pretty good. Do you compete?"

"No. Well...only with my high school team," she confessed. "But normally I don't longboard."

"Ah, a shortboarder." Trevor grinned. "Same here."

"So what are you doing at C Street?"

"My dad's hanging out with his brother, who lives in Oxnard. They're winetasting." He made a face.

Alana laughed. "Oh, I see. So you and your cousin came to the beach instead."

"Exactly." Trevor swept his gaze over the water. "I was hoping the swell would be bigger, but I guess not. At least a few waves are coming in."

"You should have been here earlier this week. It was pretty good—not firing, but good enough to pull some airs."

"Really?" Trevor gaped at her. "You can do aerials?"

Alana nodded and smiled, a bit embarrassed. "Well...kind of."

"That's sick, man. You really need to come to Trestles, you would love it there."

"Actually, I might be going in a few weeks. My friends and I are taking a surf trip down the coast."

"Nice. What spots are you going to hit?"

"Anything that's breaking, I guess."

"I hear there's supposed to be a solid west-south-west swell hitting Malibu next week. You should check it out."

"Malibu? Yeah, I'm looking forward to surfing there, but I hear the crowds are insane."

Trevor shrugged. "You get crowds pretty much everywhere nowadays."

"True," she chuckled. "Especially in the summer."

Their conversation was suddenly interrupted by the arrival of another set. "Wanna catch this one together?" Trevor asked.

She laughed. "Sure, why not." They caught the first wave of the set with ease, popping up to their feet and cruising along the shoulder. Alana bent down and trailed her fingertips along the glassy surface, noticing that Trevor was copying her movements.

"Hey," he said suddenly, "you might want to move!"

"What?" Alana straightened up and realized she was heading right towards a mini-whirlpool a few yards away. As she drew closer, the wave caused the surrounding water to recede a few inches, revealing a small rock protruding above the surface of the water.

Uh oh. Her eyes widened in horror until Trevor's voice shattered her out of her thoughts. "Quick!" he called. "Jump on!"

Alana glanced over at his board. He had shuffled backwards a few feet to make room for her on the front of his longboard. "No way!" she exclaimed. "Both of us are going to wipeout!"

"Would you rather ding your board?"

Alana's gaze shifted over to the rock. Even more water was receding now, causing the rock to stick out dangerously high. "Uh..."

"Just jump, Alana!"

Well, here goes nothing, she thought, bending her knees and taking a leap of faith. She let out a short scream as she sailed through the air. Less than a second later, she found herself perched wobbly on the front of Trevor's surfboard.

"Hang on," he laughed, grabbing her waist to keep her from falling. "There, that wasn't so bad, right?"

"Right," Alana laughed, surprised that she hadn't lost her balance. She glanced over her shoulder and saw that her abandoned longboard had passed calmly over the wave. It rested only a few feet from the exposed rock, floating peacefully on the surface of the water. She let out a sigh of relief at her narrow escape.

"Hey Alana..."

"What?"

"Think fast."

Before she could react, he suddenly did a cannonball off his longboard. With his weight no longer holding the back of the board down, Alana proceeded to purl headfirst into the water. She tumbled underwater for a few feet before resurfacing, a scowl on her face. "Oh, so now we wipeout!" she exclaimed.

Trevor merely laughed from where he was treading water a few yards away. "Sorry, I just couldn't resist."

"Yeah, whatever." Alana grabbed his longboard and pulled herself on. Instead of paddling towards Trevor, though, she stroked right past him and made a beeline for her own surfboard.

"Hey! Forget something?"

"Nope!" Alana called triumphantly over her shoulder.

"Not fair," Trevor grumbled. "Come back!"

"If you want your board, you better swim after it," she teased.

He frowned before reluctantly doing freestyle towards her. "Okay, so I guess I deserved that," he said as soon as he reached Alana.

"I got water up my nose thanks to you."

"Well, that's never fun."

Alana rolled her eyes. "You know, you're not getting your board back until you apologize."

Trevor placed his elbows on his surfboard to keep himself afloat. "Okay. I'm sorry for saving your life and your surfboard."

"Not that part, dimwit—the part about where you made me purl."

Trevor chuckled at the memory. "Sorry about making you purl, Alana."

"That's better." She smiled and slid off his board willingly.

As soon as they were back on their own separate longboards, Trevor announced, "I'd like to make this up to you."

"Hey, I was just teasing about the whole apologizing thing," Alana said. "That wipeout was actually the most fun I've had today."

Trevor grinned. "Well, then consider this a gift—I'd like to properly introduce you to Trestles."

Alana's heartbeat suddenly accelerated. "Wait, are you serious?"

"Dead serious."

"Then of course!"

"It's pretty localized there, but I can totally get you guys in."

"Wow," she exclaimed. "I don't know what to say. Thank you, Trevor."

"No worries." He grinned.

Alana felt all her anxieties about the upcoming surfing safari drift away. Now Cole would have to come—they literally just got a free pass to Trestles! There was no way he could resist that.

Trevor and Alana spent another hour in the water. When they weren't surfing, they chatted casually in between sets. During those times, he gave her his phone number and had her repeat it a dozen times until he was sure she had memorized it. Only when his cousin waved him in from the beach did they both catch their final wave of the day. They cruised as far in as they could, but since it was low tide, they had to do the rock dance the rest of the way into shore.

They bade each other goodbye and promised to stay in touch. "I'll be calling you about that Trestles offer soon," Alana promised.

"Of course. See you around," Trevor replied, giving her one last smile before heading off with his cousin. Alana quietly rinsed off her longboard by herself, wishing she could spend some more time with Trevor. Even though they had only known each other for a day, he was fun to be around and easy to talk to. In a way, he reminded Alana of Koa—always smiling, always joking around, and always having fun. She missed him already.

Chapter 9

Cole was angry. He had been angry ever since Alana went and dropped the bomb about going on a surfing safari. The idea was tempting, of course—who wouldn't want to surf epic waves while cruising down the California coast?—and Cole was actually buying into the idea until the gang mentioned using his Volkswagen. And that's when it all went downhill.

Earlier that morning, Cole had stormed out of the kitchen after another heated disagreement with his father. Blaine, as usual, had been sucking up to Mr. Anderson about the "awesome" idea of going on Alana's surf trip. Mr. Anderson immediately agreed and said Cole should go as well, so Cole immediately disagreed and said he wasn't going anywhere.

His father had been annoyed, to say the least, and went into a long lecture about why Cole needed to stop thinking about himself and start looking for the needs of others. Mr. Anderson even pulled the church card: "I can't believe you've been going to church your whole life, because it certainly looks like you don't take any of it to heart!"

"Well," Cole had retorted, "maybe that's because I don't."

That's when Cole had stormed out of the kitchen and headed to the one place he knew would calm him down—the beach. He had been tossing rocks into the ocean when he spotted a familiar surfer girl jogging down the steps, a longboard tucked underneath her arm.

His breath caught in his throat. Alana...what was she doing, with hardly any waves in the water? He watched as she exchanged a few words with one of the guys on shore. With her effortless style, she then paddled out and caught the first wave that came her way.

Cole's fascination began bordering on apprehension when one of the guys followed her into the water and struck up a conversation. Cole watched intently as they chatted back and forth on their longboards, waiting for another set. Did Alana know him from somewhere? No; from their actions, it appeared that they had only recently met.

So when the two surfers caught a wave together and the guy placed his hands on Alana's waist, Cole was perplexed. What was he thinking? What was Alana thinking? That was no move to save Alana from wiping out. Cole would know.

Appalled by the stranger's audacity, Cole didn't know why his fingernails were hurting so badly until he glanced down and saw that he was still gripping a rock—and gripping it hard. He frowned and tossed the rock into the ocean before he could do something a little more harmful with it. He took one more glance at the two surfers bobbing up and down in the water before turning around and storming up the stairs. He needed to blow off some steam—and some thoughts that had recently assailed him regarding Alana.

As soon as Alana was dressed and the longboard was safely tucked away in the garage, she settled down at the dining room table to stuff her face with food. She had scarfed her way through a turkey sandwich and an apple before her ringtone suddenly went off. She whipped it out of her back pocket and checked the caller ID.

"Hello?" she asked, her heart pounding in her chest.

"Hey, it's Blaine."

She sucked in a deep breath. "So what's the verdict?"

"Cole still doesn't want to go for whatever reason," Blaine sighed, his exasperation evident even over the phone. "Personally, I think he's still upset over the whole Volkswagen thing."

"Oh."

"Tell me about it. But the good news is, Dad's taking my side. He wants Cole to go."

"Really?"

Blaine chuckled. "If there's one thing my Dad hates, it's Cole moping around the house. Believe me, if he gets a chance to send Cole away for a little bit, he'll take it."

Alana smiled broadly. "So you guys are going?"

"We'll pick you up bright and early Saturday morning," Blaine confirmed.

Alana bit her lip to keep back a squeal of excitement. "Great! I'm so glad you guys can come! Tell your dad he's, like, my favorite person right now."

"Will do," Blaine laughed. "So listen, I've gotta go run some last-minute errands for my dad, but I wanted to let you know this surfing safari sounds epic. I can't wait."

"Me neither." Alana was bursting with excitement.

"Well, I'll talk to you later."

"Bye." As soon as they hung up, Alana let out a sigh of relief. She couldn't wait to tell the rest of the gang the great news.

They were going on the surfer!

With a massive yawn, Cole stumbled downstairs, still in his boxers and still half-asleep. He blinked slowly and glanced around the kitchen before finally coming up with a coherent thought. He plugged in the coffee maker on the kitchen counter and groggily went through the motions of making breakfast.

"'Morning," Mr. Anderson greeted, suddenly coming around the corner.

Cole jumped. "Sheesh! You didn't have to scare me."

He merely smiled and reached over Cole's back to get some bacon out of the refrigerator. "Mind if I help?"

"Um, yes."

Mr. Anderson stared in disbelief. "So you're voluntarily making breakfast right now?"

"It's five in the freaking morning. I'm only making myself break-fast."

"Language," Mr. Anderson warned.

"I don't even know why my alarm went off so early anyway," Cole muttered.

His dad raised an eyebrow. "Surfing safari? A trip down the coast? Ring any bells?"

Cole didn't reply. His father watched him for a few moments, frowning at his son's sullen expression. "Alright, I'll leave you alone. I know you don't want your old man around to bother you. Blaine should be coming downstairs any minute."

Cole remained silent, pondering what to say next. Just as Mr. Anderson was about to head back upstairs, he suddenly asked, "Do I have to go?"

"Where? On the surf trip?" Mr. Anderson laughed. "Of course. I shouldn't even have to answer that question."

Cole set his jaw. "I hate it."

"Don't be like that. Surfing is your passion; you should make the most of this trip. It's a once-in-a-lifetime thing. You and Blaine are blessed to—"

"Blessed?" Cole interrupted, rolling his eyes. "If I don't want to go, then this isn't a blessing."

Mr. Anderson wasn't startled in the least by Cole's retort. If anything, he seemed to have been expecting it. "Well, then at least have a better attitude about it," he said before disappearing up the stairs.

Cole had the sudden urge to chuck the coffee maker out the window. He wasn't frustrated at his dad; he was frustrated at himself. The whole idea of going on a surf trip with his church-happy friends was a little disturbing. The thought of driving his precious Volkswagen was appalling.

But what bothered him the most was spending almost a month with the girl who had made him feel and do things he hadn't before. She was a threat—a very attractive threat. Cole knew the bottom line was he didn't trust himself going on the surfing safari. He didn't trust his self-control. He either had to get a grip within the next hour or put up a front for his friends.

"Are you sure you have everything you need?" Dylan asked for the umpteenth time that morning.

"Yes," Alana sighed. "I've triple-checked everything in my suitcase. Don't worry."

"And you have your boards?"

She nodded impatiently.

"Did you bring enough wax?"

"Dylan!"

"I just don't want you to forget anything," he said sheepishly, tousling Alana's hair in his brotherly way. Alana rolled her eyes and wriggled out of his grasp so he couldn't further mess up her hair.

"Bye, Alana," Tammy said quietly. Those were her first words she had spoken all morning, and Alana wrapped her in a large hug as she shyly stepped out from behind Dylan.

"Oh, don't look so sad," Alana told her. "I won't be gone for that long."

"But you'll be gone for two weeks." Tammy sighed dramatically. "Who will I surf with?"

"Maybe Dylan can come down to the beach and watch you," Alana suggested, raising her eyes and giving her older brother a look. Dylan ignored her.

"I'll miss you, Alana," Tammy said. Alana could tell she was doing her best not to cry, and it nearly broke Alana's heart seeing her like this. She had no idea Tammy was so attached to her.

"I'll miss you too," Alana said truthfully before pulling away from their embrace. She gave Tammy's little hand a comforting squeeze.

"Hey, don't I get a goodbye hug?" Dylan asked.

Alana stuck out her tongue. "No." When he faked a pout, she couldn't resist laughing at how silly he looked. "Okay, okay. I guess you can get a hug too."

Just before the siblings finished their awkward hug, Alana heard two loud honks from outside their apartment. She quickly rushed over to the window and grinned when she saw who it was.

"They're here!" she exclaimed. "Bye guys!" She threw open the front door and grabbed her belongings. The gang had decided everyone could bring one suitcase, a small backpack, and up to two surfboards. When Alana struggled to carry everything down to Cole's Volkswagen, Koa and Blaine hopped out to assist her.

"Need a hand?" Blaine asked.

Alana grunted in response, and the guys obediently took her two surfboards. They strapped them onto the roof of Cole's van before helping her get situated inside.

"Am I sitting in here?" Alana asked Koa.

He nodded. "Jake is riding with Maya in her van," he explained, jerking a thumb to where Maya was driving her family's camper. She gave Alana a smile and a wave.

"Cool," Alana said. "I should've known Maya and Jake would ride together."

Koa winked. "Of course," he said, causing the two of them to crack up at their secret knowledge.

Cole honked three more times. He glared at them through the window.

"Sheesh," Alana muttered. "We're right on time. It's only six in the morning and he's already this impatient?"

"He's been in a sour mood ever since he picked me up." Koa shrugged. "Hopefully once we hit the water his attitude will change."

"Yeah, let's hope so," Alana sighed. She turned around and gave her siblings one last wave before filing into Cole's van.

"Wait, Alana!" Dylan suddenly called. Alana paused as he jogged over. "Remember what our deal was?" he asked.

"Uh..."

"You need to text me every single night and call me at least every other day. Got it?"

"Yes, father."

"Don't sass me," he said firmly, but Alana could tell by the look in his eyes that he was excited for her. "Look, Alana, have fun on this trip. Enjoy yourself and the awesome waves. But stay out of trouble, alright?"

"I will," she promised.

"Oh, and one more thing." Dylan lowered his voice. "Tell Cole he better not honk anymore, or he's gonna wake up the whole apartment complex."

Alana chuckled. "He's just giving us attitude per usual."

Dylan grinned and tousled his sister's hair one last time before backing away. "See you soon!" he called.

"Bye!" Alana waved to her siblings before taking a seat inside Cole's van, anxious for the surfing safari to begin.

Koa plopped down next to her, and Blaine slid into the passenger seat. "Is everyone buckled in?" he asked.

"Yep. We're ready to go," Alana announced. "Let's get this party started!"

"Well, in that case, I think it's time for some music." Blaine grinned and cranked up the radio. He rolled down his window, allowing the chilly morning air to rush inside the van.

As Koa and Alana rocked out to a Switchfoot song in the backseat, Alana caught Cole's steely gaze through the rearview mirror. Her smile immediately drooped when she saw how angry he looked. What's his problem now? she wondered, a little ticked off that he was acting so pessimistic.

"What's wrong?" Koa asked, noticing Alana had stopped dancing to the radio.

"Oh, nothing," Alana said quickly, but Koa wasn't buying it. He followed her gaze and saw Cole's narrowed eyes through the rearview mirror.

"Like I said, he's been this way ever since he picked me up," he muttered.

"Do you think he's upset because of this trip?" Alana was certain that Cole would liven up as soon as the surfari began, but she wondered if he would act like a jerk the entire trip. It would totally ruin it for the rest of the gang.

"Alana, I have no idea what Cole's problem is," Koa said with a dry laugh. "But let's not have it get in the way of our fun."

"Right. I'm with you there," Alana said, forcing herself to smile even though she was still bitterly disappointed. She had spent hours researching the best surf spots, swells, winds, and tides, and now Cole was going to ruin it. He had better shape up for the rest of the trip.

Suddenly, Alana felt her phone vibrate in her back pocket. She whipped it out and realized Maya was calling. "Blaine!" Alana hollered. "Turn it down!" As soon as the radio was back to a quieter volume, she held the phone up to her ear.

"Hey, we're heading to County Line first, right?" Maya asked excitedly.

"Of course."

"Then tell Cole to get his butt off the freeway!"

"Whoa, why?"

"We need to pull onto Rice Avenue in a few minutes. That'll take us to Pacific Coast Highway."

"Oh, got it." Alana quickly told Cole the directions, and a couple miles later he coasted onto the off-ramp.

Maya laughed. "That was a close one," she told Jake, who was dancing to a pop song on the radio. "We almost missed the turnoff for County Line."

"Then why aren't you leading the way?" he asked.

"I don't know. Cole is in one of his moods. I'm not going to push the issue."

A few moments later, Cole turned onto PCH. Maya followed, being careful to make her lane change slowly in the campervan. Before she knew it, they were sailing along the coast with County Line Beach only a few miles away.

Maya pulled into the beach parking lot after Cole, and the two found parking spots right next to each other. Her mixed feelings were quickly replaced by excitement as soon as she set foot on the asphalt. She hadn't been to County Line in over a year, but this beach held many memories. This was the exact spot where she had caught her first wave. This was the beach she had grown up surfing at until her family moved closer to C Street. Now, sweeping her gaze from the shoreline to the landscape behind her, she saw a few points of light rising above the distant hills. Though it was overcast, the sun was already rising, bathing the world in its bright morning glow. Maya couldn't wait to hit the water.

"Here we are," Blaine announced as he slid out of the van and stretched his limbs. Koa and Alana filed out of the backseat, eager to have arrived at their first surf spot.

Alana's eyes lit up as soon as she saw some waves crashing on the shore. "It looks small, but at least it's something," she said. "Let's go!"

As the guys started to unload the surfboards, Alana rushed down to the water's edge, making sure to pick her way along the rock-littered shore. Maya ditched the boys as well and jogged over to her friend. "Hey," she said excitedly. She grinned and buried her hands in her sweatshirt pocket. "Are you excited?"

"Well, I guess you could say that's an understatement," Alana chuckled. "This is surreal."

"I know." They let out a deep sigh at the same exact moment, their breaths coming out as white puffs in the chilly morning air. After the last wave of the set crashed on shore, they headed back to the gang and began pulling on their wetsuits. After shoving their surfboards underneath their arms, they jogged to the beach, itching to catch some waves.

"Ready?" Alana asked.

"As ready as I'll ever be!" Maya grinned and dashed into the water with Alana right on her heels. It was time to shred their first surf spot.

Chapter 10

C ole trudged out of the water at County Line Beach with his shortboard tucked under one arm. He paused at the water's edge and shook some droplets from his hair before jogging across the sand to the parking lot. Blaine and Jake were seated in lawn chairs next to the campervan, lazily tossing a football back and forth.

"'Sup," Blaine greeted his twin. "All surfed out?"

"Nah. Just tired, I guess." Cole leaned his board up against the side of Maya's camper. After taking off his wetsuit, he plopped down in a lawn chair next to Blaine.

Blaine tossed the football to Jake and said, "Hey, I think your girlfriend's coming in."

"Dude, she's not my girlfriend," Jake countered. "I don't know why you guys keep saying that."

"Because it's obvious," Blaine chuckled. "You two are bound to get together sooner or later, trust me."

"You're wrong," Jake said, but his flushed cheeks gave him away. "There's nothing going on between Maya and I."

Though Blaine didn't press the issue, he smiled slyly. Jake rolled his eyes and stood up, heading to the shoreline where Maya, Koa, and Alana were getting out of the water.

"And then there were two." Blaine gave his brother a light shove. "So what's up with you?"

"What do you mean?"

"Come on, don't play this game with me."

Cole narrowed his eyes. At times, Blaine could be just as persistent as Cole—only in a less threatening way, of course. He sighed—another wave crashed on the shore—and the smooth roar of the tide could have lulled Cole to sleep, if he didn't feel so on edge.

"You're making this way harder than it should be," Blaine said. "I don't know why you hate this surf trip, but you need to relax and let loose. Have fun. So maybe County Line doesn't have the best waves, but—"

"It's not about County Line," Cole muttered irritably, and immediately wished he had kept his mouth shut.

Blaine's smile grew wider. "I knew it!"

"Just leave me alone. I don't want to hear this crap."

Before Cole could stand up and leave, his twin quickly grabbed his arm. "Cole, I'm sorry—but this isn't just 'crap.' You of all people should know that."

Cole gave him an annoyed look. "I don't know what you're talking about."

"Sure you do. We're talking about Alana, aren't we?"

It took all of Cole's self-control not to lunge at him. "I don't know what you mean," he repeated.

"But it's true, isn't it?" Blaine was grinning from ear to ear now. "You like her. It's totally obvious."

"It is?" Cole asked weakly, sinking lower in his seat. Suddenly realizing what he had just confessed, he hastily added, "Not that I like her or anything."

Blaine raised an eyebrow.

"Look, can we just drop it?"

Blaine opened his mouth, about to say something, but quickly closed it. His gaze bored into his brother's for a few seconds before he finally said, "Okay."

"Thank you," Cole muttered.

Their conversation fell into an awkward silence as soon as the rest of the gang came within hearing distance. Jake and Koa were laughing about some wipeout they had just seen, while the girls were busy setting down their boards and taking off their wetsuits.

Cole sighed. He wasn't ready to burst headlong into another conversation—especially if it risked bordering on Alana—and he craved some alone time. Before the gang came any closer, Cole stood up and started walking. He didn't know where he was going until he glanced down and realized he'd been tramping through the sand for some time. Here, at a more secluded part of the beach, he could finally be by himself.

He stared at the ocean until his eyes started to burn from the intense light. It was one in the afternoon, the hottest part of the day, and the glinting whitecaps on the surface of the water were like missiles. Cole turned away and picked up a rock from the smooth sand. After weighing it in his hand, he brought his arm behind his head and chucked it as far as he could. It landed in the ocean with a satisfying splash.

"When did things get so complicated?" he muttered, taking a seat on the sand. He rested his elbows on his knees and gazed at the crowded lineup of surfers. He couldn't remember a time when he had felt so confused. Life had been so simple before—surf, go to school, airbrush boards, repeat. Cole's reputation meant everything to him. He always felt a twinge of pride when girls flirted with him and guys were jealous over him. He loved to party and mess around. That was what high school was for, right?

But that didn't account for why he always got a strange feeling whenever he laid eyes on Alana. If Blaine was right, and this "thing" Cole had for her was obvious, then he really needed to get ahold of himself. He was Cole Anderson. He didn't fall for girls; they fell for him. He couldn't let something as stupid as a crush ruin his entire rep.

Cole sighed and threw another rock into the ocean. As soon as it hit the water, he pushed off the sand and headed back to the parking lot. Though he wasn't in the mood to hang out with the gang, he wanted to get back before Blaine decided to spill some of his secrets.

Before he reached the camper, a bright flash of color suddenly caught his attention. He turned just in time to see a sports car zip out of the parking lot. But his thoughts were quickly diverted as soon as he came within sight of the gang. They were all seated in lawn chairs, singing along to Jake as he played his guitar.

"Here I am," he sang, "just waitin' on this storm to pass me by."

Everyone immediately joined in on the chorus: "And that's the sound of sunshine coming down!"

Jake was strumming so fast that his fingers were a blur. "You're the one I want to be with when the sun goes down. You're the one I want to be with when the sun goes down."

"And that's the sound of sunshine coming down!" Koa's off-key singing rang above everyone else's, causing Cole to crack a smile. Jake strummed a few more chords for the grand finale before taking a bow. Everyone applauded, laughing.

"You're just in time, Cole," Alana said, noticing the more moody of the Anderson twins standing on the outskirts of their little circle. "We're listening to Jake give his first concert."

"I haven't gotten any tomatoes thrown at me yet," Jake joked.

"Well, don't count on it." Cole smirked. "At least your playing doesn't sound too horrible."

"Jake, do another one," Maya piped up.

"Sure thing." Jake smiled and began playing, softly at first until the chorus picked up. The crashing of waves was a soothing background to the music.

Once the song was over, Jake placed his guitar in his lap and looked at Koa. "I think we should pray, don't you?" he asked.

Koa nodded. "Good idea."

Cole was surprised at his friends' actions. When they all bowed their heads, his was the only one who remained upright, glancing around their circle.

"God," Koa prayed, "we come before you this afternoon, excited that we get to go on this surfing safari and grateful that we get to have so much fun this summer. We pray that you will bless this trip and keep everyone safe, and we ask that no matter what happens, you will remind us that it's all for your glory. In Jesus' name, amen."

"Amen," everyone murmured.

"So what's the plan, guys?" Blaine asked, glancing around the circle. Everyone automatically looked at Alana.

"Well..." She seemed to be at a loss for words. "It's really up to all of us. We can stay at County Line as long as we want, or we can head down the coast and find another surf spot."

"I heard there's a swell coming soon," Jake said. "We should try and surf Malibu when it hits."

"Good idea." Alana nodded. "Why don't we check out Zuma Beach on the way to Malibu? On the right swell it can get pretty big and wild."

"Alright," Jake agreed. "So we'll surf Zuma tomorrow and Malibu the following day?"

Alana glanced at the rest of the gang. "How does that sound?"

Everyone—with the exception of Cole—murmured his or her assent. Alana grinned and gave Maya a high-five. "Sweet! Zuma Beach it is, then."

The sun was just beginning to rise by the time the gang arrived at Zuma the next morning. Its first rays were sweeping over the dunes of sand, making it appear as though each grain was glistening like a gemstone. Cole pulled into the parking lot with Maya right on his tail. Only a handful of other cars were there, which was surprising because the waves were a decent size.

Cole was eager to get a closer look at the water, so as soon as he turned off the engine he grabbed his sweatshirt and headed to the shoreline. The sound of crashing waves greeted him as soon as he set foot outside his van. He pulled his sweatshirt over his head and strolled across to the sand, which felt icy cold beneath his feet. He shivered and quickened his pace.

"How do the waves look?" Blaine called.

Cole didn't reply right away. Instead, he watched quietly for the next set to appear on the horizon. As soon as the first few waves broke, he turned around and said, "It looks pretty good. It's dumping, but there's still a few workable shoulders."

Blaine gave his brother a thumbs-up before heading back inside the van. He reappeared a few seconds later, his wetsuit in one hand.

Cole made the quick trek back to the parking lot and followed his friends' leads. Though they were all tired, sore, and freezing cold, they pulled their wetsuits on in expectant silence. They were eager to surf, and they would battle fatigue and freezing temperatures just to catch one sick wave.

As soon as Cole was dressed and ready to go, with a fresh coat of wax on his shortboard, he strapped his leash around his right ankle and sprinted to the water's edge. He leaped over the first whitewater wave and landed belly-first on his board. The water was chilly at first, especially since there wasn't enough sun to have properly warmed it yet, so he launched into a brisk paddle to get his blood flowing.

Four duck dives and two minutes later, he reached the lineup and sat back on his surfboard. Already the sun was significantly higher, and he watched, transfixed, as its bright rays illuminated Alana's hair from a white-blonde to a majestic gold.

But the moment was short-lived. As soon as Blaine, Koa, and the rest of the gang reached the lineup, Cole's admiration faded. He forced himself to look away from Alana before anyone noticed. He really needed to get his head out of the clouds.

"Is something the matter?" Alana asked, paddling up next to him.

Yeah—you are. Cole shook his head and folded his arms over his chest. "Nope."

She gave him a knowing smile. "Come on. The Cole I know would have given me a sarcastic reply."

He laughed in spite of himself. "Okay, you got me. I'm feeling a little under the weather, I guess."

"Oh." Alana frowned. "Are you getting sick?"

Physically? No. Emotionally...? "Maybe," he replied.

"That's a bummer. Maybe you shouldn't be surfing in this cold water, then."

Cole glanced up and saw a set was fast approaching. "Nah, I'm good. I'd rather surf and face the consequences than not surf at all."

Alana grinned. "There's the Cole I know."

He quickly paddled into position for the first wave, noticing that Alana watched him from the shoulder. He felt her eyes on his back as he stroked into the peak, popped up to his feet, and raced down the line. For some reason, knowing that she was watching his every move planted a desire within him—a desire to show her what he could really do.

As the section in front of him stacked up, Cole dug his right hand into the water and made a long, drawn-out bottom turn. He bent his knees and rotated his upper body as he neared the lip, barely skimming the top as he made a quick cutback. Then he raced back down to the trough of the wave and set up for an even bigger maneuver.

Cole could feel the wave's energy surging behind him as the whitewater frothed at his heels. Eyeing the section in front of him, he threw his arms forward to gain speed. Just as the lip began to curl over, he turned his body up so he was flying vertically up the face of the wave. Two-thirds of his shortboard went completely over the lip before he twisted his hips and snapped it back down.

The rush from his off-the-lip was exhilarating. The section in front of him was about to collapse, leaving him nothing more to work with, so he bent his knees and ducked under the lip just for fun. He was encased in a roaring barrel for a few seconds until the wave closed out, forcing him to jump off.

Once the whitewater rolled past, Cole pulled himself back onto his board, grinning from ear to ear. Though his wave hadn't been outstanding, his performance had been pretty darn good. He glanced up and saw Alana bobbing up and down in the lineup, her gaze fixed on him. He sucked in a deep breath, every fiber of his being tingling when he realized she had been watching him this whole time.

But the feeling quickly dissipated as soon as Maya paddled over to her and launched into a conversation. The action both angered and relieved him. On the one hand, he wanted to grow closer to Alana. There was this charm about her that constantly drew him in. But on the other hand, he knew that the more space he put between them, the better chance there was that his attraction would blow over.

Chapter 11

Waves crashed all around her. The sky was a dark, ominous gray. Threatening storm clouds billowed over the churning sea. Wave after wave rose up, only to slam back down in a spray of foam. Alana felt herself sinking lower and lower until she was completely swallowed by the ocean. Now the waves were no longer crashing, but spinning her underwater.

She swam furiously, not knowing which way was up and which way was down. The hazy underwater world was plunged into near-darkness. Only when her hand reached the surface did she come up spluttering, thankful to be alive. As the waves slowly receded and the storm clouds rolled back, she pulled herself onto her surfboard and rested.

In just mere minutes, calm waters replaced the churning ocean. The sun lit up the sky in a rainbow of colors, chasing away the dark storm clouds. Alana reached out and trailed her hand across the glassy water, her fingertips just barely skimming the surface. She leaned forward in amazement, causing her white-blonde locks to come tumbling over her shoulders.

She heard a splash of water and glanced up. The sun was so blinding that she could barely make out a silhouette moving towards her. Then the nose of a surfboard suddenly bumped against her leg, and she heard a low voice say her name.

"Alana."

Alana bolted out of her dream. Her heart beat erratically through the thin material of her tank top. She waited until her ragged breathing slowed to normal before lying back down, pulling the top of her sleeping bag over herself as she did so.

The churning feeling in the pit of her stomach should have told her it was a nightmare, but the sensation that had come along with it said otherwise. It had been a dream—an unusual but oddly pleasant dream.

As her eyes gradually became adjusted to the early-morning glow around her, she remembered that she was on the floor of Maya's campervan. Maya was sleeping soundly next to Alana, a lock of her brown hair draped over her eyes. Jake was positioned on the couch with Koa at his feet. On the opposite side of the camper were the Anderson twins, both of them sleeping on their stomachs.

Alana quietly propped herself up on one elbow. Reaching up with one hand, she pulled aside part of the curtain covering the window, allowing a half-inch of light to come streaming through. Judging by the soft pink glow of the sunrise, she knew it to be about six o'clock in the morning.

"Hmm." She let out a sigh when she realized she wasn't going back to sleep anytime soon. She fished through her sleeping bag until she found her well-worn Bible, the cover faded and the corners bent upwards from years of turning its pages.

Alana rolled over so she was lying on her stomach. Placing the Bible on top of her pillow, she opened up to the Psalms, where she had been reading for the past few weeks. She had made it her habit to read at least one Psalm a day, whether she found time in the morning before a surf session or at night before going to bed.

Her eyes skimmed over the verses. She was currently on Psalm 76: "The waters saw you, God..."

An image from her dream immediately popped up in her head. A tremor ran down her spine as she remembered the crashing waves, the feeling of helplessness, of danger—and then rising above the surface, only to hear someone say her name.

Alana frowned. Who is the mysterious person in my dream?

Maya suddenly shifted in her sleeping bag, causing Alana's gaze to flicker from her Bible to her friend. She rolled her lips into her mouth and thought carefully. Was it possible her dream held a deeper meaning? Usually dreams were just the product of one's subconscious, but Alana wondered if this dream, with all its clarity and reality, could be something more. It might even be a message God was trying to get through to her. The Magi, after visiting Jesus, had been warned in a dream not to return to King Herod. Joseph was given a vision that came to pass in the future when he became Pharaoh's right-hand man. God had spoken through dreams in the past, and Alana knew he could do the same now.

But what were the odds that he was, indeed, speaking to Alana? She shook her head and turned her attention back to the well-worn Bible.

"Mm...Alana?"

She glanced up and saw Maya watching her with sleepy eyes. Her hair was sticking up all over the place, and Alana fought the urge to laugh. "'Morning," she whispered, trying not to wake anyone else up.

"'Morning." Maya gave a yawn and stretched her limbs. "What time is it?"

Alana checked her phone. "Six fifteen."

Maya's eyebrows shot up eagerly. "How do the waves look?"

"Lemme check." Alana sat up and peered out the window once more, this time craning her neck so she could see the ocean. Though she couldn't make out if there was a lineup or not, she could see the unmistakable lines of whitewater rolling in. "There's definitely some swells," she said.

Maya yawned again before pushing herself up with one elbow. "Wanna head out?"

"Sure." Alana closed her Bible and carefully slipped it back inside her sleeping bag. She and Maya quietly stepped over their dozing friends and snuck out of the camper. Their eyes blinked rapidly in the ever-brightening light as they headed over to Cole's Volkswagen, where their suitcases and boards were stashed. They changed inside the surf van and were soon ready to go.

Maya grinned as she tucked her shortboard underneath her arm. "Malibu, here we come!"

The gang had pulled into Malibu late last night. The swell had been building all day yesterday while they were at Zuma. Alana smiled when she saw a decent-sized crowd already out in the water—but it wasn't the crowd that got her excited. It was the waves.

Maya and Alana kept their eyes glued to the horizon as they jogged across the damp sand. Wave after peeling wave broke around the point. The glassy, green-blue rights were like something out of a movie. They couldn't believe how blessed they were to be able to surf these waves.

Alana strapped on her leash as soon as she reached the shoreline. Then she dashed into the surf, following Maya's lead, paddling straight towards the lineup.

"Dang," Maya whistled as an outside set came into view. "Do you think we should have woken up the rest of the gang?"

"Nah. They'll be getting up soon." Alana watched in awe as the first wave of the set began to break. The lip curled over in a spray of glittering foam. A lucky surfer dropped into the peak and raced down the line.

"Wow," she breathed. Her pulse quickened as she saw yet another perfect wave start to break. It was like there was an invisible wave machine churning out endless rights.

Maya and Alana positioned themselves slightly outside of the lineup, not wanting to get stuck in the middle of the crowd. As soon as the sets began to shift a little, Maya paddled into the first wave that came her way. Alana watched as her head disappeared behind a cloud of whitewater.

The next wave was hers. Alana grinned as she stroked into the glassy peak and popped up to her feet. Just as the lip began to curl over, she drove down to the trough and angled back up. She pulled a huge snap off the lip, followed by another bottom turn and a long cutback. It seemed like the blue-green wave would go on forever. Her leg muscles were beginning to ache from turn after intense turn. Twenty seconds later, when the wave finally showed signs of closing out, she grabbed the rail of her board and pulled a carving 360 through the foaming whitewash.

"How was your ride?" Maya asked when they had paddled back out to the lineup.

"Sick," Alana exclaimed, her whole body pulsing with adrenaline. "How was yours?"

"Flawless. Absolutely flawless." Maya shook her head and grinned. "This almost seems too good to be true!"

"I know. I wish I could stay and surf all day, but my stomach's starting to grumble." Alana laughed as her stomach growled hungrily.

"Same, girl." Maya chuckled and glanced over her shoulder. "Hey, I think the rest of the gang is coming out."

"Really?" Alana turned and shaded her eyes from the sun with one hand. She spotted four tiny figures filing out of the camper. Though she couldn't make out their faces, she could tell it was her friends. "Great! They'll love these waves."

"Who wouldn't?" Maya flashed her a smile before breaking into action. She scratched into a medium-sized wave that had popped up nearby.

Moments later, Alana caught her own wave—but this time, she mistimed the end section and fell into the foaming whitewash. She resurfaced, climbed back onto her board, and paddled back out to the lineup. Jake and Maya were only a few yards away, the former's hair still dry and fresh. "Hey!" he called.

"Hey yourself," Alana replied. "It's about time you guys woke up."

"Well, maybe if someone had woken us up instead of sneaking out with Maya, we would have paddled out with you."

"Sorry. Maya and I just couldn't resist."

Jake laughed. "Well, I forgive you. At least the waves are awesome, right?"

"Better than awesome! It's like a manmade wave pool or something. I still can't get over it. The only downside is the crowd."

Jake shrugged and stroked past her. "It seems like there's always crowds no matter where you go."

"Yeah, I guess you're right."

"Hey ladies." Cole caught them by surprise as he suddenly paddled up from behind them. "Don't mind me, I'm just getting ready to snake your waves out from underneath you."

Jake snorted, put off by the 'ladies' comment. Alana rolled her eyes, but inwardly she was pleased. She remembered her little chat with Cole the other day, and how he had seemed down in the dumps about something. He'd said he was feeling under the weather, but that couldn't be the truth. Something was definitely up with him. At least he had taken a turn for the better this morning.

"Hey, Alana, whatcha waiting for?" Maya's shrill voice snapped Alana out of her thoughts, and she quickly glanced up to see that Maya, Jake, and Cole were already a few yards ahead of her. Her eyes connected with Cole's for a brief second before he suddenly glanced away.

Alana felt a little put off. What was that all about? She sighed and began paddling after her friends. Was Cole sinking back into his foul mood again?

She looked up, suddenly feeling a warmth spreading over her bare face and hands. She realized two clouds were parting overhead to let the sun through. She let out a deep breath and smiled. Who was she to worry about Cole? She was here to surf and have fun—that was the whole point of this trip. And here were perfect, peeling rights for her to carve all day long! There was no reason for her to be down just because Cole was moody. She had some waves to catch.

With this new mentality firmly fixed in her mind, Alana set out at a faster rate for the lineup. There was no worrying about Cole or wondering about her dream. It was just herself, the gang, and the epic Malibu waves.

The sun was just starting to dip below the horizon when Alana trudged out of the water. Every bone in her body was sore from two straight days of surfing. Though the waves had been perfect, nearly twenty hours in direct sunlight and saltwater had taken its toll. Her throat was parched and her arms could barely hold up her shortboard. Despite her fatigue, the twinkle in her eyes showed that she was still raring to paddle back out. The only thing holding her back from surfing was her exhaustion.

Alana set her shortboard down and collapsed into a folding chair next to Maya. She groaned as she leaned her head back and closed her eyes.

"Rough day, huh?" Maya joked.

"Yeah. Surfing epic waves for two days is hard work."

"I hear ya." Maya chuckled and unscrewed a bottle of water. She guzzled nearly half of it before handing it over to her friend. "Here. Drink some of this."

Alana reluctantly opened her eyes and took a swig. As soon as the cool water hit her parched throat, she guzzled more. "Thanks," she said as soon as she had finished off the bottle. "I didn't realize I was so dehydrated."

"Well, what's the plan now? Are we spending another day in Malibu?"

"I dunno." Alana squinted into the hazy sunlight and watched the waves still rolling through. "I could surf for hours if my body would let me."

"Same here. I really don't want to leave Malibu, but none of us can even hold up our heads without feeling exhausted. I think we need a break."

Alana watched as a surfer pulled a huge floater over a section, the whitewater thundering around him like a whirlpool. She reluctantly tore her gaze away from the ocean. "Yeah," she sighed. "You're right."

As the rest of the gang shuffle into view, it was clear that everyone was fatigued. Even Jake, who usually had more energy than the rest of the gang, stripped off his wetsuit and announced that he was going to hit the sack.

Sleeping sounded like an excellent idea to Alana, whose mouth involuntarily opened in a large yawn. Just then, Maya tugged impatiently on her arm. She held up her iPhone for Alana to see. "Take a look at this," she urged. "It's called Paradise Cove. It's a nice little beach with a pier and some shops just a couple minutes up the road."

"What?" Alana leaned forward and peered at Maya's phone. There was a picture of a rustic-looking house called Paradise Cove Beach Café. Her stomach growled at the thought of eating a nice home-cooked meal instead of the sloppy PB&J sandwiches the gang had been sharing for the last few days.

"I think we should check it out. It would be a nice break for all of us," Maya suggested. "Plus, it's only a few minutes of backtracking up the coast."

"Sure. We can talk it over in the morning." Alana gave her a tired smile as she stood up and stretched her limbs. "Right now, though, I'm gonna change into some warm clothes and curl up in my sleeping bag."

Maya turned off her phone and copied her friend's movements. She let out an ear-splitting yawn. "Sounds good to me. See you in the morning, chica."

Chapter 12

After everyone in the gang got a long, much-needed night of sleep, they ate a quick breakfast of bagels and fruit while deciding their next plan of action. Since no one was feeling quite up to surfing after being in the water all day yesterday, they agreed to go with Maya's plan and check out Paradise Cove. The promise of eating lunch at the seaside Beach Café was appealing, so by eleven o'clock everyone was packed and ready to go.

They arrived at Paradise Cove in less than five minutes. Since the sun was shining and a few small waves were lapping the shore, the beach was already thrumming with activity. Tourists were spread out on towels and walking the pier. Kids splashed in the water and collected seashells near the shoreline. It was a picturesque setting of the perfect beach day.

"Alright!" Jake exclaimed as soon as they pulled into the parking lot. "Food, here we come!"

However, by the time they reached the Paradise Cove Beach Café, they were bummed to see a long line streaming out the door. It seemed like the Beach Café was the spot to grab a bite to eat, and nearly everyone within a quarter-mile radius was eager to get lunch.

"Dang it," Blaine muttered as the gang hesitantly got into line. "I guess we have to wait." He flagged down a waiter that was rounding the corner and asked him how the line was going to take.

"About half an hour, maybe twenty minutes," the waiter said, smiling apologetically.

Blaine frowned. "Great. What should we do now?"

"Well, I don't know about you guys, but I don't really feel like eating another PB&J sandwich," Alana said, making a face. "Let's just wait it out. It'll be worth it." She glanced around the group. Everyone nodded his or her head in agreement.

"How about this?" Maya suggested. "Let's do rock-paper-scissors to see who gets to stand in line and who doesn't."

The looks of confusion crossing their faces prompted Maya to continue. "Look, what if only one of us waited in line while the others took a walk on the beach? It would help pass the time. Every ten minutes someone else can trade places with the person waiting in line. It would go much faster."

"Sure. I'm up for it." Alana held out her hands, ready to battle Maya in a game of rock-paper-scissors. She ended up beating her two out of three times, securing Alana's freedom. By the time everyone had battled it out, Cole was left as the unhappy person forced to hold the gang's spot in line.

"This is stupid," he muttered, crossing his arms over his chest. "Why do I have to be the one who stands in line?"

"Because you lost," Maya deadpanned. "Don't worry, I'll switch out with you in ten minutes."

"You better." Cole glared at her.

Blaine rolled his eyes at his brother's behavior. "Look, guys, I'll just wait in line with Cole to keep him company. The rest of you can go do whatever you want."

"Are you sure?" Alana asked.

Blaine nodded and motioned for them to leave. "Go, on get out of here. We'll see you in ten minutes."

Alana smiled and mouthed a thank-you. Before she could link her arm through Maya's, Koa suddenly came in between them with a mischievous smile. "Come on," he said. "Follow me."

"Where are we going?" Alana asked.

"Oh, you'll see."

When Alana glanced over Koa's shoulder, she saw that Maya and Jake were strolling away from the twins hand-in-hand. She suddenly realized why Koa had wanted to get away from them.

"Oh," she laughed. "I see. You're just giving the two lovebirds some space."

"Exactly." He winked.

Alana turned towards the pier and burst into a quick jog. "Come on!" she called over her shoulder. As they zigzagged their way through the crowd, Alana's flip-flops suddenly went from smacking on the pavement to thumping on the hollow wooden slats of the pier.

"Where are you going?" Koa wheezed.

"Over here," she said in between breaths. She finally slowed, took a look at her surroundings, and found an empty seat on a nearby bench. Koa plopped down next to her, and they watched the tourists flocking around the beach for a few minutes as the gentle sea breeze cooled them down.

As Alana and Koa walked away, Maya and Jake immediately gravitated towards each other.

"Well...I guess this means you're stuck with me," Maya said, causing Jake's heart to do a little flip.

"Oh, what a bummer," he replied. She laughed.

As they melted into the crowd, drifting away from the Anderson twins, Jake felt Maya reach out and grab his hand so that they wouldn't be separated. His heart pounded in his chest as they made their way towards Paradise Pier. He thought back to their sunset walk on the Promenade and to Maya's kiss on his cheek. They liked each other; that much was sure. Jake only wondered if Maya was ready to make it official.

Once they emerged from amongst the crowd, the pair threaded their way down to the sand and paused underneath the pier. The wide strip of shade provided by the structure was like a slice of heaven, and they eagerly kicked off their flip-flops to enjoy the cool sand. The sound of the swishing tide seemed magnified underneath the pier as it lapped against the sturdy pilings.

Maya released Jake's hand, but simultaneously gave him a smile, as if to make up for the lost contact. She stepped towards the water. "Let's see how cold it is."

Jake gratefully stepped into the ocean, allowing the tide to pool around his ankles. After marveling at the tiny shells and clinging mussels around them, Jake instinctively pulled Maya closer, his heart thudding. "Can I ask you something?" he said tentatively.

"Of course."

"What do you think? About us, I mean?"

Maya bit her bottom lip, trying to keep her smile from growing larger. "I think you're straight and to the point."

He rolled his eyes.

"Okay, okay...I think I like you."

"You think, or you know?"

"I know I like you."

The words were spoken with such sincerity and not the slightest bit of hesitation. Jake beamed. "Then I like you too."

Maya cocked her head to one side. "So...?"

"So what?"

"So obviously there's something else you want to say. What is it?"

Jake sucked in a breath. It was now or never. "Do you think we should give us a try? You know, as a couple?"

Maya turned and gazed at the ocean. "Is that what you want?"

"Only if that's what you want."

She pursed her lips. To Jake's anxious heart, her silence was unnerving. A few swells pitched over and broke against the pilings of the pier, causing her to suddenly jerk back to the present.

"What?" Jake breathed, leaning forward to hear her better.

"Yes," she repeated, quietly.

Jake closed his eyes—his heart was full.

"But I'm not sure what we do now," Maya admitted, turning to face him.

"We don't have to do anything," he replied, taking her hands. "We just take it day by day."

She nodded and smiled. Then, moving forward, she nestled her head in the crook of his shoulder and breathed deeply. "Is this what people call 'defining the relationship'?" she mused.

Jake laughed. "I guess so."

Satisfied, Maya pulled out her phone and checked the time. "I think we should get back before Cole becomes even more impatient waiting in line," she suggested.

"Oh, you're right." Jake's face fell at having their moment interrupted, but he quickly masked it with a smile. "Look, I'm glad we're giving this couple thing a try."

"Me too, Jake."

The Anderson twins stood in an awkward silence as they waited in line. After a painful ten minutes, Maya and Jake finally returned.

"Have fun?" Blaine asked.

"Yep, and we're ready to surrender our freedom." Jake stepped forward and motioned for Blaine to move. "Now it's your turn to explore."

"All right!" he said, grinning. "We'll see you guys soon. The line should only take another fifteen minutes or so."

"Sounds good," Jake agreed, taking his place. He and Maya fell into a relaxed conversation as the Anderson twins made their way to the beach, eager to get moving and do a little sightseeing before lunch.

Suddenly, Cole spotted an abrupt movement out of the corner of his eye. He turned just in time to see a cherry-red sports car zip into the parking lot. For some reason, the whole situation seemed a bit off. He paused, watching as the car pulled into a spot. Moments later, the door opened, and the driver stepped out.

"Um, Blaine?" Cole said. "I need to use the bathroom. I'll be right back."

Blaine was busy studying the water, so he merely shrugged and said, "All right, I'll wait for you here."

Cole immediately sped off in the direction of the Beach Café. He rounded the corner, pretending he was heading to the bathroom, before quickly swerving left. He made a beeline for the parking lot.

Oh no. There she was. Cole swallowed nervously as he made his way over to the red sports car. After a furtive glance over his shoulder, he casually stepped up to the driver.

"Taylor," he said calmly. He was trying to play it cool while his thoughts were running rampant. What in the world was she doing here?

"Cole." She smiled sweetly and took off her sunglasses. Her arms were outstretched, ready to wrap him in a hug, but when she realized Cole wasn't going to move any closer they dropped to her sides. She cleared her throat. "Nice little beach town, isn't it?"

"Tay..." Cole shook his head. "Can you skip the small talk and get to the point?" He glanced over his shoulder to make sure Blaine still hadn't spotted him. "I mean, why are you even here?"

Taylor seemed surprised by his straightforwardness. "Wow, I thought you'd be happy to see me."

"You know our relationship is...different."

"So what?"

"You still haven't answered my question."

She smacked her gum loudly. "I just wanted to see you."

"That's it?"

"For crying out loud, Cole!" She threw her hands in the air. "It's like you don't even care about me."

He raised an eyebrow. Where was all this coming from? Why was Taylor suddenly running to him, when usually it was the other way around?

"Look," Taylor sighed, "I've been doing some thinking lately."

Cole crossed him arms. "About?"

"Us."

He swallowed. "Oh."

"See, this is what I was afraid of when you said you were going on some surf trip down the coast! It's like you're trying to avoid me or something."

"You know it's not like that—"

"We haven't even texted or called since you left."

"Jeez, Tay, I'm sorry. I didn't know it meant that much to you." It usually didn't.

Taylor reached out and grasped Cole's hand. It was a move that was meant to pull him closer, but to Cole, the air suddenly seemed suffocating. He jerked his hand out of her grasp, surprising both of them.

"Is everything alright?" Taylor asked, trying to hide her disappointment. "What's up with you lately?"

What a great question, Cole thought. What a complicated question.

"Cole!" Taylor irritably snapped her fingers in front of his face. "This is exactly what I'm talking about. You're the one coming between our relationship. I'm starting to think you don't even like me anymore."

Cole gave her his best apologetic look before glancing over his shoulder again. "Look, babe, I'm sorry. Can I call you later? I told my brother I was off to the bathroom, so I should really get back before it's too late."

Taylor narrowed her eyes. "Oh, I see how it is. You don't even want Blaine seeing you with me. Have you ever thought about how that makes me feel?"

"Well..." He took a few steps backward. "Can we talk about this later, Tay? It's a bad time right now."

"Yeah, sure. Whatever." Taylor gave him a disgusted look and yanked open her car door. "I have half a mind to dump you right now, you know."

Cole almost opened his mouth and dared her to do it. They had broken up a handful of times already, so what could one more hurt? Instead, he shrugged his shoulders and said, "I'm real sorry, Taylor, but I have to go. I'll call you later."

She revved her engine in reply. He watched as she backed out of the parking lot and sped away, a fierce expression on her face. Cole scratched his head as he strolled back to the Café, wondering what in the world had just happened. Usually he was trying to hook up with Taylor, not the other way around. What had caused them to flip?

Chapter 13

Flicking on his blinker, Cole pulled off PCH into a small parking lot buzzing with activity. A sign positioned at the entrance read Topanga State Beach. Swerving around a Mini Cooper idling near the curb, he pulled into a parking spot and put his Volkswagen into first gear. He turned the key in the ignition and hopped out.

Above his head, white clouds billowed across the vibrant blue sky. He stood on his tiptoes and peered above the cars in the lot to get a better look at his surroundings. To his left, he could see the rugged strip of coast fringed by a stretch of sand and the blue-green ocean.

"How's it look?" Blaine asked, coming up next to Cole.

"Pretty crowded, but there are plenty of waves to go around. The swell is definitely fading, though."

Blaine nodded. "At least it was good while it lasted. I hear a new west swell is going to peak over the next couple days."

"Nice." Cole could feel his frustration over Alana and Taylor slipping away as he studied the breaking waves off in the distance. Now that they were all running on full stomachs, surfing seemed like a pretty good idea. Cole stretched his arms and realized they were still sore, though not as bad as that morning. He gave his brother a grin. "Wanna hit the water?"

"Yes!" Cole could tell by Blaine's tone of voice that he was hungry for waves. The twins quickly suited up and waxed their boards. They were ready to go in record time, with the rest of the gang hot on their heels. As soon as the vehicles were closed and locked, the six of them dashed to the beach.

They jogged across a long stretch of sand bordered by a rocky shoreline. A nice little set rolled around the point, providing some crumbly but fun two-footers. A decent-sized lineup was positioned beyond the breaking waves.

After a short paddle around the impact zone, Cole plopped down on his shortboard and adjusted his leash. He sucked in a deep breath and let it out slowly. It was time to relax and put his mind at ease. He was tired of all this girl drama. So, with his face turned towards the bright sun and his arms resting on his thighs, he closed his eyes and relaxed. His feet drew lazy circles in the water while small ripples lapped at his surfboard.

"Hey, Cole!"

He groaned. "What?" he sighed, reluctantly opening his eyes and turning to face the person who had so rudely interrupted his relaxation.

"Hey," Alana said brightly, casually stroking over to him. Her hands rested on the nose of her shortboard.

"Hi," he said dully.

"How'd you like the food at the Café? Pretty good, right?"

Though Alana shot him her brightest smile, the corners of Cole's lips didn't twitch a centimeter. "Yeah, great food," he said without emotion.

Realizing that she wasn't going to get anything out of him, Alana sighed and let her smile fall. "Look...can I talk to you?"

He held out his hands, palms facing up. "I guess."

"I'm just trying to help. I don't know what your problem is, but you need to let me—let us—help you. We're all worried." She gestured towards the rest of the gang, scattered throughout the water. "It seems like you're not really a part of our group anymore. You keep yourself distant from the rest of us, and we don't know why."

He avoided eye contact. "Why do you even care what I do anyway?"

"Because we're friends, Cole. Friends care about each other and make sacrifices for one another. I know you weren't exactly thrilled to go on this surfing safari, but now that you're here, you have to admit it's been pretty fun. So what's with the attitude?"

Cole stayed silent. She did have a point.

Alana paddled closer into his line of vision. The ends of her white-blonde hair just barely touched the water. "Something's bothering you," she stated, making it sound like more of a fact than just a mere observation.

Cole opened his mouth to respond, then quickly closed it. What good would it do to lie? They had already had a similar conversation back at Zuma. He knew Alana was hot on his trail. If it was blatantly obvious that something was bothering him, then why argue the point?

"Okay," he sighed, averting his gaze from hers. "I just have something on my mind, that's all."

"Do you want to talk about it?"

Of course! I would love to tell you all about my relationship problems with Taylor. Oh, and did you know I've become randomly attracted to you over the past week? Cole shook his head to chase away those thoughts. "Not really," he muttered.

"Okay, well, just know that I'll be praying for you." Alana gave him a slight smile before paddling away.

Prayer? Cole snorted. Yeah, like prayer was going to help. What he needed was to get Taylor back to normal—and his own self back to normal. And when the girl sitting a few feet in front of him was the source of his problems, obviously distance was the solution, not prayer.

"Outside!" a surfer hollered. Cole glanced over his shoulder and saw everyone scrambling to get into position. A set was looming on the horizon, and no one wanted to get stuck in the impact zone—Cole included.

He lay down on his stomach and paddled towards the oncoming set. Though the waves were small, they had the tendency to snap over due to the low tide. He wasn't expecting the first wave to break so quickly. The two surfers who took off on the peak were quickly swallowed in a spray of whitewater. The wave unpredictably dumped over, leaving a small shoulder open—right in front of Cole.

He had a split-second decision to make. Since he was a good distance to the left of the lineup, no one else was in position to catch the wave. But the wave itself was dumpy and crumbling at the lip. Was it even worth paddling for?

"Ah, screw it," Cole muttered, whipping his board around. He dug his hands deep into the water and stroked into the wave. Since he was about to do a late takeoff, he popped up to his feet early and drove down to avoid the breaking lip.

The crumbling two-foot wave had next to no power. He threw his arms forward and pumped his legs to gain speed. Twisting his hips, Cole banked his shortboard off the whitewater and continued racing down the line. He leaned back, one arm trailing in the water, and pulled a big roundhouse cutback. Just as he snapped his board in the pocket of the wave, he overextended and dove headfirst into the whitewash. After the wave rolled over him, he swam back up to the surface and grabbed ahold of his board.

Okay, so clearly a big roundhouse cutback wasn't going to work on this two-foot slop. As Cole arched his back and paddled towards the lineup once again, he spotted a petite figure dropping into an outside wave. He could clearly see Maya's dark brown hair knotted into a tight bun on the top of her head. He watched as she twisted her hips and pulled a nice snap off the lip. She made long, fluid carves that sent arcs of spray flying everywhere. When her ride closed out, she merely rode to the top of the wave and dove off her board.

The rest of the waves were fairly similar. Jake ended up taking off on one of the bigger set waves, allowing him to walk the nose and hang ten for an impressive amount of time. Blaine pulled a carving 360 on one of his rides. But it was clear who surfed the best in the gang—Alana.

She could execute some pretty tricky maneuvers, but performing them on slow, small, dumping waves was a completely different matter. She jerked her body forward, arms flying in front of her, to generate speed. With every turn, she bent her knees and twisted her hips faster than it appeared possible. The result was smooth, solid turns that made her rides look flawless.

It was obvious to everyone in the water that Alana was the best. Cole could tell by the awestruck (and sometimes jealous) looks she received that others were aware of her skill. He overheard a few striking up conversations with her during lulls in between sets. She just acted like her usual fun, relaxed self, despite the many compliments from different surfers. No matter the situation, she appeared oblivious to her natural talent.

It would be an understatement to say that Cole was awestruck as well. Not only was her style of surfing a wonder to observe, but also the way she carried herself in the water was amazing. She laughed and talked as if she had known the surfers in the lineup her whole life. To put it simply, Alana was fun to be around.

Cole felt his stomach twist into a knot as he watched her carve up another wave. His thoughts flickered back to the times when he had seen Alana and Koa together. They were always laughing, smiling, enjoying each other's company. Could it be possible that he wasn't the only one who liked Alana in that way?

He scowled and turned his attention back to the horizon. The sun was setting now, illuminating the sky with bold streaks of colors, but it did nothing to lighten his spirits. What was the use in fighting against his feelings? The harder he pushed Alana away, the stronger she drew him in.

His thoughts suddenly took a new turn. He was treading unfamiliar waters. What if—he dared to ask himself—what if he actually gave in to his feelings? What if he pursued this relationship? As far as he knew, Alana already considered him a friend, and that was the first step in moving toward a deeper relationship.

Cole's heart had softened. It thudded loudly in his chest, louder than the waves breaking just a few yards away. The blood pounded in Cole's ears, and he knew that there was no going back. He would no longer push his feelings away.

But if Alana's charm continued to affect other guys, then he had to move quickly. He wanted to be the first one to get her attention. It all depended on how he played the game, though. He needed to reel her in. And he needed some advice...

PCH was starting to feel like home to Cole. It seemed like wherever the gang went, Pacific Coast Highway could take them there. Cole smiled to himself as he pulled off the highway onto Venice Boulevard. It was eight in the morning, and already the skies were a cloudless blue. It looked like it was going to be a hot one today.

He raised his cup of coffee to his lips and took a swig. According to the GPS on his phone, Muscle Beach was only a few stoplights away. At every intersection he found himself peering at the strange but wonderful buildings lining the street. A few people, mostly runners and walkers, were streaming down the sidewalks, and Cole knew those same sidewalks would be packed later on today.

He made a right on Pacific Avenue before turning down Windward. "Here we are," he murmured, pulling into the parking lot. Blaine stirred from where he was sitting next to Cole in the passenger seat. Cole quietly opened his door and slid out into the warm morning air.

A few moments later, Maya's campervan rumbled into view. Jake was driving, and he flashed Cole a thumbs-up before pulling into a nearby parking spot.

Cole yawned. Though the evening surf session at Topanga had been fun last night, he was itching to surf some bigger waves. Already the good times at Malibu seemed to be slipping away.

He took another sip of coffee as he reflected on the past week. He had gone to sleep thinking about how he was going to get Alana's attention (a.k.a. The Plan). But seeing as his relationships with girls rarely lasted longer than a week, he knew he was going to need someone else's input.

Cole turned at the sound of someone slamming a car door shut. "Blaine!" he greeted his twin. "Just the guy I was looking for."

Blaine gave him a startled look. "Well, good morning to you too. It's been a while since I've seen you so cheerful."

"Listen." Cole lowered his voice and glanced over his shoulder to make sure no one else had come outside yet. "I need your help."

Blaine's eyebrows automatically shot up in surprise. "Did you say what I think you just said?"

Cole rolled his eyes. "Look, are you gonna help me or not?"

"That depends. What exactly do you need help with?"

Cole sucked in a deep breath. "Well, it's kind of...complicated."

"Is this about Alana again?"

"No," Cole said automatically. "I mean...kind of." He dropped his gaze. "Yes."

Blaine let out a low whistle. "I'm glad you finally manned up to tell me. But this is Alana we're talking about."

"I know. And she probably isn't remotely interested in me. But..." Cole sighed and squeezed his eyes shut. Dang it. This conversation had gone so much more smoothly in his head. He didn't know how to make his brother understand.

Blaine studied his twin for a few moments, taking in all of Cole's frustration and anxiety. "Okay," he said after a lengthy silence. "I can tell she means a lot to you."

That's an understatement, Cole thought.

"I'm just hesitant to see how this will play out. What if Alana has no interest in you?"

"That's where you come in. I want you to help me change that."

Blaine shook his head. "I don't know, man..."

Cole let out a frustrated sigh. "I'm not looking for another fling or another Taylor. I'm over that. I just can't get Alana out of my head, and it's driving me crazy. I need to do something to get her attention."

At the mention of Taylor, Blaine stiffened, but the rest of Cole's words struck home. "Here's the deal," he said. "I'll help you, but you have to promise me that this isn't another game of yours. It's obvious that you have feelings for her—"

Cole cringed.

"—but do those feelings run deeper than 'just a fling'? Are you positive this is different than the rest of your track record?"

"I already told you—I'm over Taylor. And as for my...ah..." Cole's face reddened. "As for my feelings, let's just say I've never felt this way before." He ducked his head in embarrassment. Well, there went his pride.

Blaine gave him a small smile. Placing one hand on Cole's shoulder, he said, "Okay. I can see it in your eyes. You're falling hard, bro."

Cole winced. "Yeah."

"If you're positive that Alana means this much to you, then we need to get one thing straight." Blaine looked his brother squarely in the eye. "You have to understand that life isn't all about girls."

Cole could have rolled his eyes, but kept his gaze locked onto Blaine's.

"I know that you have more experience with girls than I do," Blaine said, causing Cole to smile, "but that's totally different from having a true, lasting relationship with a girl. And that goes for friendship or romance."

"Okay, okay, I get it." Cole held up his hands. "Alana is different, trust me. And besides—when have I ever come to you for advice about a girl?"

Blaine studied him carefully. "Can I ask you something?"

"Go ahead."

"Why Alana, of all people?"

Cole felt his face grow warm. "Well...she's...Alana. You know, a great surfer, a fun person to be around..."

He fell silent. Why did he like Alana? He had always found the gang to be a little annoying—and weird—with all their talk about God and Jesus and church. Alana was no different. But things had suddenly changed.

"I don't know," Cole confessed. "I don't know why I like Alana."

Blaine laughed. "Oh, I think you do."

Chapter 14

Alana emerged from Cole's Volkswagen yawning. She stretched her limbs and blinked up at the vibrant blue skies overhead. "So this is Venice," she murmured, sweeping her gaze over her surroundings. The city had an expectant feel to it, as if everyone was preparing for the hordes of tourists to come swarming in later that day.

Just then, she heard two voices talking excitedly. She stepped around to the front of the van and saw the twins, their heads bowed together. They were conversing in hushed voices, so she tried to back away quietly, sensing that they didn't want anyone to overhear them.

Too late. Blaine jerked his head up when he heard Alana's feet shuffle on the pavement. "Alana?" There was a worried tone to his voice. "Oh, hey, good morning!"

She glanced from Blaine to Cole. They both had the same anxious look mirroring their faces. "Um...hi," she said uncertainly. "Sorry if I interrupted something. I was just getting some fresh air."

"No problem," Blaine said quickly. "Cole and I were only talking. We're thinking of going for a morning surf before walking the shops at Muscle Beach."

Cole gave his brother an indecipherable look. Despite what Blaine said, Alana knew she had interrupted something important. "Oh, yeah, that sounds cool." She gave them a halfhearted smile. "I'll go tell the others."

She quickly turned and headed back inside the van. Koa was dozing in the backseat, so she lightly shook his shoulders until he woke up. "We're here," she said softly. "We're in Venice. The twins want to go for a morning surf."

"Sure," Koa said gruffly, his voice thick with sleep. "Now?"

"Most likely. I'm gonna go see what the lovebirds are up to."

At the mention of Jake and Maya, Koa's face automatically lit up. He cracked a smile. "Alright."

It took about half an hour for everyone to rub the sleep out of their eyes and get going. By the time the gang had scarfed down a meager breakfast and pulled on their wetsuits, the sun was blazing overhead. Alana could tell it was going to be in the mid-nineties later. For only eight in the morning, the cool water already sounded inviting.

The gang snaked down the sidewalk to Ocean Front Walk. Though they could see a few whitewater lines off in the distance, a huge stretch of sand lay before them.

"Yikes!" Jake exclaimed. "Look at all that sand!"

"I'm looking at the skatepark," Blaine said, gazing off to the right. "I should have brought my skateboard."

It took them nearly ten minutes to make the long trek across the sand. The soles of their feet were burning by the time they finally reached the water. Alana glanced behind her and saw that the beach stretched as far as the eye could see. There was nothing but blue-green water, a wide expanse of sand, and inland buildings for miles and miles.

"Ready?" Maya asked, nudging Alana with the nose of her short-board.

"Totally." Alana grinned and finished strapping her leash around her ankle. The two of them dashed into the water side-by-side. Alana felt a pair of eyes on her back, but when she glanced over her shoulder, she saw Cole quickly look away.

Though the waves at Muscle Beach were bigger than those at Topanga, they were still dumpy and unpredictable. Nevertheless, the gang had a productive surf. After two hours of shredding waves, they made the long trek across the glittering sand back to Maya's camper. Once there, they took turns showering and cleaning up to get ready to walk the shops of Muscle Beach.

Alana threw a tank top and shorts over her bikini. She stuffed her feet into a pair of flip-flops and brushed out her hair while she waited for the rest of the gang to finish getting ready.

Once everyone was dressed, they set off to do some sightseeing. Since it was a typical hot Southern California day, all the tourists swarming Ocean Front Walk were wearing swimsuits or tank tops and shorts as they cruised through the different shops.

"Hey, look at these!" Alana jogged over to a rack of eccentric-looking sunglasses. Picking out a neon orange pair with slits on the eyes, she placed them over her nose and turned to face the gang. "How do I look?"

"Like you have laser vision," Koa joked.

"How about these?" Maya asked, putting on a huge green pair with antennas sticking above each eye.

"You look like an alien," Blaine laughed.

Alana whipped out her phone and took a few pictures of her and Maya trying on dorky sunglasses. Once they were all laughed out, the guys led them over to an outdoor gym. A bright blue fence marked off the perimeter with signs reading Muscle Beach, Venice, California.

"Let's go check out the weightlifting," Jake suggested. The guys were immediately drawn to the competition going on around the corner.

Alana wrapped her fingers around Maya's wrist. "Well, we would love to join you guys," she said, "but we're going to take a look around."

The guys shrugged, clearly more interested in the bodybuilders than anything the girls wanted to do.

"We'll catch up with you later," Alana said as she and Maya pulled away from the group. After they were out of earshot, she heaved a long sigh. "Finally! It gets old being surrounded by guys 24/7, doesn't it?"

"Yeah." Maya sounded indifferent. From the look on her face Alana could tell there was a certain guy that didn't fit that category.

"I'm glad for a little girl time," Alana said, giving Maya a sly grin. "Come on." She pulled her friend towards Jack's Surfboards. They wandered up and down the aisles before approaching the back of the store.

Maya ran her hand down a sleek white rail of a surfboard, one of many leaning up against foam-covered racks. She headed down the row of surfboards and studied each one carefully. "So, I have a feeling you didn't bring me in here just to have 'girl time,'" she said slowly.

Alana grinned. "You got that right."

"Then what are we doing? Just getting away from the guys?"

Alana's grin widened. "No, just getting away from one guy in particular."

Maya rolled her eyes. "Don't play matchmaker, Alana."

"I'm not! I'm just stating the obvious."

Maya quickly turned away from her friend so Alana wouldn't see her blushing. "I don't know what you're talking about."

"Oh, come on. Why are you and Jake acting so coy? I mean, it's kinda obvious that you two are in love." Alana dragged out the last two words to emphasize her point.

Maya sighed and turned to face her friend. "Okay, so maybe there is something between us."

"Then why are you guys keeping it a secret?"

Alana's own words echoed in her ears. Why are you keeping it a secret?

Why was she keeping her past a secret? And why was she keeping her dream—her vivid, haunting dream—a secret even from her best friend? She was always pushing Maya and Cole to open up about their feelings, yet never demanded the same from her own self.

Alana quickly shook her head and brought herself back to the present. Maya pursed her lips, and Alana could tell the conversation was making her a little uncomfortable. She put a reassuring hand on her friend's shoulder. "It's okay. I'm sorry if I pushed you. I was just itching to find out what was going on between you and Jake because it's been driving me crazy!"

Maya smiled. "Understandable."

Alana mirrored her smile, simultaneously pushing her doubts away. If Maya was keeping secrets, then Alana had every right to keep her own.

The girls rounded the corner to check out some more surfboards and meandered through the different aisles until it was time to meet up with the rest of the gang. Once they regrouped at Ocean Front Walk, they decided to grab a quick bite to eat and go for another surf session.

Alana could feel the beginning of a sunburn on her cheeks. She carefully rubbed in some extra sunblock before paddling out for the last surf sesh of the day. The wind had picked up throughout the afternoon, so the waves were a bit more crumbly than earlier. Naturally, that didn't stop her from ripping.

Alana loved the rush she got whenever she dropped into a wave or pulled a satisfying snap. It felt amazing to be in the cool water, bobbing over swells until the right wave came through. Though her arms ached and her eyes were tired from watching the sunlight glint off the water, she pushed through and ended up surfing until six in the evening.

When the gang eventually trudged out of the water, their energy sapped and their arms feeling like noodles, it took everything they had just to make the long trek across the sand. By the time they finally reached Cole's Volkswagen and the camper, they were thoroughly exhausted.

Maya had the genius idea of eating at an Italian restaurant she had found online. After giving Cole directions, the gang headed a few miles south to eat their fill of garlic bread and spaghetti. It was the most delicious carb-filled meal they had ever eaten.

It didn't surprise Alana when Maya ended up sitting next to Jake at their booth in the restaurant. While Alana was sandwiched between Cole and Jake, she glanced over Jake's shoulder every now and then to see him holding Maya's hand under the table.

Alana smiled as she remembered her conversation with Maya. Now she knew for sure that there was something going on between her and Jake. What puzzled her was why they were trying to keep it a secret. Koa obviously knew, and Alana sensed the twins had their suspicions...

"Alana." Cole's deep voice interrupted her scheming. She turned to face him, her fork paused in midair. "Can you, um, pass the Parmesan?" he asked.

"Sure." She set her fork down and reached over for the tube of cheese. "Here you go."

Cole's eyes kept flitting from Alana's face, to the cheese, and back to Alana. She laughed nervously.

"Oh." He shook his head. "Sorry—I don't know where my head is."

Alana gave him a hasty smile as he took the tube of cheese, his fingers brushing against hers just a second too long. She felt her stomach do a little flip. Forget about Cole—where was her head?

The gang's time in Muscle Beach, Venice, soon came to a close. With a west swell slowly building, they wanted to time it just right so they could surf Huntington Beach when the swell peaked. They still had two surf spots to go before reaching Surf City, however.

One of those spots was Redondo. Nestled between Hermosa Beach and Palos Verdes, it was perfect for receiving a mid-period west swell.

The gang pulled into Redondo Beach early the next morning, chasing the sunrise. Alana caught herself dozing off during the twenty-minute drive, but every time she glanced up, Cole had one hand firmly gripping the steering wheel and the other fingering his coffee mug.

It was eerily quiet when they stepped out of their vehicles. The only sound was the monotonous swoosh of the tide and the crashing of waves. Alana wrapped her jacket tighter around her body as she observed the conditions. It was going high tide, so the waves were a bit slow to break, but the eight surfers who were already in the water were all shortboarders. Alana waited until one of them caught a wave before turning back to Cole's Volkswagen. The surfer had made a quick cutback before racing down the line and pulling a big floater.

It was good enough for Alana. She stuffed a banana into her mouth and pulled on her wetsuit. Since her fullsuit was still damp from yesterday's session, she opted to wear her springsuit instead. Her arms were completely covered, as well as her torso, but the thick neoprene material ended right at her legs. It was like wearing a long-sleeved vest paired with bikini bottoms.

She tucked her board underneath her arm and jogged across the sand. Her hair was pinned up in a tight bun to keep any stray tendrils away from her face. As soon as she felt the first ripples of water touch her toes, her mind kicked into surfing mode.

Alana was the first of the gang to reach the lineup. She did a few light stretches while sitting on her board, loosening up her arms and back. But she quickly got down to business as soon as a set appeared on the horizon.

The first two waves were taken by other surfers, so she wait-ed until she was in a good position—just slightly behind the peak—before paddling into the third wave. She was barely able to scratch into the mushy whitewater. As soon as she popped up to her feet, she threw her arms forward and pumped her legs to gain speed. Since the wave wasn't quite stacking up yet, she did a few cutbacks to stay in the pocket until the lip began to show.

Once the wave began hollowing out a bit more, Alana angled down and set up a snap with a nice bottom turn. She twisted her hips, which in turn twisted her upper torso and then her shoulders, causing her surfboard to whip around and send arcs of water flying into the air. She ended up back in the whitewash, maximizing her rotation by allowing her tail to slide a few extra inches.

That was all this wave had to offer, unfortunately. Alana ended her ride by attempting to do another snap, but the section in front of her closed out before she had time to generate enough speed. She kicked out of the wave and paddled back to the lineup, where she spotted Maya and Jake bobbing up and down on their surfboards.

Alana smiled. "Hey guys! Good morning."

"'Morning," Maya chirped. "How was the drive?"

"Same as usual. Koa and I conked out in the backseat while Cole drove." She paused. "How was your drive?"

"Fine," Maya said.

"We almost crashed," Jake deadpanned.

"Did not!"

"You tried to change lanes without a blinker or checking the mirrors."

"No one uses a blinker anymore."

"It's the law."

"You guys are perfect for each other," Alana laughed. That made them shut up.

Alana spotted Blaine bobbing up and down in the water a few yards away, and immediately paddled over to him.

"Hey," he said. "Did you..." He lowered his voice. "Did you get a chance to talk to Cole yet?"

"About what?"

Blaine quickly masked his surprise. "Oh, you know, I just thought that you of all people could snap him out of his attitude."

Alana nodded. "I spoke to him a few times, basically saying that we cared about him and we didn't want him to stay distant. I reminded him that we're here to help."

"And what did he say?"

"That he had something on his mind."

"That's it?"

"Yeah."

"Oh." Blaine's eyebrows knitted together in a look of concentration. "Well, I guess if he doesn't want to talk about it, then he doesn't have to."

"What if you talked to him?" Alana pressed. "I mean, you're his twin. Don't you share the same feelings or thoughts or whatever?"

Blaine cracked a smile. "I wish. It's more like I can sense what he's feeling. We can read each other really well. And yeah, I've talked to him—more than once, actually—but he hates opening up about things."

Alana swallowed. "Did he say anything in particular?"

"Just that his problem was...uh..." Blaine scratched his head as he searched for the right word. "Personal."

"Oh."

"Don't worry about it. You have a habit of stressing over people, Alana. Cole needs to figure this out on his own."

Alana forced herself to smile. "Right. So, do you want to take this wave?"

A new set was quickly approaching, and Blaine turned his board to get into position. "Sure, but not unless you want it."

"Really?"

"It's all yours."

Alana grinned and spun her board around. Digging her hands deep into the water, she stroked into the peak and popped up in one fluent motion. Her mouth dropped open when she saw Blaine scratch into the shoulder. "Hey! I thought you said this wave was all mine!"

"It is!" he shot back, quickly popping up to his feet.

"Then why did you drop in on me?"

The duo raced to the bottom of the wave side-by-side. The whitewater roared around them.

"Sharing is caring," Blaine said, laughing.

Alana bent her knees and swerved around him. She pulled a snap off the lip just as Blaine made a bottom turn. They continued to do figure eights around each other until they almost collided at one point. Alana shrieked when the noses of their shortboards missed each other by mere inches. She and Blaine laughed in relief and rode the wave almost all the way into shore. They kicked out at the same time, huge smiles on their faces.

"On your next wave," Alana promised him, "I'm dropping in on you."

Blaine grinned. "Fair enough."

Chapter 15

Ever since Cole had humbled himself to ask for his brother's advice at Venice Beach, Blaine's words kept echoing over and over in his mind, like a playlist on repeat. The bottom line: Cole had to change.

"If you want to get Alana's attention," Blaine had said, "then you have to start with yourself."

"What do you mean?"

Blaine had looked long and hard at his brother. "Think about it," he'd finally said. "You said yourself that you weren't looking for another fling. You said Alana was different. So in order for your relationship with girls to change, you need to start by changing your attitude."

Cole caught his brother's gaze in the rearview mirror. Blaine was sitting calmly in the backseat next to Alana, who was scrolling through a playlist with her headphones on. Meanwhile, Koa was busy watching the scenery from where he sat in the passenger seat.

Blaine gave his brother a quick nod in the mirror before looking away. Cole refocused his attention on the road, popping his van into third gear and easing off the clutch. The vehicle immediately slowed as he rounded the corner, turning into a parking lot off to the side of PCH.

For the third time that morning, it dawned on Cole that he had an awesome brother. How had he not realized it before? Not only had Blaine agreed to help him, but he had also agreed to keep Cole's feelings for Alana a secret. This would have been perfect material for Blaine to use as blackmail against his twin.

Cole shook his head. No—Blaine wasn't like that. Blaine was respectful, loyal, forgiving. Everything Cole needed to be.

I need to change. That was easier said than done, Cole realized. Outward change always began with inward change. Cole needed to start thinking differently in order to start acting differently.

He pulled into a parking spot and popped his Volkswagen into first gear. After turning the key in the ignition, he hopped out. "Let's take a look at the waves," he announced.

Cole strolled across the asphalt with the rest of the gang on his heels. In front of them, a wide stretch of sand—almost as far as Muscle Beach—stood between them and the glittering ocean. As soon as they reached a section of fire pits, they climbed on top of one to get a look at the waves.

Though Cole's eyes were scanning the lines of whitewater breaking a football field's-length away, his thoughts were some-where else. He glanced over at Alana out of the corner of his eye. She was studying the waves in silent fascination, her lips slightly parted and her white-blonde hair blowing around her shoulders.

"—do you think, Cole?"

"Huh?" Cole jerked his gaze away from Alana, only to realize that Jake was staring at him.

"What do you think?" Jake repeated.

"About...?"

"Come on, man, where's your head?" Jake laughed. "What do you think we're talking about?"

"We're trying to decide if we should paddle out or not," Alana said, coming to Cole's rescue.

"Oh. Right. What's the verdict?"

Jake rolled his eyes. "That's what I was trying to ask you."

Cole ignored him and studied the waves for a few more seconds. They were about chest-high and came in multiple sets. He knew there was a long paddle out to the lineup—but where was the lineup? No one was even sitting in the water. Though he saw a few shoulders here and there, they were rarities, with the majority of the waves closing out or offering a racy section.

"Nah," he said. "Too inconsistent. We should try somewhere else."

"Where's the next spot?" Koa asked.

Cole shrugged. "South."

"How about the Cliffs?" Maya suggested.

Cole pursed his lips. The gang had already driven through Palos Verdes, past Long Beach, and right by Seal Beach. They were currently standing in Sunset Beach, but the waves weren't offering much. "How far away are the Cliffs?" Cole asked.

Maya looked up the answer mere seconds after whipping out her phone. "About five miles away."

"Let's go," Cole said automatically. Anything would be better than this mush.

They flew past Bolsa Chica, which was choppy and walled out. Maya parked her camper directly next to Cole's van as soon as they entered Huntington Beach. The gang strolled out into the bright sunlight and peered over the edge of the Cliffs.

Cyclists, runners, walkers, skaters—people of all shapes and sizes darted past them as they checked out the waves from behind a metal railing. The Huntington Cliffs dropped down in a rugged stretch of rocks, where they faded into a smooth curtain of sand before tapering off into the ocean.

Though the waves looked similar to those at Sunset, they had a bit more consistency to them. They even came in sets, with some nice lulls in between, allowing a horde of surfers to make the long paddle out to the lineup. The waves were definitely rideable and rippable.

"What do you guys say?" Cole asked, turning to face the gang. The looks on their faces spoke volumes: Let's do this.

They were suited up and ready to go in record time. With the hot summer sun beating down on their backs, they jogged down a steep walkway, across the sand, and into the surf. Even though they were in top condition from surfing every day for over a week, the paddle to the lineup was still long and difficult. Cole duck dived under at least a dozen waves before he finally made it through the impact zone, arms aching.

Fortunately, the waves rewarded them for their tiring paddle. They were surprised to see some nice head-high swells with fairly workable corners on the first set that rolled through.

Jake took off on the first wave, leaving the rest of the gang to fend for themselves. While Maya and Alana went into a paddle battle for the second wave, Cole dug his hands deep into the water and set his sights on something else. Another wave was looming to his left, overshadowing the rest of the set. He kicked and paddled as hard as he could, not wanting to get caught inside when it broke. He spun his board around just as the lip curled over. Then he popped up to his feet and took the drop.

He could feel spray kick up on his face as he raced to the bottom. The wave was surprisingly slow and crumbly for its large size, so he made a quick cutback to stay in the pocket. He rode the wave for a few yards until it began to hollow out on the inside. Then he began to pull some snaps and carving turns. He kicked out only when he realized how far he was riding the wave in. He didn't want to have to face another long paddle to the lineup.

After plopping down on his stomach, Cole lifted his eyes and saw Blaine scratching into the last wave of the set. Cole quickly duck dived under a small wave and resurfaced, his gaze automatically connecting with his brother's ride. He saw Blaine pull a nice combination of maneuvers, smiling the entire way.

Cole watched until he realized another wave was heading straight towards him. He paddled quickly over the breaking lip and coasted down onto the other side. Then, relaxing his muscles, he calmly stroked over towards the gang. It was time to catch another ride.

And it was time to set Blaine's plan into action. If Cole needed to change, then he was sure as heck going to change. The only problem was, he didn't know where to start.

Cole had never been so hungry in his life. When he trudged out of the water at Huntington Cliffs, he realized he hadn't eaten anything save for a small breakfast of fruit and yogurt that morning. He was beginning to feel lightheaded and sick to his stomach.

"Dude, are you okay?" Blaine asked worriedly. He jogged over to his brother.

"I need something to eat," Cole croaked. "Badly."

"Okay." Blaine stayed by Cole's side as they headed back up the walkway to the top of the Cliffs. As soon as they reached Maya's camper, Blaine jerked open the door and tossed Cole a bagel. "Eat this," he said. "I'll find a nearby grocery store and get us some more food. We're running low."

Cole scarfed down the bagel. His lightheadedness vanished immediately, though his stomach still growled for more. "What time is it?" he asked.

Blaine checked his wristwatch. "4:12."

"Oh man." Cole's eyes widened in surprise. "No wonder I'm starving."

Blaine nodded. "You should take Alana out tonight."

"Yeah. Wait, what?"

"You should take Alana out tonight," he repeated.

"I heard you the first time."

"Then what's the problem? You're hungry, aren't you? Just find a nice restaurant and bring Alana. It's not like it's a date or anything—it would just give you some time to work on The Plan. To strengthen your friendship and connect with her. You guys need to have a conversation, you know?"

"Oh." Cole furrowed his brow in concentration. "But what if she doesn't want to go with me? Alone?"

"Don't worry, I'll handle that part."

"What are you thinking?" Cole asked suspiciously.

"I can take Jake, Koa, and Maya in the camper to pick up some food at the supermarket while you and Alana grab a bite to eat. Then we could all meet up in Huntington Beach later."

"Alright," Cole agreed. "If you think it'll work, let's do it."

Moments later, the rest of the gang came into view. Blaine sauntered over to Jake and Koa and casually worked his way into their conversation. "We're running low on food," he said. "I think we should head to the grocery store and pick up a few things."

"Sure, I'll go," Koa agreed.

"Count me in," Jake added.

Maya perked up her ears upon hearing Jake's assent, and immediately walked over to the trio. "Where are you going?" she asked.

Blaine filled her in, and Maya's consent was instantaneous. "Alana!" she called. "Hey, do you want to—"

But Koa cut her off. "What about Cole?" he asked.

"He doesn't feel too good," Blaine admitted. "He needs to rest a bit and get some food in him."

Everyone turned to look at Cole, who averted his gaze and stared down at his bare feet.

Alana was the first to speak. "I'll stay with him," she volunteered.

"You will?" Cole asked, dumfounded.

She shrugged. "Why not?"

"Look, why don't you two meet up with us in Huntington Beach?" Blaine suggested. "After Cole rests a bit, you guys can get some food and then catch up with us later."

Alana agreed, and the gang began taking off their wetsuits and piling them in the back of Cole's Volkswagen. After stuffing their surfboards into their bags and strapping them to the top of the surf van, Alana and Cole waved goodbye to the gang as they pulled out of the parking lot.

"Do you need to rest?" Alana asked. Cole noticed her slight manner of tucking a stray of hair behind her ear. It was cute.

"Yeah, just for a few more minutes. I'm gonna close my eyes and get out of the sun."

Alana nodded and slipped inside the Volkswagen. Meanwhile, Cole kicked back in a lounge chair with a pair of sunglasses over his eyes. Though he tried to relax and pretend like he was resting, his thoughts were flying all over the place. Where was he going to take Alana? How could he make the rest of the evening go smoothly? And would Alana see right through his intentions?

Ten minutes of worrying later, Cole whipped off his sunglasses and muttered, "I'm starving." He leaned forward and called, "Alana, wanna find someplace to eat now?"

"Sure," came her muffled reply. She stuck her head out the window a few seconds later. "How are you feeling?"

"Better. I need to get something in my stomach, though."

"Then what are we waiting for? Let's go."

Cole didn't need any further encouragement. After folding up his lawn chair, he stashed it in the backseat and whipped out his keys. He slid into the driver's seat and let the van run for a few seconds, mulling over his options. He guessed his safest route would be to ask Alana what she wanted.

"Anywhere that's good," she replied.

Cole pulled out his phone, his fingers flying across the screen. As he scrolled down the list of nearby restaurants, he had a lightbulb moment. "Hey! Let's go to Ruby's."

"Ruby's?"

"Take a look." He tilted the screen in her direction.

Alana smiled at the picture of the old-school American diner. "Cool," she said. "Let's go. Hamburgers sound great."

Cole smiled. "Did you see where the restaurant is?"

"Um...Huntington Beach?"

"At the end of the pier."

Alana's mouth dropped open. "No way!"

"Yeah. Awesome, right?" He quickly backed out of the parking spot and sped onto PCH. Alana was rattling off what she wanted to get—either the Classic Rubyburger or the Bacon Cheeseburger, according to the online menu—and Cole was having a hard time trying to keep the smile off his face.

"Hey, I think I'll call Maya," Alana said suddenly.

"Why?"

"To see if she and the others want to meet us there."

Oh, no... Cole racked his brain for a plausible excuse. "Actually, Blaine told me they were going to find some fast food place for dinner. You know, after getting some groceries. It's probably fine if we meet up with them afterwards."

"Are you sure?"

"Yeah, I'm sure," he confirmed. To emphasize his point, he pressed on the gas a tad more, sending them shooting even faster towards Ruby's Diner.

"Alright. If you say so."

Chapter 16

Palm trees overshadowed the glowing streetlights. Buildings loomed up on both sides of the street. Cole knew he was nearing the focal point of Surf City, Huntington Beach. He grinned when the pier itself finally came into view. A red building could be clearly seen on the end of the pier, with a large sign reading, Ruby's Diner.

"Bingo." He nodded his head towards the restaurant, and Alana followed his gaze. Her expression brightened.

The streets were packed with cars, whether parked or waiting at red lights. The intersections were flooded with surfers and tourists crossing the street. Cole had to circle the block a few times before he finally found a metered parking spot. He paid enough quarters for two hours' time. Afterwards, Alana helped him place all the surfboards inside the van. He made sure his precious Volkswagen was locked before joining Alana in the walk to the pier.

They felt like tourists amidst the crowds of people. Some were walking home from work, while others were navigating through the throngs of people on beach cruisers. Cole smiled when he spotted a few surfers, still dripping wet, holding their shortboards underneath their arms.

Though he was still a bit lightheaded from not eating, he wished the walk across Huntington Pier would last longer. He was in no rush to get to Ruby's. It seemed like he and Alana were only inches apart, their hands dangling at their sides next to each other. But Cole knew he had to take this slowly.

His lips curved up into a soft smile when Alana darted over to the side of the pier. Cole joined her over at the railing, and they watched some surfers carve up the beautiful Huntington waves.

"The swell's definitely at its peak," Alana said. "I can't wait to go surfing tomorrow."

"Me too."

His stomach suddenly growled with hunger, causing Alana to burst out laughing. "Sorry, we should probably head over to Ruby's now," she said. "I forgot you needed to eat."

After a short walk, they reached the end of the pier, where they promptly placed themselves at the back of the line for Ruby's and scanned the menu hungrily. As soon as it was their turn to be seated, they followed a waiter to the inside of the restaurant. He led them to a booth sandwiched between a family with sulking teenagers and another booth with a young couple. Alana and Cole slid in across from each other, and the waiter handed each of them a menu. "Can I start you off with anything to drink?" he asked.

After the waiter took their orders and left, Cole cleared his throat and glanced around the restaurant. They had a window seat that faced the south side of the pier, so they sat in silence for a few minutes, quietly watching the surfers.

He let out a deep breath that whistled through his teeth. "So...I guess I owe you an apology. Or two."

Alana raised her eyebrows. "Wow."

"I know, it's not what you were expecting..."

"Not at all." She smiled. "But please, go on."

Cole took a deep breath. "Look, Alana...I know I haven't been the most happy person lately. I know that you and the gang have been a little worried, and I'm sorry for not being willing to open up about it."

"Oh, Cole, that's all in the past—"

"But it isn't," he interrupted. "I still owe you an apology. You've always cared for people without anything in return. I like that soft side of you."

Warning bells immediately went off in his head. That was too sentimental—way too sentimental!

Cole ducked behind his menu, hoping Alana didn't think he was a complete freak. There went the smooth apology he was aiming for. "Uh, what I meant to say was, I think it's time someone repaid you for your kindness. You know, actually thanked you for it."

"Um, you're welcome?"

"No, I mean it." He looked her directly in the eyes. "Alana, I'm sorry for acting like a complete jerk to you and the rest of the gang. I hope you'll forgive me so we can finish this surfing safari with both of us in better spirits." He dropped his menu and stuck out a hand. "Friends?"

Alana stared at Cole's outstretched hand, a smile forming on her lips. "Cole, you know we've always been friends," she said. "But yes, I forgive you." She laughed as they shook hands dutifully.

"Good," Cole said. Once they let go, a shiver of delight racing up his arm, he leaned back and let out an anxious breath. At least that was over with.

It was much easier to relax, put on a nice smile, and have an entertaining conversation now that things were patched up between them. Cole felt like a weight had been taken off his shoulders. The Plan was going smoothly so far.

After the waiter delivered their drinks, Alana and Cole ordered their meals. Cole didn't even know he was so faint from hunger until the waiter slid a delicious bacon cheeseburger under his nose. Cole ate the whole thing in under three minutes and ordered another one.

"Do you always eat like this?" Alana asked, her own hamburger only a quarter of the way finished.

"Maybe." Cole wiggled his eyebrows and began digging into his fries. A meal had never tasted so darn good.

After eating their fill at Ruby's, they headed out of the restaurant full and content. On their way out the door, a bright red gumball machine grabbed Alana's attention, and she scurried over.

"You know, if you get a red gumball you can exchange it for a root beer float," Cole told her.

"Really? How do you know?"

He smiled. "I have my ways."

"I'm gonna try it." Alana fished around in her wallet for a quarter, but Cole grabbed her wrist to stop her.

"Here. Let me pay." He handed her one of his quarters with a smile. It was the least he could do, since Alana wouldn't let him pay for both their meals earlier. Though he had insisted, she wouldn't hear of it. He hoped a quarter would suffice.

"Thanks." Alana grinned and stuck the quarter in the machine. She turned the knob and watched as a yellow gumball rolled down the rack and into her palm. "Bummer. Here, you can have it if you want."

"No, it's fine." Cole handed her another quarter instead. "Try again."

"If you say so." Alana repeated the motions, and she nearly jumped for joy when a red gumball rolled down the rack. "Yes!" She cupped the gumball in her hand and shot Cole a grin.

"Are you getting a root beer float?" he asked.

"Of course I am!" Alana rushed over to one of the waiters and showed him the gumball. He told her to wait a few moments, and soon she was happily sipping on her treat.

Cole and Alana strolled out of Ruby's into the crisp night air. The sun was slowly setting behind them as they walked down Huntington Pier, staying close to one other to keep warm. Alana kept switching her drink from hand to hand so they wouldn't get too cold.

"Want some?" she asked, holding out her root beer float to Cole.

"Oh, no, it's fine. I'm good."

"I see that look in your eyes." Alana smiled mischievously. "Come on."

Cole shook his head.

"Either that or I'm throwing it away." She held the drink over a nearby trashcan. "I'm stuffed. Do you want it or not?"

"Well, if you insist..." Cole snatched the drink from her hand and took a long sip.

"Thanks for tonight," Alana yawned, surprising Cole by leaning her head against his shoulder. Though she was tall for her age, Cole was still a good inch taller. He wondered if now would be an appropriate time to drape his arm around her waist.

"No problem," he said casually. "I'm glad to have gotten that off my chest."

"Cole, I will always forgive you. That's what friends are for."

"Thanks." He decided not to do the arm-thing, and instead just relished in the feeling of her head in the crook of his shoulder. He smiled and took another sip of her root beer float. Tonight had gone well.

Chapter 17

"So how did dinner with Cole go last night?" Maya asked as she pulled a rashguard over her bikini top. It was bright and early on Sunday morning. Cole and Alana had met up with the gang late last night after their dinner at Ruby's.

Alana smiled. "It was good, actually." She grabbed her vest and yanked it over her head.

"What, no teasing? No attitude? That doesn't sound like Cole."

"I know. It was a little weird, to say the least, but in a good way." A very good way, Alana thought. Her heart beat a little faster.

"Why? How did he act?"

Alana fumbled for the right words. "Well, he was acting different, I guess, but in an honest way."

"Honest? Are you sure this is Cole we're talking about?" Maya grinned.

Alana ignored her. "In so many words, he said he was sorry for acting like a jerk. So I forgave him."

Maya's jaw dropped open. "That's it?"

"Yeah. I'll admit he caught me off guard, but I'm glad he's coming around. I've been praying for him ever since this surf trip started."

"How in the world did you get him to apologize?"

Alana shrugged. "It wasn't me."

"That's so uncharacteristic of him."

"Tell me about it." Alana smiled at the memory. "He was such a gentleman, though. I don't think I've ever seen him go a single night without smirking or making fun of someone."

"Well, it's a start. Let's see if it lasts for the rest of the trip." Maya tossed her tube of sunblock at Alana. "Meet you outside."

Once Alana was done covering every inch of exposed skin in sunblock, she stuck the tube in Maya's backpack and headed out of the camper. She tried to stifle a massive yawn as she joined the rest of the gang in the parking lot. They were busy unstrapping their surfboards and waxing up.

Her eyes met Cole's as she slid her shortboard out of its bag. He nodded at her, a half-smile on his lips, and she couldn't help but smile back. Maya's words had really affected her. What was the cause of Cole's apology? He couldn't have apologized because his conscience finally got the best of him—or could he? It certainly didn't sound like the Cole Alana knew.

Not that Alana was complaining. She squatted down and began waxing the center of her shortboard, the spot where she always planted her front foot. On the tail of her board was a neon pink pad to match the pink fins on the bottom.

As she dragged the stick of wax back and forth, creating a bumpy texture to keep her feet from slipping off, she immersed herself in her thoughts. She was so lost in the memory of last night that she didn't hear Koa come up behind her.

Koa's fingers trembled as he helped the guys unstrap their surfboards.

"You okay, man?" Blaine asked, noticing Koa's distraught face and shaking hands.

Koa slowly stopped what he was doing and backed away from the surf van. "Yeah...I just need to take a walk."

"No problem. Maybe drink more water, too. You might be dehydrated."

Koa forced a smile, though he knew dehydration was the least of his worries. He muttered a thank-you anyway and headed over to where Alana was waxing her shortboard. He let out a shaky breath and paused a few feet away from her. What was he doing? He was going to sound crazy...

Crazy or not, Koa knew that the intense feeling he had experienced all morning wasn't something to ignore. He felt sick to his stomach just thinking about it.

God, if this is what you want me to do, then please help me. Koa squeezed his eyes shut as he prayed, hoping that by some miraculous event the feeling would go away.

It didn't.

With a frown, Koa knew what he had to do. He quietly came up behind Alana and cleared his throat. "Um, hey, Alana."

She jumped, dropping her stick of wax and letting it clatter on the deck of her board. "Oh, you startled me."

"You alright?"

She nodded and tucked a lock of hair behind her ear.

Koa could tell her smile was forced. He squatted down next to her and picked up the wax between his fingers, rubbing it back and forth. "Um, listen...I don't want this to come off as crazy—even though it will—but I really need to pray for you."

"For me?"

He glanced over his shoulder, but no one else had overheard their exchange. "I just have this overwhelming sense that something is going to happen. I can't explain it, Alana, it's just there." Koa seemed at a loss for words, but the urgency behind his tone was good enough for her.

She studied him for a few seconds. "Okay," she said, wrapping her hand around his, wax and all. "Maybe God's trying to tell you something."

"Yeah, but it's about you," he stressed.

"It doesn't matter. If God's putting it on your heart to pray, then we need to pray."

Koa nodded, and they bowed their heads.

Alana could feel Koa's hand trembling beneath hers. Honestly, she was a little scared as well. It wasn't like him to be so shaken up over something. "Father," she began, closing her eyes, "thank you for this new morning and the great waves. Please give us peace and reassurance—and give Koa the right words to say."

Koa squeezed Alana's hand thankfully. He let out a shaky breath before adding, "And Lord, though I don't understand why I feel this way, I ask that you would give us peace of mind and protect us today. Keep us from harm and help us, Lord. We need your protection. Amen."

"Amen," Alana murmured. She glanced up and met Koa's gaze. Though he still looked rattled, he wasn't as anxious as before. She hoped some of the weight had been taken off his chest. "Well, that's all we can do for now," she said. "We just need to pray."

Koa nodded and stood up, causing their entwined hands to fall to their sides. "Thanks, Alana."

"Thank God. You were starting to scare me there for a bit." Actually, Koa was still scaring her. Asking for protection was something he normally didn't include in his prayers. And "keep us from harm"? Did Koa sense something Alana didn't? As she swept her gaze over the clear blue skies and rolling waves, she couldn't imagine any harm coming to them today. But if God had put it on Koa's heart, then prayer was the best thing to do.

Alana tossed her stick of wax into the backseat of the Volkswagen. As she tucked her shortboard under one arm, she glanced up to see Cole staring at her. His gaze flickered from Alana's face to Koa's, as if to say, What's the problem?

"We just need prayer," she said quietly.

"Who doesn't?" he replied, though the question sounded forced, rather than mirroring his true thoughts. Alana turned away, feeling his eyes on her back as she made her way to the sand.

A cool sea breeze tousled her hair as she fell in step with Maya. The girls followed Jake and Blaine down a flight of steps next to the pier. Tall palm trees rose up on either side, creating a cool shade underneath the warm summer sun. The foursome paused to let a few joggers and cyclists pass before dashing across the sidewalk and onto the sand. They jogged past some sand volleyball courts on one side, and the sturdy mussel-encrusted pilings of Huntington Pier on the other.

"What's the matter with Koa?" Maya asked, her tone grave. She glanced over her shoulder at their dark-skinned Hawaiian friend. Cole was trailing only a few paces behind him.

"I don't really know," Alana admitted. "He has a feeling something is wrong—and now I do, too."

Maya nodded thoughtfully. "I don't think I've ever seen Koa so anxious."

Me neither, Alana wanted to add. A wave of nausea washed over her. She had felt fine when she woke up that morning. Why had

Koa, of all people, felt the sudden urge to pray for her? And why did she have an uncanny sense that he was right?

Suddenly, Jake hooted and fist-pumped the air. Alana glanced up and saw an overhead wave breaking outside. A lucky surfer dropped into the peak and pulled a beautiful bottom turn.

"Aw yeah!" Maya whistled. "Now that's what I'm talkin' about!" She turned to face Alana excitedly.

Alana swallowed her apprehension and forced a smile. "Let's do this."

They strapped their leashes around their ankles and dashed into the surf. They paddled out directly underneath the pier, taking advantage of the rip current that brought them to the lineup. Once they were through the impact zone, Alana paddled between two large pilings and found a spot in the crowd. Though she still couldn't shake the nervous feeling that had settled in her chest, the sun on her skin and the salt in her hair were a refreshing reminder that she would be fine. She was in her element, and it was time to shred some Huntington waves.

The gang earned some pointed looks from a couple locals, but they brushed it off, knowing that as long as they stayed out of the locals' way they wouldn't cause any trouble. The gang let the best waves of the set go by and settled on catching some of the medium-sized swells instead.

Jake and Koa, the two longboarders in the group, shared a nice little A-frame that rolled through. Being the goofy footer, Koa went left and had a long noseride, while Jake angled right. Alana watched them in fascination.

"Alana, outside!" Maya called. She pointed to the horizon, where a new set was rapidly approaching. The girls were forced to duck dive under the first wave, which broke directly on top of their heads. Alana kicked hard and dug her hands deeper in the water to get in position for the second wave. She spun her board around, about to stroke into the peak, but another surfer was already on the inside. He dropped into the wave and forced her to pull out.

Alana frowned and watched as the wave broke behind her, carrying the surfer with it. Oh well—there would always be another one.

Suddenly, Maya's shrill voice cut into Alana's thoughts. "Alana!" she cried. "Watch out!"

Alana turned and saw another wave, this one easily overhead and walled out all along the length of the beach. But it wasn't the sheer size and power that scared her—it was the tall surfer paddling into the peak. The pointy nose of his shortboard was heading straight for her.

Time seemed to slow down as the surfer got to his feet. He never once glanced down the wave, where Alana was watching his every movement with wide eyes. Why isn't he pulling out? I'm right in his path!

It was an unofficial rule that a surfer riding a wave must look out for others paddling in the vicinity. Clearly, the surfer heading straight towards Alana was oblivious to that rule. She had a split second to yell, "Watch out!" before ditching her board and diving as far underwater as possible.

What happened next was a blur of water, a surging of the wave as it passed overhead, a tug on Alana's ankle as her surfboard was swallowed by whitewater, and a sudden zap of pain that shot down her left hamstring. She let out a yelp as she struggled underwater, the sound escaping her mouth in the form of air bubbles. She instinctively grabbed the back of her left leg as the wave picked her up and threw her to the bottom. She felt her foot hit the sandy seafloor and the rush of water as it spun her in all directions.

The pain in her hamstring was so intense that she couldn't scissor-kick her way to the surface. Instead, she did an awkward one-legged swim until her head popped above the water. When she finally broke through, she sucked in a huge gulp of air and immediately looked for another wave. Fortunately, that had been the last of the set, and the ocean was once again calm in the midst of a lull.

Alana winced as she slowly let go of her leg. The water around her immediately turned bright red.

"Alana!" Maya paddled over to her friend, worry etched on her face. "Crap, did you see that guy? He nearly ran over you! Are you okay?"

The look on Alana's face must have been clear, as Maya let out a sudden gasp. "He did run over you! Oh my God, Blaine! Cole! We need help!"

The twins, who had been slightly in front of the girls and hadn't seen Alana's accident, immediately turned around. A few other surfers in the area had heard Maya's cries and were stroking towards them as well. In any other situation, Alana would have rolled her eyes at the unwanted attention. But the only thing she could think about was the throbbing pain in her leg and the bright red water encircling her.

"Oh no. This is bad." Maya was clearly panicking, but she suppressed her emotions the best she could and helped Alana onto her surfboard.

Alana felt lightheaded. She could hear her own breaths coming out in short gasps. "M-Maya," she said. "How bad...?"

"You're bleeding a lot. It's hard to tell in the water, though," a deep voice replied. Alana rested her head against the cool surface of her board as a hand gently touched her wound. She lifted her eyes and saw Cole gazing at her worriedly. "I can't believe that freak ran over you," he muttered. "What was he thinking?"

"There's no time to be mad," Maya scolded. "We need to get her into shore. Tell Jake to get his butt over here."

Black dots danced across Alana's vision. Though her hand was still resting against her hamstring, Cole's hand was on top of hers, keeping pressure on the wound. Alana didn't know how much time had passed before Jake showed up and transferred her onto his longboard.

"I'll take her," Cole said. No one argued. Though Alana was still lightheaded and couldn't make much sense of what was going on, she could feel someone lie down behind her and start paddling. "I got you," came Cole's voice. "Just keep breathing, Alana. We're heading into shore."

"It's—h-hard—to breathe," she stammered, her fingers twitching. Now that she was out of the water and resting on Jake's longboard, she could feel the blood seeping out of her wound. It was a dizzying, warm feeling. She shuddered.

"Keep talking," Cole ordered.

"I'm lightheaded." Her voice was faint.

"It's okay. We'll get to shore soon. Just hang on."

"He was in my way."

"I know. He's an idiot."

Alana's vision became more blurred with each second. "I c-couldn't get out of his way."

Cole said something in response, but his words were swallowed by a roar of whitewash as they suddenly lurched forward. Alana realized a whitewater wave was pushing them to shore. She forced herself to keep her eyes open and not concentrate on her wound. The warm blood against her fingertips was making her woozy.

Once again, she couldn't make out how much time had passed. She felt herself slipping in and out of consciousness as someone lifted her off the board. Something tight was wrapped around her upper leg, and she was laid down on the sand. She blacked out just as she was being lifted onto a stretcher.

"Hang in there, Alana," Cole said, his words sounding light years away as everything faded into darkness.

Chapter 18

Waves crashed all around her. The sky was a dark, ominous gray. Threatening storm clouds billowed over the churning sea. Wave after wave rose up, only to slam back down in a spray of foam. Alana felt herself sinking lower and lower until she was completely swallowed by the ocean. Now the waves were no longer crashing, but spinning her underwater.

She swam furiously, not knowing which way was up and which way was down. The hazy underwater world was plunged into near-darkness. Only when her hand reached the surface did she come up spluttering, thankful to be alive. As the waves slowly receded and the storm clouds rolled back, she pulled herself onto her surfboard and rested.

In just mere minutes, calm waters replaced the churning ocean. The sun lit up the sky in a rainbow of colors, chasing away the dark storm clouds. Alana reached out and trailed her hand across the glassy water, her fingertips just barely skimming the surface. She leaned forward in amazement, causing her white-blonde locks to come tumbling over her shoulders.

She heard a splash of water and glanced up. The sun was so blinding that she could barely make out a silhouette moving towards her. Then the nose of a surfboard suddenly bumped against her leg, and she heard a low voice say her name.

"Alana."

Alana shot up in bed, causing a bolt of pain to run through her leg. It throbbed in sync with her heartbeat. When she reached out to touch the bandage tightly wound around her thigh, she realized there was no more blood.

Her breathing slowed as she took in her surroundings. She noticed she was on a small cot inside an air-conditioned, gray-walled room. First aid posters and medical supplies were the only decorations. Despite the appearance of a hospital ward, something told Alana that she was in a similar, yet slightly different, place.

A drop of water landed on her shoulder. Her hair, she noticed, was stringy and slightly damp. She held a strand in front of her nose and realized it still smelled like salt.

Slowly, the memory of the accident came back to her. She remembered trying to paddle out of the surfer's way, ditching her board and swimming as deep as she could, and feeling searing pain shoot down her left hamstring.

"Alana!" a voice gasped. "You're awake! Are you okay?"

Alana smiled as Maya, who had been sitting on a chair at the opposite end of the room, dashed over to her.

"Of course I am," Alana laughed. Maya wrapped her in a tight hug, being carefully not to lean against Alana's leg. "How long was I out?"

"About twenty minutes," she replied.

"Oh." It seemed like much longer. Alana's mind was in a fog, and she wondered if this was what jetlag felt like. She rubbed her eyes and sat up straighter, being careful not to move her leg too much. Though she could bend her knee with no problem, her left hamstring was still quite sore.

Suddenly, a tall lifeguard wearing a white T-shirt and red board-shorts entered the room. Maya stepped aside and let him take her place.

"Hello, I'm Jeremy," he said, giving her a warm smile. "How are you feeling?"

"Groggy."

"That might be because we gave you some medicine," he explained. "You were unconscious when one of your friends pulled you out of the water."

"Oh," was all Alana could say.

"You were in shock. Though you lost some blood, I was able to bandage the wound quickly. I've already changed it once and gave your friends some extra bandages. The wound should stop bleeding soon."

Alana gingerly ran her hands over the lump on her left leg. "How bad is it?" she asked quietly.

"Not very deep, actually." Jeremy smiled. "But it's five inches long, which is why you were bleeding so much."

"So...no stitches?"

"No stitches."

Alana breathed a sigh of relief.

"Since you don't have a concussion and your wound is fairly easy to treat, I'm able to let you leave with your friends as soon as you're ready. I just need you to fill out a few papers before you go."

Alana sat upright and followed his instructions, filling out a few sheets of information with a pen. Jeremy helped her ease out of bed, stand up, and take a few tentative steps towards the door. Once he was confident she would be fine, he escorted her outside.

Maya quickly ran to her side. "I'm so glad you're okay! That guy in the water really snagged you bad."

Alana's face darkened at the thought of the surfer who had ran over her. "It was his fin, wasn't it?"

"Yeah. He said he didn't see you until it was too late. He felt like he ran into a thick patch of seaweed and one of his fins got caught," Maya explained. "He face-planted into the water a few yards behind you. When he realized you were injured, he followed Cole into shore and has been hanging out with us since. He's sitting in the parking lot with the rest of the gang right now, actually. He feels really bad."

"Kook," Alana muttered.

Maya laughed. "Yeah, tell me about it. He admitted this is only his first year surfing. Even though it's hard, we've all been trying to give the poor guy some slack."

Alana frowned and hobbled over to the parking lot, where she saw Cole's Volkswagen waiting to pick her up. She felt horrible. She hadn't even gotten a chance to catch a single wave! The thought was dispiriting. But even more depressing was the fact that she had passed out from the shock, rather than the pain, of the accident. She couldn't believe she had been out for twenty minutes!

"Need some help?" Maya asked, allowing her friend to lean on her arm. "I don't think you should be walking so fast."

"I'm fine."

"Jeremy said you need to rest and reapply your bandages every few hours. I don't think—"

"There." Alana smiled, a little faintly from her lightheadedness, as she placed all of her weight on her left leg. The throbbing pain had now subsided to a dull ache. She could handle this.

Maya sighed and helped her the rest of the way to the Volkswagen. "Guess who's awake?" she called as they came within earshot of the gang.

"Alana!" four voices cried in unison. Blaine, Koa, Jake, and Cole all jumped up at the sight of their friend. They immediately rushed over, relieved upon seeing the smile on Alana's face.

"I'm okay, guys," she said. "Just a little dizzy."

"It's only natural after losing some blood," Blaine replied.

"Yeah, thanks for attracting sharks," Jake teased.

Alana laughed and patted her bandage. "It doesn't seem to be bleeding that much anymore."

"Good. I don't think we would have taken the injury so seriously unless you passed out," Maya said.

"Well, I didn't pass out from the pain, if that's what you were thinking." Alana winced at the memory of the fin slicing across her leg. "I mean, it hurt like crazy, but it was all the blood that freaked me out."

"At least you're here." Koa grinned and gave her a high-five. "The lifeguard said you can be back in the water in another week."

"Another week?" Alana laughed. "I don't think so."

"Don't push it, Alana," Maya warned.

Just then, Alana noticed a wiry kid standing behind Jake and Blaine, looking extremely uncomfortable. He was wearing a gray wetsuit and still had water droplets in his hair. When his gaze connected with Alana's, he offered a small smile. "Um...hi."

The rest of the gang turned at the sound of his voice. "I'm Ben," the kid said, stepping forward and reaching out a hand. "I feel so bad for running you over. I can't believe I was stupid enough to go for that wave without looking." He dropped his gaze.

"Oh." Alana shook his hand politely. "Ben, it's fine. We've all made mistakes."

"I'm really sorry about your leg. It must suck not being able to surf for a week."

Alana laughed again. "Oh, believe me, it won't take that long to recover. I'll be back in the water in no time."

Cole rolled his eyes. "Judging by the five-inch scar on your leg, I think Ben is right. You need to take care of that wound or it'll get worse."

"We'll see." Alana grinned. "Thanks for your help, Cole. You were the one who brought me into shore, right?"

His sea-green eyes flooded with relief. "Yeah, that was me."

"Sorry to break up the reunion, but your phone has been ringing nonstop after I told your brother about the accident," Blaine said, handing Alana her phone.

"Oh. Yeah, I should probably talk to him." She carefully sat down in a lawn chair next to Maya and dialed Dylan's number. He picked up after the first ring and immediately launched into a myriad of questions. Alana tried to downplay her injury as best as she could.

"Dylan, I know you're worried about me, but I'm fine. I'm in good hands," Alana told him.

"Are you sure you don't need stitches? Or a hospital? I have no problem driving down there to see you," Dylan said anxiously.

"For the last time, I'm fine. Why else would the lifeguards leave me? It's just a fin gash. It'll heal. My wound has already stopped bleeding."

She heard her brother suck in a deep breath. "Okay. But take it easy, alright? I don't want you coming home with an even worse injury."

"I'll be careful, I promise," Alana reassured him.

"Good," he said. "But tell me—are you really all right?"

"Dylan..."

"I know when something else is bothering you. It's my job as an older brother."

Alana sighed. She knew she would recover from the accident, but there was another accident—one hidden deeper in her past—that she knew she would never recover from. An image came to mind of blood—her blood—seeping into the ocean and mixing with the white waves. She shuddered.

"Alana?" Dylan said.

"I'm fine," she urged. "I'll call you later."

He persisted, but finally gave in after Alana said she needed to get going. "Have fun," he told her. "Be safe. I'll see you in another week or so, right?"

"Right. Love you." After they said their goodbyes and hung up, Alana turned her attention back to the gang. Ben, nervously bouncing on the balls of his feet, apologized one last time before hurrying away. As soon as he left, the gang grabbed their Bibles and rearranged their lawn chairs in a circle next to Alana.

"What's going on?" she asked.

"We thought it was time for a Bible study," Blaine said. "It's been over a week since we've been to church, we thought we should get in the habit of reading our Bibles together."

"Especially after this recent accident," Koa added. "Prayer and Bible study isn't something that should be ignored."

Alana smiled. "That's a good idea."

"Should we start?" Jake asked.

"I think we should read the Psalms," Blaine suggested. "How does that sound?"

They all nodded. As they took turns reading verses starting in Psalm 1, Alana's thoughts slowly drifted back to the accident, and back to the dream she had just before waking up.

Alana frowned. There was that dream again. It was the second time she had dreamt that exact scene—the stormy ocean changing into a calm sea. What could it mean? And why did it keep coming back to her?

Blaine's voice rose above the sound of cars, voices, and crashing waves as he read the beginning verses of Psalm 1. "'Blessed is the man who walks not in the counsel of the wicked, nor stands in the way of sinners, nor sits in the seat of scoffers; but his delight is in the law of the Lord, and on his law he meditates day and night.'"

When Maya's quiet voice picked up where Blaine left off, Cole found himself tuning out her words. His eyes locked on the text in his Bible: "Blessed is the man..."

Who walks not in the counsel of the wicked...

Cole automatically thought of Taylor. He gulped.

...nor stands in the way of sinners...

Again, he thought of the crowd that he usually hung out with at school. When he wasn't with the gang, he tended to drift towards Taylor and her friends, who weren't exactly the best role models.

...nor sits in the seat of scoffers...

This time, Cole thought of himself and winced. He knew he wasn't one to shy away from sarcasm and mockery.

...but his delight is in the law of the Lord, and on his law he meditates day and night.

Now his thoughts did a 180-degree turn. Verse 2 was a perfect description of the people around him at that very moment. Blaine, Maya, Jake, Koa, and Alana—they had all brought their Bibles with them on the surfari, and they all read them daily. Cole realized that maybe there was something to their faith.

"'He is like a tree planted by streams of water that yields its fruit in its season, and its leaf does not wither,'" Maya read. "'In all that he does, he prospers.'"

Cole glanced up and looked over at Alana. Her piercing blue eyes were hidden behind a veil of golden hair, but he could tell her gaze was focused downwards. Her fingers lingered on one of the pages of her Bible. She quietly turned the page as Jake began to read.

Cole lifted his eyes to the ocean. A cool sea breeze tainted the air with a salty spray. He made a mental note to read Psalm 1 again later. In whatever he does, he prospers. Now there was something to think about.

Chapter 19

Cole placed his hands flat on the deck of his board and pushed. As the power of the wave helped him surge forward, he popped up to his feet and raced down to the bottom. A cool spray of saltwater hit him in the face as he zoomed around a section of whitewash. Once there was a clean shoulder in front of him, he threw his arms up and twisted his hips to pull a satisfying snap off the lip.

Cole allowed his momentum to carry him down the wave and set up for another turn. This time, he made a roundhouse cutback that brought him back into the pocket. He finished his ride with an attempt at a huge tail slide that nearly caused him to wipe out.

He carefully lay down on his surfboard and let the whitewater carry him into shore. As soon as he was in shallow water, he stood up and wrapped his leash around the tail of his board. He saw Alana emerging from the water farther down the beach, squeezing the saltwater out of her hair. The bulky bandage wrapped around her left thigh was visible from beneath her wetsuit.

Cole didn't know whether to catch up with her or just hang back and play it cool. He stared dumbly at Alana's figure as she headed across the sand. Aw, screw it. He quickly jogged over to her. "Hey," he said, trying to sound as casual as possible.

"Oh, hey!" Alana grinned. "Great waves today, huh?"

"Yeah." Cole glanced over his shoulder at the rolling lines of swells. The wave height had increased over the past few days. Most sets were now easily overhead.

"How's your leg doing?" he asked, gesturing to Alana's hamstring.

"Better—but it's starting to itch."

"That's not keeping you from shredding, apparently." Cole grinned. Even though it was her first time in the water since the accident, she was surfing just as beautifully as before—even though Cole could tell she was favoring her right leg over her left. But she was still making good progress after only resting her hamstring for one day.

Alana laughed. "True," she replied. "Nothing can hold me back from surfing."

"You either go all out, or don't paddle out."

"Exactly."

Cole was relieved at their brief connection. They smiled in unison and continued walking towards the parking lot. He let out a deep breath, glad that The Plan was still working. He had over the past few days that it was easier to be nice and friendly than it was to be selfish. He regretted acting like a jerk during the first week of the surfing safari.

The gang had been a little wary of Cole's attitude change, but that was expected. Even Blaine had been a little surprised, as if he didn't expect his twin to take his advice seriously. But Cole wasn't going into The Plan halfhearted. You either go all out, or don't paddle out.

The temperature suddenly dropped a few degrees when a large cloud blocked the sun overhead. Being the hottest part of the day, it was still fairly warm. To keep his shortboard off the sand, Cole stuck it in between his legs while he unzipped his wetsuit. He slipped the material down to his waist, allowing his bare chest to soak up the warm sunrays. It felt good to feel the cool sea breeze on his back.

After grabbing a quick bite to eat, the gang decided to stay in Huntington Beach for the rest of the evening since the waves were still firing. They had been pumping for three straight days, but now it was time to check out the next spot south—Newport. They agreed to have an evening surf session by the pier before heading to Newport Beach tomorrow morning.

"I heard the southwest swell is getting some reinforcements," Blaine said as he and Cole suited up for their last surf sesh in HB.

"You think it'll be bigger in Newport?"

"Hopefully. The waves are faster compared to Huntington, so it'll be fun."

"Good."

"It looks like The Plan is working for you."

Cole laughed at his brother's obvious change of subjects. "Yeah, it is."

"You're different now—in a good way, of course." Blaine tilted his head thoughtfully. "It's hard to explain, but it seems like you're happier. More lighthearted."

"And I intend to stay that way."

"Alana seems to be warming up to you, just like the rest of the gang."

"It won't be long now," Cole said hopefully.

"We'll see. Not to rain on your parade or anything, but The Plan might not work to a certain extent...if you get my drift."

Cole sighed. "Yeah, I know."

"It depends on how Alana feels about you." Blaine nodded in the direction of said surfer girl as she pinned her hair up in a messy bun. She had exchanged her fullsuit for a vest and bikini bottoms, the same outfit she had worn when the accident happened. A new bandage was around her left hamstring, but this time no blood was seeping through.

"Come on, guys! The waves wait for no one!" Jake hollered. He sprinted past the Anderson twins, hooting all the way across the beach. Blaine and Cole laughed and jogged after him.

"How does he run so fast with a longboard?" Blaine asked.

Cole shook his head. "Beats me."

"I guess it's the motivation to surf."

"Probably."

Cole smiled when he reached the water's edge. The tide pooled around his ankles, completely calm except for the huge waves breaking near the end of the pier. That was his destination. He knew it would be a long paddle and many duck dives before he made it through the impact zone, but the dozen awesome rides that awaited him were worth the hassle.

He waded into the surf and began paddling alongside his brother. "Let's do this!"

It took every ounce of Cole's energy just to keep his eyelids open, let alone drive his Volkswagen. His whole body was sore—in a good way, of course—from surfing Huntington. Last night's surf session had been amazingly fun, but they had all paid the price when they woke up this morning.

The sun was shining bright as the gang zoomed down PCH. A few wisps of clouds were still floating across the sky. Cole felt dehydrated and guzzled an entire water bottle while driving to Newport, even though his body craved coffee with a passion. He promised to treat himself to a coffee shop after one more surf session.

He circled a few blocks in Newport Beach, mainly 52nd and 54th streets, before finally securing a parking spot. Maya wasn't so lucky and had to park in a metered lot since her campervan was so big. The gang was a salty, smelly, yawning mess as they made their way to the beach to check out the waves. No one really felt up to surfing, yet all of them wanted to surf. Cole was resigned to let the wave quality do the deciding.

They were greeted by the sound of crashing waves as soon as they set foot on the sand. Instead of making the trek to the shoreline, they climbed onto a short brick wall near one of the beachfront houses to see the waves. Rights and lefts were breaking along the entire distance of the beach. The best rides were near the jetties, thick strips of rocks jutting out to sea.

Jake hooted when he saw a surfer get barreled. The surfer barely made it out of the tube before the lip slammed down. "It's dumping!" Jake declared.

"It looks low tide," Maya said. "No wonder the waves are hollowed out."

"Should we try it?" Blaine asked. "I'm only game to paddle out if you guys are."

They glanced at each other. "Let's go," Alana said. "I think the tide's only gonna drop more, so we should have an hour to surf, max. Then we can come in to eat and shower."

"Sounds like a plan." Maya smiled, and the two girls took off for Cole's surf van. The gang worked together to unstrap the surfboards from the roof. Instead of pulling on their fullsuits, they decided to go lighter and wear springsuits. It would be less of a hassle and made more sense since they were only planning to surf for an hour. By the time they made it to the shore, ready to paddle out next to the 54th Street jetty, the waves were practically sucking up nonexistent water.

"How low did you say the tide was?" Cole asked Alana.

"I didn't say," she replied, "but from what I read on Surfline, it's dropping to a negative 0.6."

"Oh." He made a face as a surfer went for a late takeoff and got slammed over the falls. "Not much of a water cushion to land on, then. We better be careful."

"Yeah, if you want to take it easy." Alana grinned and dashed into the surf. "I'm going on the wild side!"

"Of course you are," Cole muttered. But it was hard to not feel reckless on this warm summer day. There was hardly any wind, the waves were spitting barrels left and right, and there were only a handful of surfers in the lineup. Since the waves were faster than those at Huntington, it would give Cole a chance to work on his speed and takeoffs.

He was grateful for the short paddle to the lineup. The gang timed it just right by paddling out in between sets. Cole stroked over a few unbroken waves and plopped down on his surfboard, ready to prove he was worth his salt. His adrenaline was buzzing as soon as the first swell appeared on the horizon. The first two waves of the set were walled out, so he decided to go for the third one. He paddled slightly in front of the peak to ensure that he would make the section, but just before he popped up, he got a glimpse of the swirling sand at the base of the wave. There was nothing but a five-foot drop to the trough and only a foot or two of water below the surface—hardly enough to cushion a wipeout.

He quickly pulled out. The lip broke on his head and tried to suck him over the falls, but he held on and resisted the force of the wave. He didn't realize he was breathing hard until the wave broke behind him in a spray of foam.

"Dude!" Blaine exclaimed. "That was your wave!"

"I wouldn't have made the section," Cole called back.

"Yeah, whatever you say." Blaine shook his head and turned his attention back to the lineup.

Cole swallowed nervously. He knew he should have just gone for it, whether he wiped out or not. But with the negative low tide and the dumping waves, he had a feeling there were going to be some brutal wipeouts today—especially for the longboarders. Jake and Koa looked uneasy as they sat in the water. They only paddled for the smaller waves, and even then, they caught them on the shoulder. They weren't taking any chances.

And then there was Alana. During a bomb set, she paddled into the biggest wave and air-dropped a good three feet. She nearly lost her balance, but raced to the shoulder anyway. She ended up squeezing into a tube and rocketing out onto flat water, a triumphant smile on her face.

She made it look so easy.

Cole's competitive side immediately stirred, and right then and there he made a decision to go for the next wave he saw. But it wasn't the smartest decision, considering the next wave happened to be a six-foot, slurping wall with only a foot of water beneath it.

Yet Cole was determined. The wave picked him up like a toothpick, and he dropped down at a 45-degree angle to avoid plummeting headfirst into the sand. He narrowly missed being impaled by the lip as it shot over his head. He instinctively crouched down, putting pressure on his front foot to maintain speed, and quickly swerved towards the beach when the section in front of him collapsed. The patch of water up ahead was choppy and uneven, and it took all the balance he had not to fall off. He stalled and let the whitewater run past him as soon as the wave lost power.

I'm alive. That was the only thought running through Cole's head as he paddled back to the lineup. Though that hadn't been the biggest or deadliest wave he'd surfed, it was still lethal. It was like Cole had felt its power surging around him as he narrowly escaped a brutal wipeout.

"Now that's how it's done!" he declared, giving Blaine a high-five. But when Cole turned to face Alana, the words died on his tongue.

She hadn't even been watching.

Chapter 20

Cole learned, in just a few short minutes, there was nothing a glazed donut and a cup of coffee couldn't fix. He was currently sitting in his Volkswagen with his feet propped on the dashboard. In one hand he held a Styrofoam cup of cold milk, and in the other a half-eaten glazed donut.

He knew it wasn't the healthiest snack, but it hit the spot. After the scary surf session that morning, he was gearing up to shred a better—and less dangerous—spot. That meant he needed fuel. Not even six slices of pepperoni pizza from Papa John's was going to cut it. He was determined to get Alana's attention at the next surf spot, so he needed all the energy he could get.

Cole wasn't content with merely talking to Alana every now and then. Though she had certainly warmed up to him, especially after his help during her accident at Huntington Pier, their relationship hadn't moved on since then. The sought-after couple status Cole was planning on didn't even seem to be on the radar. If they kept going at this rate, Cole was sure to be friend-zoned for the rest of his life—or slowly whittled out of Alana's life altogether.

I have to do something drastic, he thought as he took another bite of his donut. Something eye-catching. Something Alana will love.

Therein lay the problem. What else did Alana love except surfing? She enjoyed reading her Bible and going to church, but Cole wasn't a church type of guy. Having a Bible study wasn't his thing.

He was running out of ideas.

Cole narrowed his eyes as he studied the waves in front of him. He was currently parked at Blackies, in direct view of the ocean. Technically he was still in Newport Beach, just eight lifeguards stands away from where the gang had surfed that morning at 54th Street jetty. The now-rising tide and shape of the beach helped to create some smaller—and safer—conditions at Blackies. The semi-choppy waves rolling in actually looked pretty fun. *Maybe I should paddle out after I finish this donut...*

Cole guzzled the last of his coffee and stuffed the rest of his donut in his mouth. Wiping his sticky fingers on his boardshorts, he slid out of the van and walked around to the other side. The guys were messing around with Jake's guitar while Alana and Maya were playing cards.

"Anyone up for a surf?" Cole asked.

Everyone's head immediately shot up. "Sure, but the waves aren't that exciting," Blaine replied.

Jake stopped strumming his guitar. He peered at the waves for a few moments. "Eh, why not. I'll paddle out."

"Me too." Alana grinned, and Cole felt a smile of his own spreading on his face.

He unzipped his board bag, pulled out his 5'8", and fastened the leash around his ankle. "See you guys in the water," he called.

The trek across the sand took a mere thirty seconds—nowhere close to the immense distance of Venice or Huntington. The paddle to the lineup was just as quick. The waves were a fun, playful size, with quite a few surfers out. The afternoon sun glinted golden off the whitecaps in the water.

Cole paddled away from a large group of surfers to a less populated area of the lineup. The waves seemed to be breaking fine the entire length of the beach. Once he discovered where the peaks were popping up, he got into position and dropped into a clean three-footer. He made a few quick cutbacks before setting up for a closing maneuver. Just as the section in front of him collapsed, he twisted his hips and pulled a deep bottom turn. This set him up for a vertical off-the-lip that he narrowly executed. He rode the whitewater back down to the trough and hopped off his board.

After paddling out for more, Cole got a glimpse of the gang waxing their boards on the sand. When Cole saw Alana glance up, probably searching the water for him, he quickly got into position for another wave. Now that she was watching, he had a greater incentive to show what he could do.

The wave Cole stroked into was a peaky four-footer with a crumbly section. He popped up a tad inside the peak and dropped to the bottom. Using the speed from his takeoff, he raced up to the lip, leaned back, and dug his right hand deep into the water. The tail of his board automatically slid out a few feet. He grinned as he straightened back up. If that wasn't a killer layback snap, he didn't know what was.

Cole finished off his ride with a little floater, then dove off his board. When he resurfaced, he saw Blaine give a thumbs-up from where he stood on shore. Alana was smiling next to him. Yes!

Cole didn't care that her smile was more of a "nice try, but I've done better" smile than a "great job, Cole" smile. He was just glad that she had seen him.

He bobbed up and down on his board for a few minutes, deep in thought. Then he heard the rest of the gang before he could see them. They appeared over an unbroken swell right behind him, laughing and talking excitedly.

"Sick move," Blaine said, giving his brother a high-five. However, his words were swallowed by a peal of laughter from Alana as she accidentally collided with May and Koa while paddling over the top of a wave.

Cole rolled his eyes, trying to hide the bitterness stirring in his gut. Was it possible Koa was on a deeper level with Alana than "just friends"? Could they even be best friends? The thought of being second best to another guy made Cole sick. That needed to change—and fast.

"What's on your mind now?" Blaine asked quietly.

"Nothing," Cole said automatically. Blaine gave him a look, so Cole added, "Well, it's more like what's not on my mind. I need to think of something that will bring Alana and I closer."

"You're already friends," Blaine pointed out.

"I know, but the whole point of The Plan is to move past being friends."

"That isn't gonna happen overnight."

"I figured," he grunted, "so what's something I can do? Something big and dramatic?"

Blaine pursed his lips. "Well, how about the Wedge?"

Cole gaped at him. "Are you for real?"

The Wedge was a spot known for its big, peaky waves, both dangerous and fascinating. Though many had died there, either crushed by the waves or driven against the rocks, it still drew thousands of onlookers to its shores.

"I'm not saying we could surf there," Blaine explained, "but we should definitely go and watch. The waves at the Wedge are killer."

Cole immediately knew Alana would love it. He pictured them standing on the beach, side-by-side, watching huge waves pound the shore. It would be a once-in-a-lifetime opportunity and the perfect chance to bond with her. After all, the one thing surfers did bond over was waves. "You're a genius," he said to Blaine.

"You're welcome."

The vibrant blue skies the gang had been used to all summer were suddenly a bleak gray. Though wind was conspicuously absent, the way dark clouds billowed overhead made it appear as though a thunderstorm was approaching. Even the slightly cooler temperature made it feel like a rainy winter day instead of a warm summer morning.

Alana hungrily bit into her taco as the gang pulled away from Great Mex. There was nothing like authentic Mexican food for brunch—especially on a moody day like this one. When she had woken up that morning, the waves had been small and crumbly with crossed-up peaks. Though a good-sized lineup had formed by nine o'clock, hardly anyone was getting decent rides. The swell that had peaked in Huntington Beach was finally ebbing away. But there was one more beach that the Anderson twins assured the gang would be breaking.

They pulled up to the Wedge just as the first rays of the sun began peeking out from the clouds. Alana smiled as she stepped out of the Volkswagen, but the gusty sea breeze that nearly knocked her over wiped it right off her face.

"Weird weather we're having," Maya remarked as she slid out of her camper.

"Tell me about it." Alana grabbed a sweatshirt and pulled it over her head. "I thought this was summertime."

"The surf must be good since all these people are here." Maya gestured to the surrounding streets and parking lot. They were packed bumper to bumper.

"Well, this is the Wedge," Blaine mused. "I wouldn't be surprised if most of these people are photographers and tourists."

Cole, Koa, and Jake joined them as they made their way down the street and across the sand. As soon as they came within sight of the ocean, they paused in amazement.

The waves crashing on the shore were huge, twenty- to thirty-foot walls of water. When they broke, they left nothing but a few meager feet of water between the surface and the seafloor. The cushion was so shallow that one could see long tendrils of sand being sucked up with each swell.

The way the waves broke was unnatural as well. Instead of tapering off into a shoulder, they would jack up into one huge, pointed peak—a "wedge," hence the name—and break for a few seconds before closing out. Once the wave ran into another peak, it would explode in a furious crash of whitewater, swallowing anything—or anyone—in its path.

Alana felt something lodge in her throat as she watched wave after massive wave pound the shore. A lone surfer dropped into a peak, but he didn't even get a chance to stand up as the water beneath him suddenly disappeared. He air-dropped fifteen feet onto the sand, and milliseconds later the entire force of the wave slammed on top of his head.

"Blaine!" Jake exclaimed. "Did you think we were gonna surf this? Are you out of your mind?"

"No," Blaine said quickly. "If the waves were smaller, maybe, but I didn't expect it to be anything like this."

"It's insane," Maya breathed. Her eyes grew wide as a bodyboarder dropped into a second wave. This time, the guy was fortunate enough to make the drop, but before he could race back up the wave and bail out, the section of whitewater in front of him closed out.

The immediate reaction from the crowd was one giant wince. There were at least a hundred spectators on shore, and the closer the gang got to the water's edge, the harder it was to walk—not only because there were so many people, but because Alana's footsteps were becoming heavier with each step. Her heartbeat accelerated when she saw another monstrous set roll through. Combined with the gloomy skies and clouds overhead, it was a nightmarish scene. The sky was a dark, ominous gray. Threatening storm clouds billowed over the churning sea.

Alana tried to swallow the lump in her throat, but it was to no avail. She forced herself to look away from the ocean. Waves crashed all around me.

The next set began to break, one by one. Wave after wave rose up, only to slam back down in a spray of foam.

It suddenly became hard to breathe. Images flashed across the forefront of Alana's mind. She shut her eyes and willed them to go away, but the incessant pounding, pounding, pounding, of the ocean waves held her in fear. I felt myself sinking lower and lower until I was completely swallowed by the ocean.

"Alana?" Someone placed a comforting hand on her shoulder. "Hey, what's the matter?"

Alana opened her eyes and saw Cole standing beside her. He had a worried expression on his face. "My God, you're pale. What—"

She didn't stick around to hear him. The crashing waves and gasps of the crowd were like blood throbbing in her ears. Now the waves were no longer crashing, but spinning me underwater.

She couldn't breathe. She couldn't watch the waves anymore. She couldn't stay here. With one final look at the churning ocean, Alana turned and ran. She pushed her way through the crowd, not really knowing where she was going, but driven on by a single thought: I need to get away.

Her blonde hair whipped around her shoulders as she sprinted away from the beach. Before long, her bare feet were smacking loudly on concrete as she dashed across the street. She slowed down only when she realized there as a dead end ahead of her. Leaning forward, she placed her hands on her knees and stopped to catch her breath.

You're acting like a baby, Alana told herself, but the reminder of the huge waves crashing on shore overruled her thoughts. Her breath caught in her throat as the tears began to fall. Her vision became blurred through a veil of tears, and she angrily wiped them away.

"Alana!"

She turned around and saw a figure running towards her. She could barely make out Cole's anxious expression. An image of a wave rearing its gray, foamy lip and slamming down on shore flashed through her mind.

The tears fell faster. She sprinted in the opposite direction of Cole, ignoring his cries. All she could think about were the waves—the churning, crashing waves, full of deadly power. It consumed her.

Alana ran and ran until she couldn't physically run any farther. Her breathing was erratic, and beads of sweat had formed on her brow. She slumped down against a short wooden fence in front of a house, not knowing where she was. She waited until her tears subsided before resting her head in her hands, allowing her heart rate to return to normal.

"Oh, God," she choked out. In between shaky breaths and sniffles, she murmured a quick prayer. Even though she knew what had come over her, she was still scared. She thought she had pushed those memories into the deepest corners of her mind.

No. I can't think about that. Alana forced herself to dwell on something—anything—other than the Wedge. But the image of those lethal waves was so firmly engraved in her mind that she couldn't toss aside the memory of them. It was overwhelming.

"Alana, where are you?"

She raised her head at the sound of Cole's voice. "Over here," she called, her voice cracking.

Cole rounded the corner a few moments later. "Alana!" he exclaimed, sprinting over to her. His eyes were wild and his breaths haggard. "Thank God I found you. What's going on? Why did you take off like that?"

Alana let out another shaky breath, unwilling to let herself meet his gaze. Cole crouched down, his breath hot on her arm. Alana could feel his eyes boring into hers. After a few seconds, he gently took her chin in his fingers and turned her head so she could look at him.

"Alana, talk to me."

"I can't." With a heavy sigh, she pushed a few strands of her now-tangled hair out of her eyes.

"Come on, talk to me. The gang is worried about you. Was it the waves? Are you scared for the people in the water?"

Alana shook her head.

Realizing she wasn't going to talk, Cole switched topics and leaned in closer. "Hey, you've been crying." He gently wiped a stray tear from her cheek. "Are you okay?"

No, she thought automatically. "I'm fine, I guess."

Cole didn't respond. He quietly sat down next to her, their shoulders touching as they leaned against the wooden fence. Alana hugged her knees to her chest, trying to summon enough strength to push past her emotions. But every time she thought she was ready to move on, she remembered the sheer size and power of the waves, and her mental walls broke down.

They stayed seated for a long ten minutes. Neither of them said anything, but Alana was glad for Cole's company. She felt as if he was her lifeline, keeping her cemented to reality while her thoughts ran wild.

"Hey," he said softly, lightly touching her arm, "do you remember what you told me at Topanga?"

"What?"

"You said that we were all friends." He chuckled softly. "I was acting like a jerk, and you told me to lighten up. Do you remember that?"

She nodded.

"You said that friends care about each other, and friends open up to each other." Once again, he lightly touched the bottom of her chin, turning her head to face him. "But friends are also patient and understanding."

She stared at him, searching his face, searching for something in his eyes. Was now the right time? Her thoughts drifted back to her past, to the moment she had opened the front door and saw two police officers standing outside, bringing condolences...

Cole let his fingers drop from her chin. "Hey, I know this cool little place just down the coast. Do you want to head back to the van with me?"

Alana nodded and let go of her knees, allowing her legs to stretch. "Yeah, let's go." Her eyes felt puffy and wet, so she quickly brushed any remaining tears away before getting to her feet. She was glad that Cole didn't ask her any questions on the way back to his Volkswagen. They walked in silence to the parking lot. It didn't feel awkward in any way—it was the most comfortable silence Alana had experienced in a long time.

Chapter 21

Alana was glad for the short drive to Corona del Mar. If it had been any longer, she probably would have died of embarrassment. Though the gang sensed she needed some time to herself and were too considerate to bombard her with questions, she could tell they were itching to ask what had happened.

And Alana knew exactly what had happened. She shuddered and slid deeper into her sweatshirt. She didn't want to remember, not after working so hard to forget, but the sight of those waves was too raw. Too powerful.

Cole parked on the corner of Ocean and Poppy. A gust of wind—the first they had experienced all day—hit them in the face when the gang stepped out of their vehicles. Below a stormy gray sky, the ocean stretched as far as the eye could see, fringed by a rocky coast. Large houses were positioned at the edge of cliffs leading down to the beach.

"It's beautiful," Maya said.

Alana nodded. "It really is."

The sound of her voice broke the spell. Everyone suddenly began talking and moving at the same time. "Okay, we need to bring shoes and wetsuits," Blaine instructed.

"We're going in the water?" Jake asked. "Now? But it's freezing!"

"Well, technically we aren't surfing," Blaine replied vaguely. "We're gonna do a little exploring and we may have to get wet." He smiled slyly.

Alana numbly pulled on her fullsuit and a pair of booties, being careful not to aggravate her scab in the process. The wind whipped her hair in front of her eyes, so she pulled it back in a tight ponytail. She was cold and hungry—two more things to add to her list of complaints. Though the shock from the Wedge was wearing off, it had been replaced by embarrassment. She felt like a coward for running away from the gang.

Alana pursed her lips. No, she hadn't been running from the gang. She had been running from her past.

Another chill ran down her spine, though it wasn't from the cold wind. She forced herself to think happier thoughts and not dwell on the events of that morning. The Wedge was behind her. They weren't going back. There was no reason for her to be so afraid.

But the fear hanging over her like a dark cloud felt like shackles on her wrists, pinning her down, forcing her to remember what she tried so hard to forget.

"Alana."

Maya's voice shattered Alana out of her thoughts. Alana realized she was breathing hard. "Oh, sorry," she said, mortified.

"It's okay. Um, the gang is leaving..."

Alana caught a glimpse of a cherry-red sports car zipping around the corner, music blaring. As soon as the noise subsided, she said, "I'm coming!" She tried to ignore the worried tone in Maya's voice as they ran to catch up with the others.

They passed a sign reading Corona del Mar State Beach before descending a steep driveway to the beach. For a bleak summer day, there were lots of people on the sand and splashing in the water. Though the waves weren't suitable for surfing, some kids were swimming or riding bodyboards. Most of the people were climbing near the tidepools on the shore, curiously studying the sea life at their fingertips.

"Where are we going?" Koa asked, voicing everyone's thoughts.

Blaine grinned. "You'll see. We have a twenty minute hike ahead of us, but it'll be worth it."

Maya and Alana exchanged glances, but when Alana saw the worry laced through her friends' eyes, she looked away. Fear churned in the bottom of her stomach. As the sand slowly gave way to rocks, and rocks to jagged cliff faces adjacent to tidepools, Alana could feel the questions among the gang hanging in the air. The tension was almost tangible. Every so often Alana would slip on a rock or take a wrong step in the tidepools, and someone's hand would be on her arm, asking, "Are you alright?" It was hard to miss the double meaning in their words.

Before long, the rocky shoreline gave way to another beach. Only a few people were climbing on these rocks and tidepools. Alana was amazed at how beautiful and untouched this part of the coast appeared. There were small islands that had been carved into rugged arches from water erosion. Yawning caves of all sizes had been etched out of the cliff face. It was a different type of beach from the rest the gang had visited, and Alana liked it.

She was glad that Blaine had instructed them to wear shoes. A second stretch of sand quickly turned back into rocky tidepools. The gang picked their way among the shallow pools of water and rocky cliffs before a large island suddenly loomed out of the water.

"There it is," Blaine announced. "Cliff Island—or, as I like to call it, the jumping rock."

Only a handful of people were swimming out to the island, climbing up its steep surface, or jumping off the edge into the ocean.

"Sweet!" Maya exclaimed. "How did you know about this place?"

"I Googled it," Blaine said simply. "So who wants to jump off a cliff?"

They all laughed. Jake and Koa shouted, "Me!" at the top of their lungs. One by one, the gang carefully made their way through the tidepools until the water was just deep enough to swim. Every so often a large rock would protrude above the surface of the water, and they would have to either climb over it or swim around it. Before long, they reached the base of Cliff Island. Alana glanced up and saw a few people climb over the top precipice and disappear from view.

"How do we get up there?" Maya asked.

"We rock climb," Cole said in a "duh" voice. Like a mountain goat, he deftly swung himself up onto the lowest ledge and began climbing. Since the island was made out of crude ledges and jagged rock, he had no trouble making his way up to the top. The final ledge was a bit harder to climb over, as it jutted out farther than the rest of the rock, but Cole heaved himself over the edge with his brute strength.

A few seconds later, his twinkling green eyes could be seen peering down at them. "Who's next?" he called.

The guys wasted no time in following Cole. The girls weren't far behind them as they hurriedly climbed Cliff Island's thirty-foot face. Alana made sure to follow the three points of contact rule—having two feet and one hand (or two hands one foot) on a ledge at all times. She was glad for the quick burst of energy that kept her mind off the Wedge, if even for a few minutes. By the time she reached the final ledge, she was breathing hard and excited from the endorphin rush.

Suddenly, Cole's face appeared directly above her as she struggled to pull herself over the top ledge. "Need a hand?" he asked.

Alana glanced at his outstretched arm. Her lips curved up into a tight smile. "Thanks," she grunted as he helped heave her over the ledge and onto the top of the island.

"No problem." He flashed her a smile and got to his feet, brushing off some dirt from his wetsuit. "It's pretty nice up here. Come check out the view."

Alana stood up and looked around her. While climbing Cliff Island, she hadn't realized how high she actually was. She seemed to be much higher than just thirty feet from the surface of the water. She could see the rocky coast stretch across the entirety of her peripheral vision. Tidepools, thriving with miniature sea life, shimmered blue-green from the hue of the ocean. There was nothing but rocks and tidepools directly below her, but when she walked to the opposite side of the island, she realized there was a large sandbank perfect for jumping. The water was clear and empty of any rocks or obstructive objects except for a large clump of seaweed a few yards away.

"Awesome," she breathed.

"Who wants to go first?" Koa asked. He stood on the edge of Cliff Island, ready to jump.

"Why don't we all go at the same time?" Maya suggested.

"Aw, that never works," Jake said.

That was good enough for Koa. He let out a yelp as he bent his knees and jumped over the edge. He hit the water with a loud splash, and seconds later his curly head popped above the surface. "That was awesome!" he hollered.

Blaine and Jake exchanged glances, both of them daring the other to go first. As soon as Koa swam out of the way, they sprinted forward and leaped off the rock. At the last second, Maya darted behind them and grabbed Jake's hand, screaming as she, too, jumped into the chilly water.

Alana laughed. "Well, I guess that leaves us."

Cole grinned and took a step forward, poised to jump. "Ready?"

"You bet I am." She peered over the edge of Cliff Island, causing her stomach to squirm in anticipation of the long drop. It was different from taking off on an overhead wave—instead of having a board under her feet, there was nothing but air.

An image of a surfer attempting a late takeoff at the Wedge flashed through Alana's mind. She sucked in a deep breath, remembering how he had air-dropped fifteen feet into the water, and tried to push it away.

"Hey, are you alright?" Cole asked.

She snapped back to reality. "Yeah, I'm fine."

"Are you scared of heights?"

"No, it's not that." Alana squared her jaw and leaned forward. "Let's just jump."

Cole grinned. "Whenever you're ready."

Alana counted down from three, and both of them took a flying leap. She felt Cole wrap his hand around hers as they sailed through the air, her ponytail streaking high above her head. She closed her eyes and waited for the impact of water, which happened a few seconds later. In one moment, she and Cole had been flying in midair, and the next they were underwater.

Alana felt Cole remove his hand from hers. As the chilly water rushed into every pore of her body, she had a fleeting thought of the Wedge...the monstrous, pounding waves...and her dream.

My dream...

Instinct took over, and Alana quickly scissor-kicked her way to the surface. She burst through, but the cold feeling that had settled in her chest wasn't from the water.

"That was fun, wasn't it?" Cole asked, his eyes flashing with excitement.

Alan nodded and forced a smile.

Taylor drummed her fingers lazily on the dashboard. She skimmed through the messages on her phone one more time, even though she had just checked them thirty seconds ago. She hated waiting—but she hated the thought of losing Cole even more.

"They should be here soon," she murmured to herself, glancing over the rims of her sunglasses to peer down the street. Cole's Volkswagen and Maya's campervan were still parked next to the curb. Cole and his stupid friends were nowhere in sight.

Taylor groaned in frustration. It was growing darker by the minute. They were taking forever at Corona del Mar State Beach. What were they doing, and where had they gone? She watched the tiny hordes of people swarming over the rocks like little ants. A few playing in the water created miniature splashes that were almost indistinguishable from Taylor's distance.

She settled back in her seat and cranked up the music. Just as she was about to text one of her friends, movement caught her attention in the corner of her eye.

She smiled. There they were—Cole's deliciously muscled chest followed by his twin and the rest of the gang. Taylor waited until the gang was finished drying off and piling into their separate vehicles before starting her car. As soon as the Volkswagen and campervan pulled away from the curb, she pulled out of her parking spot as well, making sure to keep a safe distance so she wouldn't be spotted.

Let's see where these surfers go next.

Chapter 22

"Hey Maya! Come check this one out!" Jake yelled through the shop. The owner, who was seated behind the cash register, frowned at Jake before turning his attention back to his magazine.

"How do you like it?" Jake asked when Maya walked over to him. He held up a long-sleeved shirt with a Laguna Beach logo emblazoned across the chest.

Maya pursed her lips. "I don't know."

"Come on, I thought dark pink was your favorite color."

"Actually, it's maroon, which is supposed to be more of a brownish-red."

Jake rolled his eyes. "Okay, okay. I genuinely thought you would like this one, though."

Maya bit her lip and watched as Jake placed the shirt back on the rack. Her eyes lingered on the Laguna Beach logo. The gang had stopped for a quick bathroom break, but Maya and Jake had decided to look for a few souvenirs before piling back into the Volkswagen. Alana was the only one who had stayed in the van.

Maya's heart immediately went out to her friend. "Do you think Alana's okay?" she asked quietly.

"Yeah, why wouldn't she be? She seemed better this morning."

"I don't know. She seems a little...distracted, maybe."

"She's probably still spooked from her accident at Huntington, and a little scared from the Wedge. I'll admit I was pretty scared myself," Jake said. "Come on, let's go check out the next shop, seeing as you're so picky with clothes."

Now it was Maya's turn to roll her eyes. "Alright." She looped her arm through Jake's, but her thoughts were still concentrated on Alana. She hadn't been able to get her best friend alone, and she was aching to talk. She wanted to know if Alana was really, truly okay. Maya knew whatever was on her friend's mind wouldn't blow over in just a single day.

"Let's go in here," Jake said, oblivious to Maya's apprehension.

Maya quickly snapped out of her thoughts and headed inside the store. She quietly wrapped her hand around Jake's. She wanted to make the most of their time alone together and enjoy the moment before it was too late.

When it would be too late, she didn't know. She wanted to have fun while she and Jake were away from the gang, but it was hard not knowing where their relationship was headed. Would the gang accept them as a couple, knowing how deep Maya and Jake's feelings ran for each other? Or would it drive a wedge between their tight-knit group of friends?

It was a question Maya had ran through her head many a time. She didn't know if Jake felt the same way, but it didn't matter. If their relationship was doomed to hit a dead end, why start it in the first place?

The gang was nearing the two-week anniversary of the surfing safari. Twelve days ago they had left C Street, Ventura for County Line Beach. At a glance, it only felt like a couple days, but after

Cole thought back on how many places he'd surfed and how much he had changed, it felt he had been on the road for a month. His head span just thinking about how far they had traveled.

The gang planned to make San Onofre—about fifteen miles south from where they were—the turn-around point. By the time they made it to San O, they would be at the two and a half-week mark. Since they didn't want to prolong the surfari to over three weeks, they would only surf a couple spots up the coast on their return trip. Their vacation was officially coming to a close.

Cole finished waxing his shortboard and took a step back. He examined the bumpy white texture and thin grooves for a couple seconds before his thoughts were interrupted by a beep from his cell phone.

He stood up and walked over to his beach bag. After glancing at his phone's screen, he scowled and turned it off. That was the tenth time Taylor had texted him in the past day. He knew it was his fault for not replying, but she was getting to be so darn annoying. Cole thought he had gotten her off his back at Paradise Cove. Hadn't she even threatened to dump him?

He sighed and tossed his beach bag inside his Volkswagen. A salty sea breeze, rather calm compared to the gusts of wind he had experienced all day yesterday, brought thoughts of surfing to mind. The gang was currently in Salt Creek, a famous surf spot known for its great waves and solid southwest swells. Though the waves weren't expected to get over shoulder-high, Cole knew it was going to be a fun day.

But they had to move quickly. If they wanted to reach San O before the middle of next week, they only had a few hours to surf

Salt Creek. Cole was bummed, but it motivated him to make the most of this surf session.

Once everyone was suited up and ready to go, they descended a steep walkway to the beach, where they were greeted by the sight of beautiful lines of waves. They broke for a good distance along the shore, with crowds of surfers at each peak. The rising sun made the water shimmer a bright blue-green, illuminating its glassy surface. Cole was stoked.

However, the one member of the gang who was usually the first in the water was missing. Cole frowned and swept his gaze up and down the beach, then turned around and stared up at the cliffs. Where was Alana?

Koa, Jake, and Maya were too busy talking and goofing off to notice their friend was missing. Apparently Blaine and Cole were the only ones who realized they had left without Alana.

"Do you know where she is?" Cole asked his brother.

Blaine shrugged. "I thought she was right behind us."

"I'll go back and see if she's okay." Cole stuck the nose of his shortboard in the sand and hurried back to the parking lot. As soon as he came within sight of his Volkswagen, he saw Alana bent over near the curb, her surfboard wedged between her legs so it wouldn't fall.

"Hey!"

Alana glanced up at the sound of Cole's voice. "Hey," she called back.

"What's the matter?" He watched as she struggled with the zipper on her wetsuit, blindly trying to zip it up.

"This," she grunted. "I give up. The darn thing keeps getting stuck on my swimsuit."

Cole smiled and walked over to her. She obediently turned around and swept her hair over her shoulder so it wouldn't get caught in the zipper.

"Sorry we left you," Cole said sheepishly.

Alana laughed. "No worries. I was going to tell you guys to wait up, but you seemed eager to hit the water."

"Yeah." He finally freed the zipper from her bikini strap. "It's a bummer we only have a week left."

"And yet you were the one who didn't want to go on this trip in the first place."

Cole could hear the smug satisfaction in Alana's voice, and he couldn't help but shake his head and laugh. "Yeah, I was a jerk."

"We all have our days."

"But I had months."

"Okay, I can't argue with that," she chuckled. "At least you came around, though. You've brought new energy and spirit to the gang."

"Spirit? Really?"

"You know, energy. Motivation."

"Me—motivating? Now you're just pulling my leg," Cole laughed.

Alana grinned and glanced over her shoulder to see his progress. "So how's the zipper coming?"

"I think I got it." Actually, the zipper had been fixed long before they had gotten on the topic of his improved attitude. Only now did Cole zip it all the way up and fasten the Velcro at the nape of her neck. His fingers lingered on her warm skin for a few extra seconds.

Alana's breath hitched. Cole's fingers quickly withdrew, and he swallowed nervously. "Well, there you go," he said. "All fixed."

"Thanks." Alana tossed her hair back over her shoulder and picked up her shortboard. She avoided Cole's gaze as they descended the walkway to the beach.

Cole's nerves were a mess when he reached the sand. As Alana made a beeline for the water and began paddling to the lineup, he took his time getting his leash on, trying to put as much distance between them as possible. He felt like a fool.

Blaine, observant as always, came over to him. They walked into the water together and reached the lineup in silence. Neither the cloudless blue sky, nor the warm glassy water, helped to improve Cole's spirits.

Blaine sighed. "Well?"

"Well what?"

"What went wrong this time?"

"I don't want to talk about it." Cole set his jaw and turned to paddle away from his brother. "Can we just surf and go into details later?"

Blaine shrugged. "If that's what you want."

"Thank you," Cole muttered, glad to have his brother off his back. He glared at the horizon, the hot sun burning into his vision. During the next few sets he went agro on all the waves he could find—even if it meant dropping in on some unsuspecting surfers. He found himself catching more rights than lefts, since he was a regular footer, and drifted slightly down the beach away from the gang. They were now one peak apart from each other—and Cole was glad for the distance.

Every so often he would glance over and see someone from the gang drop into a wave. Usually it was Blaine or Alana, since they were the ones catching the most waves. Cole's stomach twisted into a knot whenever he spotted that familiar shock of blonde hair and Ripcurl springsuit. But what surprised him was the fact that her looks were starting to become less important. He was caught off guard by the realization. For nearly the entire surfing safari he had been trying not to let his affection show, but now her appearance wasn't the main focus of his attention. Not even the slight touches and brief contact they made on occasion were highlights. He just couldn't get away from the fact that Alana was becoming more to him than a cute surfer girl. He wanted her; he wanted all of her.

The thought terrified him.

"Dude!"

Cole was startled by the sudden exclamation. He turned around and saw a surfer paddling towards him. "Dude," the surfer said, shaking his head, "I can't believe you let that one go by."

It took Cole a few seconds to realize what the surfer was talking about. While Cole had been stressing out over his thoughts about Alana, he had unknowingly let a perfect little A-frame slip by. He watched as it broke behind him, the lip curling over in a sheen of offshore mist.

"Oops," was all he said.

The surfer laughed and sat down on his board. "It happens to all of us, man. Where was your head?"

"Somewhere."

"Yeah, I'll say. Hey, are you gonna take this next one?"

Cole glanced up and realized a second wave was coming. It didn't have a nice peak and shoulder like the one before it, but the racy section looked perfect to wake him up. "Yeah," he said, "I'm going for it."

The surfer watched as Cole got into position and popped up to his feet. Cole cruised down to the bottom, around a section of whitewater, and pulled a clean off-the-lip. He heard someone hoot with approval as arcs of whitewater flew from the tail of his board.

Cole's thoughts were now entirely concentrated on the glassy shoulder in front of him—well, almost entirely. Part of him was still thinking about Alana. He pictured her making a bottom turn, going vertical off the lip, grabbing her front rail, and executing a flawless aerial.

He narrowed his eyes. Focus, he told myself. He set himself up for the maneuver by maintaining speed in the pocket with a few cutbacks. As soon as the wave stacked up on the sandbar, he drove down to the bottom and raced back up to the lip. With his speed at its maximum, he extended his legs and grabbed his front rail. He got a glimpse of the wave as it churned below him, part of the lip broken from his launch. He felt himself rotating in air, his hips turned and his knees bent, until the tail of his board landed back on the top of the wave. As whitewater roared around him, he let go of the rail and eased back into an upright position.

He'd landed it. He'd landed a frontside reverse. Man, did it feel good!

Cole glanced over his shoulder to see the same surfer still watching him. His jaw was now hanging open, as if he didn't expect a teenager to pull of a stunt like Cole did.

Cole smiled smugly. He plopped down onto his stomach and rode the whitewater into shore. As soon as it was shallow enough to stand, he picked up his board and walked up the beach until he was directly in front of the gang. Though they hadn't seen his successful aerial, it had given him the confidence he needed. He had regained his self-assurance and was ready to confront his next obstacle, Alana, even if that meant sitting next to her in the water and engaging in slight conversation—nothing too demanding or awkward; just a simple, "Nice wave you caught."

Yeah, he could do that.

As long as he didn't let his heart get ahead of his brain, that is.

Chapter 23

The drive to Doheny Beach was slow but scenic, with PCH winding its way over cliffs and past ocean views. Cole drove the entire way with his window rolled down, relishing in the feeling of the cool sea breeze running through his short curls. It kept him fresh and alert while a certain surfer girl in the backseat kept glancing at him through the rearview mirror.

They had acted as normal as possible in the water, pretending like nothing had happened between them. And nothing had, really—at least, nothing of consequence. But they both felt it. Fortunately, no one in the gang suspected anything...except Blaine, of course. But when didn't he suspect something?

Through his peripheral vision, Cole saw Alana glance at him in the rearview mirror. She was curled up in the backseat listening to her iPod, but something told Cole her thoughts were focused elsewhere. He could only hope that The Plan hadn't backfired.

"Cole!"

"What?" he snapped.

Koa held up his hands in surrender. He leaned forward in the passenger seat to get a better look at the side mirror. "Relax, man, I just wanted to point out that you missed your turn."

Cole's grip loosened on the steering wheel. "Sorry," he muttered, flipping on his blinker and making a U-turn. He pulled into a small parking lot on the right-hand side.

"We made good time," Blaine piped up from the backseat. "We still have three hours to go before sunset."

"Time to whip out the longboards!" Koa declared. He grinned at the sight of small, glassy waves breaking next to a jetty.

"Good thing I brought my longboard," Alana said. She yanked her headphones out of her ears and stuffed her iPod in her backpack. She didn't make eye contact with anyone as she hopped out of the van onto the asphalt. Cole took a deep breath and slid out as well, hoping that the evening would go better than expected.

He glanced up at the sound of a loud motor. It turned out to be Maya and Jake in the campervan. As soon as she parked the massive vehicle, they hopped out and walked over to their friends. Not feeling like socializing, Cole busied himself by rummaging through his beach bag. His fingers automatically found his phone, and he frowned when he realized he had turned it off.

"Oh, right," he murmured, remembering how Taylor had been blowing up his texts over the past few days. He sighed. How desperate was she? And what was motivating her to get ahold of him, anyway? She had never been this clingy.

"—there's a McDonald's and a few other places just up the street, remember? We passed them on the way here."

"Why don't we just wait until it gets later? It's not even six o'clock."

"We're all pretty hungry. We skipped lunch again."

"That's what the snacks are for."

"Well, maybe some of us want real food."

"Fast food isn't real food."

Cole groaned at Jake and Maya's voices, which were rising in pitch with every sentence. "Guys!" he exclaimed, rounding the corner of his Volkswagen and coming within sight of them. "What's going on? Are we getting more food?"

"Jake here thinks we need to get something to eat," Maya said. "I'd rather go surfing."

"Yeah, like we haven't been surfing every single day for the past two weeks." Jake rolled his eyes.

Cole couldn't help but chuckle at their petty argument. "Trouble in paradise, eh?"

Maya pursed her lips and avoided making eye contact.

"Look, why don't I go and get something for all of us to eat?" Cole suggested. "I'll bring it back to the beach, and you guys can come in from surfing and chow down whenever you want."

Jake and Maya glanced at each other. "If you're up for it," Jake said with a shrug, "that'd be awesome."

"Yeah, I don't mind." In fact, it would give him some time to plan a strategy for Alana. He twirled his keys around his finger. "I'll be back in a few—after we unload the boards, of course."

The rest of the gang helped unstrap the surfboards from Cole's surf van. After explaining where he was going, Cole pulled out of the parking lot and headed back down Dana Point Harbor Drive. He cruised through the intersection, scanned for restaurants left and right, and decided his safest bet was to get something from McDonald's like Jake had suggested.

No sooner than he pull into the McDonald's parking lot that he realized a familiar red sports car was idling in front of the entrance. He sucked in a deep breath and tried to whip his Volkswagen around for a quick escape, but slammed on the brakes against his better judgment. What was he doing? Trying to run away from his problems? Cole had spent enough time working on his attitude to know that wasn't the best option.

He closed his eyes, took a deep breath, and let it out slowly. Okay. He figured he might as well deal with her right here, right now, and get it over with. He swerved into a parking spot and hopped out. He was running out of patience for the girl who had followed him down the coast. If all went to plan, this conversation would be over and done with quickly.

Taylor, who was sitting in the driver's seat of her cherry-red sports car, finally looked up from her phone. Her eyes widened when she saw Cole storming towards her. She turned off her engine and slid out, her demeanor suggesting she hadn't come to hassle him like the last time. Now Cole was the one who was going to do all the hassling.

"Taylor," he growled, "you better give me a straight answer. What are you doing here?"

Jake strapped his leash around his ankle and glanced at the incoming waves. They were small and glassy, perfect for a quick longboard sesh. He glanced to his left and gave Maya a cheeky grin. "Still sticking with the shortboard, I see?"

Even though she knew she would have a hard time catching waves, Maya had opted to take out her shortboard. Unless the waves were very, very small, she would always stick with her shortboard.

Jake knew she had been in a strange mood for the past couple days. Since the day they visited Paradise Cove, his feelings for Maya had blossomed. He just couldn't take his eyes off her. He had to touch her; he had to be with her every minute. He didn't know if Maya felt the same way, especially since she was preoccupied with worrying about Alana. That was the only reasonable explanation for her behavior, wasn't it? Jake had thought over all the possibilities, and he was certain Maya was anxious because of Alana's injury and her episode at the Wedge.

But then why would Maya be angry at him? Jake hoped he hadn't done anything to personally offend her. They had squabbled a few times over stupid things, like clothes and food, but their relationship couldn't be stilted because of that, could it?

"Hey," he said softly, lightly touching Maya's arm. As the rest of the gang dashed into the ocean, he scooted closer to Maya. "Want to talk?"

"We can't talk here," she said curtly.

Jake sighed. "Why not?" he asked, biting his tongue to keep himself from adding, "Why are you doing this to me?"

"We just can't. Not with our friends here."

"Of course we can. They're too busy watching the waves."

He moved closer, but to his surprise, Maya took a step away. "Not now, Jake," she said.

His heart fell. "Maya..." He stared into her brown eyes, wishing she would look up at him. "I'm sorry if you don't feel as strongly about this as I do. I'm sorry if we're moving too fast, if we're pushing our relationship too hard."

She finally glanced at him, puzzled. "You think we're moving too fast?"

Now it was Jake's turn to be confused. "Well...yeah. Isn't that why you're upset with me?"

A ghost of a smile flitted across her face. "I'm not upset with you, Jake."

The words were like music to his ears. "Then why...all of this?" He gestured to the space between them.

"I'm nervous. I don't know what our friends will think of us."

"You mean, if they find out?"

Maya nodded, and Jake's lips formed into an O as he realized what was going on. "So that's why you've been upset. You think we shouldn't keep this a secret any longer."

"Do you think we should tell them?"

Suddenly, Blaine yelled something from the water, causing both Maya's and Jake's heads to snap up at the sound. "Hey!" Blaine shouted. "You guys coming out?"

"We'll be right there," Jake called back. Turning to Maya, he gave her a reassuring smile. "Look, I don't see a problem with telling them. I know they already suspect something anyway."

"'Suspect' is an understatement," Maya said with a roll of her eyes.

"But they don't know for sure. I think it would come as a bit of a shock if we told them we were full-on dating."

"But we're not full-on dating, remember? We're just giving this a try."

Jake was flustered at his careless blunder. "Right. I mean, they would be shocked to find that we were—"

"Hey." Maya placed a finger over his lips, shushing him. "Jake, listen to me. Do you want to date? Do you want us to be a couple?"

It took every ounce in Jake's body to hold back the words, "Of course!" from his mouth. He glanced down at the warm sand. "Like you said, this is a risky move. I think we should tell the gang first."

"If we tell them," Maya corrected. "When would be a good time? What would we say? Talk about an awkward conversation."

"Yeah." Jake looked out towards the water, trying to conceal the emotions bottling up inside him. "I guess we should go. They're waiting for us." He glanced back at Maya before standing up. "After all, we don't want them to suspect anything, do we?" The question came out short and clipped.

He brushed the sand off his wetsuit and grabbed his longboard. Before he took a single step, Maya suddenly grabbed his arm. "Jake, wait."

When he turned around, he was stunned to see a few glistening tears in her eyes. "Whoa, what's wrong?" He immediately dropped his board to wipe the tears from her cheeks. "Hey, don't cry. Please don't, Maya."

"I'm sorry," she murmured. "I feel like such a mess. I don't want to tell the gang because it could ruin everyone's friendships, but at the same time I—" She suddenly paused.

"You what?"

"I like you, Jake." Maya placed her hands on both sides of his face, her thumbs brushing against his lips. "I really like you."

"But you don't love me?" he joked.

"I think it's a bit too early for that." She laughed softly. "But seriously, Jake—ever since we went on our first unofficial date that night at C Street, I realized my crush for you wasn't just a crush. It was something more. I don't know where we should go or what we should do with our relationship—or even if you feel the same way—but I'm so scared of telling our friends."

"Maya, listen to me." He kneeled down on the soft sand. "I like you too. I'm not sure if this is love either, but I'm absolutely positive that there's no more 'seeing if this will work out.' We made a deal to try this relationship back at Paradise Cove, but I think we're beyond that now. We will work out. Telling our friends is just a roadblock we have to figure out."

"You really think so?" Maya's tears had stopped running, and she gently let go of Jake's face. "I was kind of hoping you'd say that."

"What? The part where I said I liked you or the part where I promised we would work out?"

She smiled. "Both."

"Then you know we have to tell them sooner or later, right?"

"Yeah." She sighed and glanced down at her hands, which were now folded in her lap. "What are we going to say, though?"

Jake smiled cheekily. "That you're my girlfriend."

"Jake, you haven't even asked me!"

"Then will you be my girlfriend?"

"I'm not sure if that even counts." She laughed and rolled her eyes, but the way Jake was staring at her confirmed his question. He wanted to pursue their relationship. He wanted them to be a couple more than anything in the world.

"Yes," Maya said softly. "But only if you'll be my boyfriend."

Jake snorted. "I think that's a bit rhetorical."

She rolled her eyes again and picked up her shortboard. Jake copied her movements, and they walked to the water's edge together. "So when should we tell them?" she asked.

"When the moment is right." Jake squeezed her hand. "And I'm only going to ask you one more time—are you sure you want to bring a shortboard?"

Maya's reply was a splash and a stubborn, "No way!" They both laughed and hopped onto their surfboards. They knew there was nothing better than the feeling of peace and contentment—especially when glassy waves and good relationships were added to the mix.

But mostly glassy waves.

Cole could not believe he was having this conversation right now. "What are you doing here?" he demanded, the veins in his neck bulging.

Taylor suddenly looked very, very small. "Look, Cole, I can explain—"

"You know why I haven't been answering your stupid texts?" he fumed, slamming his hands down on the hood of her car. "It's because you can't take a hint. I left on this trip to have fun with my friends and go surfing, but here you are, ruining it with your desperate attempts to get me back."

She opened her mouth, only to close it when she didn't know how to respond. Cole could see the emotions flickering across her face, ranging from surprise to anger to bitterness. "You know what?" she exclaimed, finally finding the right words to say. "I've spent all this time following you because—you probably guessed this already—I want you to come back."

"And you thought I couldn't figure that out?"

"I thought you liked me!"

"I did," Cole stressed. "But we've been through this before. We're not a couple, Taylor, and we never have been. There's nothing going on between us."

She glowered at him. "Cole!"

"It's true. So do you mind answering my question like I asked?"

They stared at each other for a full six seconds before she finally sighed and dropped her gaze. "Fine," she muttered. "I'm here because I want to see you. And I was kind of hoping you would want to see me too."

"That's not all, is it?"

She raised her eyes and glared at him. Speaking through gritted teeth, she added, "And I wanted us to get back together."

"Is that it? You seriously like me that much, after all we've been through?" Cole was getting fed up with Taylor's lame excuses. There was something else she wasn't telling him, but he couldn't put a finger on it.

Taylor's face bottled up in a mixture of emotions. She clenched her fists at her sides, gripping her phone so tight that her knuckles turned white. "Fine!" she exclaimed. "I've had enough. I can't do this anymore."

"I can't either," Cole sighed, exasperated. "If you won't tell me what's going on, then just—just—leave."

"Maybe I will." Taylor fixed one last glare on him before ducking back into the safety of her car. Cole could make out the faint glimmer of a tear in the corner of her eye as she sped out of the parking lot, fingers shaking on the steering wheel. He watched her red sports car disappear down the street until it was completely out of sight. Then he let out a deep breath, running a hand through his salty hair.

She wasn't coming back—that much Cole knew for sure. But now that both of their emotions were drained, he felt an odd sense of remorse. He had planned to come out hard, and he'd definitely accomplished that, but had it really been worth it? Taylor had looked heartbroken when she drove away.

Cole felt horrible the more he thought about it. He knew he shouldn't have yelled at her. He knew he shouldn't have pressured her into running away—even after she had followed him down the coast.

Cole groaned as he pushed open the door to McDonald's. A wave of air conditioning hit him smack in the face as he shuffled over to the front counter. You want Alana, his thoughts echoed, yet it was Taylor's troubled face he saw in his mind's eye.

Chapter 24

Alana drew out her legs from underneath her and popped up into a standing position. The small, glassy wave remained unbroken as she put all her weight on her back foot and turned the longboard. Now that she was angling right, she cross-stepped up to the nose and put one foot over the tip. She crouched down, trailed one hand in the water, and smiled.

Koa hooted as he paddled over the shoulder of her wave. "Cheater five!" he called.

Alana stood back up and cross-stepped down the board. The lip began to curl over in a gentle splash of whitewater, so she pulled a small floater and attempted to hang five again. This time, she wasn't as fortunate to have an open shoulder in front of her, and she mistimed her cross-step. She laughed as she rode straight off the wave into calm water, landing flat on her butt.

Alana swept her gaze from the lineup, to the long jetty on her right, all the way over to the uncrowded beach. The palm trees planted near the parking lot swayed gently in the soft breeze. Fortunately, the ocean was calm and glassy, and Alana hoped it would stay that way for the rest of the evening.

"Is that the best move you got?" Koa teased when Alana reached the lineup.

"What—hanging five?" She grinned. "I've got more tricks than that."

"Then let's see 'em."

"Do I sense a challenge?"

He snorted. "No, I just want to see what other 'tricks' you can do on a longboard."

"Yeah, sure," Alana laughed. "Or maybe you don't want to challenge me because you know you're going to lose?"

He dismissed her comment with a wave of his hand. "Please. We both know I'm the better longboarder between the two of us."

"We'll see about that." As soon as the next wave appeared, Alana turned her whole body around without turning her board. Now she was facing the beach, but she was sitting on her board backwards, with the tail in front.

Koa laughed. "Good luck with that."

"I don't need luck," she shot back with a teasing smile. She dug her hands into the water and glided into the wave. As the water receded beneath her board, its long single fin became visible, and she popped up to her feet. She leaned back onto her heels, automatically causing her longboard to swivel around. The entire board did a complete 180-degree turn so that the tail was in the back of the wave where it should be.

"How's that for a trick?" she called over her shoulder. Koa just gave her a thumbs-up and that trademark Hawaiian smile of his.

They continued to surf until sunset, when sky and water were illuminated with bold streaks of color. However, as dusk descended on the beach and the waves became harder to see, the only good thing that happened was the increase in wave size. The wind picked up to ten miles an hour and misty clouds began covering the sky. It looked like another storm was fast approaching.

After catching a wave in and changing into a warm sweatshirt and pants, Alana eagerly devoured one of the hamburgers Cole had bought. The rest of the gang chowed their dinner as well while they discussed the plan for tomorrow.

Alana wiped her mouth with a napkin and picked up her phone. "Upper Trestles is the next best spot," she said.

"And with this storm coming in, the waves are sure to double in size by tomorrow morning," Blaine added. "The swell is peaking. I agree—Uppers is our best bet."

"Should we get there first thing tomorrow morning?" Maya asked.

Blaine nodded. "Definitely."

Alana quietly swept her gaze over her friends' faces. When Cole glanced up and met her eyes, she looked away, the skin on the nape of her neck tingling.

"Wait," she said suddenly. Five heads turned to stare at her, Cole included. "I think we should surf Lowers instead."

Silence, thick as smoke, descended on their little circle. Then—

"What?" everyone exclaimed in unison.

"Lowers," Jake deadpanned.

"You guys are telling me you don't want to surf Lower Trestles? Are you nuts?" Alana laughed. "I thought you would be excited about this."

"But it's so localized," Blaine said, voicing the rest of the gang's thoughts. "I would give my right arm to be able to surf there, but I know it's not going to happen. There are too many locals and not enough waves."

"Then what if I told you I personally knew one of the locals?"

"I wouldn't believe you."

Alana smiled wryly. "Well, luckily for you, I'm telling the truth."

"You've got to be kidding." Blaine's jaw dropped open.

"Where do you get these connections?" Jake asked.

Alana assumed an air of importance. "I have my ways." Picking up her phone, she added, "Now if you'll excuse me, I have an important phone call to make."

She quietly walked away from the group, punching in the numbers she had memorized nearly a month ago. On the third ring, a familiar voice answered the phone.

"Hello?"

"Trevor? Hey, this is Alana. Remember that favor you said you would do for me...?"

Though the air was biting cold and the first rays of the sun had barely begun to show, the gang dutifully suited up for Trestles. Trevor, thrilled to hear from Alana, had given her directions to parallel park along Cristianitos Road near the San Diego Freeway. Dozens of other cars were already parked there, but none of them were Trevor's. Alana checked her phone for the umpteenth time that morning.

"Relax," Maya said, startling Alana out of her thoughts. "He'll be here soon."

"I'm just excited," Alana confessed.

"We all are. I've gotta say, none of us expected to surf Lower Trestles. That was a nice card you pulled last night."

"It wasn't me. Trevor and I had met at C Street awhile back, and he was the one who told me to call him when we were in the area."

Maya grinned. "I can't wait to meet him."

"Yeah. He's chill." Alana busied herself for the next couple minutes by waxing her shortboard and checking her leash. She stood up and stuffed her hands into the pocket of her sweatshirt. Her wetsuit had been pulled down to her waist, keeping her legs covered but her feet exposed. She stuffed her hands into the pocket of her sweatshirt just as a large silver truck roared into the parking lot.

"That's him!" Alana said excitedly. Trevor pulled into a nearby spot and hopped out with a few friends of his.

"Alana!" he called. "Hey, how are you? It's been a while."

They embraced for a few seconds, both of them smiling. "I'm good," Alana replied. "You?"

"Couldn't be better. The waves are supposed to be firing today."

"I heard. This is gonna be awesome!"

"It'll be unlike any place you've ever surfed."

"Then what are we waiting for? Let's go!" Jake exclaimed.

Trevor and Alana laughed. "After you," she said, stuffing her shortboard and a towel underneath her arm. The gang followed Trevor and his friends down a dirt path, across railroad tracks, and underneath the freeway. It was a good twenty-minute hike before they reached the beach.

Everyone's eyes immediately lit up when they saw the waves. Peak after peak rolled through in glassy, A-frame perfection. Though the lineup was packed for only six-thirty in the morning, they knew the crowds would be worth it.

"Wow," Alana breathed, watching as a surfer dropped into a set wave, pulled a strong bottom turn, and executed a beautiful layback snap.

"I think I'm in heaven," Maya said.

Trevor just laughed.

After they set down their towels, zipped up their wetsuits, and strapped on their leashes, the gang dashed across the sand into the water. Alana felt like she was in a dream as she made the long paddle to the lineup. The water was warm, the sky was blue, the conditions were glassy, and the waves were epic.

"This is amazing," Koa said, gliding up next to her on his short-board. For the first time in a long time, he and Jake were ditching their longboards, because Trestles was too crowded and too big for anything longer than a six-footer.

"Now that's an understatement," Alana laughed. "I can't wait to catch one of these waves."

She and Koa were practically drooling as they watched a beautiful A-frame slip by unridden. A lone surfer had dropped into the peak and gotten stuck behind the section, leaving both shoulders wide open. Their insides stirred with anticipation.

"Hey, not to burst your bubble or anything, but remember what Trevor told us," Blaine said.

Alana nodded. "Yeah, I know." They reached the lineup and sat down on their boards.

"Even though we're with Trevor and he's a local, that doesn't mean the other locals are willing to give us waves." Blaine crossed his arms over his chest, seemingly reading Alana's thoughts. He knew how excited she was.

"Don't worry," she reassured him. "I'm not gonna drop in on anyone."

"I didn't say you were. I just think we should play it safe and go for the smaller waves that roll in."

Their conversation was cut short by the arrival of a new set. Jake hooted as the first of seven waves broke outside, causing most of the surfers in the lineup to scramble out of the impact zone. The sets were shifting, and nobody wanted to get caught in front of a torrent of whitewash when the waves broke.

One of Trevor's friends dropped into the second wave. It was a beauty. The gang cheered him on as he pulled a nice carving 360, eliciting some hoots from a couple locals as well. The rest of the waves went to some more locals, excluding Trevor, who had positioned himself on the inside next to the gang.

The remaining surfers didn't have to wait long for the next set. Jake and Blaine dropped into one of the smaller waves, followed by Trevor and another local on a medium-sized swell. Meanwhile, Alana set her sights on a set wave rapidly approaching. Since the peak had shifted slightly in her direction, she knew she was in the best spot to catch it.

She dug her hands deep into the water, concentrating on pulling hard with every stroke. Just as the lip of the wave began to curl over, she spun her board around and launched herself into the pocket.

The wave was unlike anything Alana had ever experienced. She felt a rush of adrenaline, accompanied by a sheen of saltwater, as she dropped to the trough and pulled a bottom turn. She had so much speed from dropping down the eight-foot face that she almost caught an edge and wiped out. After regaining her balance, she trailed her right hand in the water for leverage and angled back up the wave. She twisted her hips and made some long, sweeping carves to stay in the pocket.

The ride itself felt like the product of a wave machine. With each turn, Alana felt the surging power of the wave, all the way until her final maneuver where she did a little frontside grab. That was by far one of the most fun waves she'd ever surfed.

Alana couldn't stop the exhilaration thrumming inside her. "Did you see that?" she exclaimed when she paddled back out to the gang. "Did you see my wave?"

"It was sick!" Maya declared.

"You were crazy to go for that set wave," Blaine said.

"No one else was in position for it," Alana argued. "It was all mine."

"Sick!" Trevor exclaimed, paddling closer to Alana. "You short-board even better than you longboard." He glanced down at her surfboard, which was free from any stickers or logos. "Why aren't you sponsored?"

"Aside from my high school surf team, I've never competed," she replied.

"But you're definitely good enough. You should seriously con-sider it."

"Maybe. I've never really thought about it." Her stomach twisted into a knot, and she forced herself to smile in return. "I'd rather just surf for fun, you know?"

"Yeah, there's nothing wrong with that. And believe me, since we surf here year-round, we've seen lots of surf talent—but you're one of the best. It's crazy to think that no one from your high school team has noticed your potential yet!"

His words warmed Alana to the core, but the unsettling feeling in her gut was immovable. "Thanks, Trevor," she said.

"No worries." He began paddling towards his friends, but paused a few feet away to call over his shoulder, "Oh—and you totally lied to me, Alana."

She was confused. "About what?"

"About saying you couldn't do airs."

A genuine smile blossomed on her face. She laughed. "You got me there."

Chapter 25

T restles continued to fire the rest of the day. The gang surfed sunrise to sunset, only coming into shore to get some food or to take a quick break. Everyone's legs were sore and arms throbbing long before the sun fully disappeared behind the horizon. They were parched, hungry, and exhausted; but it was worth it. As soon as the locals had watched Alana take off on that set wave, she had no problem earning her spot in the lineup. The locals soon warmed up to the rest of the gang as well. They were having the time of their lives—this was one day they didn't want to end.

During a lull in one of the sets, Alana found herself shading her eyes from the glare of the setting sun, which shone with full force on the water. It lit up the sky in a rainbow of colors, from pink to blue to orange. It was breathtakingly beautiful, the way the colors reflected on the water and illuminated the glassy waves.

She reached out and trailed her hand across the placid water. If it was any clearer, she could probably see her reflection. She leaned closer and let the fringes of her hair touch the surface.

Alana heard a splash of water and glanced up. The sun was so blinding that she could barely make out a silhouette moving towards her. The nose of a surfboard suddenly bumped against her leg.

"Alana," he said.

She realized they had drifted apart from the rest of the gang. Normally, she would have paddled back into position, but she feared that the slightest movement would disturb the pristine conditions. Dipping her hand into the cool water, she said, "It's beautiful."

A lock of hair tumbled over her shoulders, but before she could fix it, he reached out and tucked it behind her ear.

"You're right," he said, "it is beautiful."

They drifted a few feet apart, admiring the colors enflamed across the sky. Finally, Alana turned sideways, out of the blinding sun, and stared at him.

It was Cole. Without another word, he caught the next wave that came their way and rode it all the way into shore. As the last rays of the sun slowly dissolved into the dark mass of the sea, Alana reached up and touched the lock of hair that had been tucked behind her ear. What just happened?

Once the waves became too dark to see, the remaining surfers in the lineup scrambled to catch a final ride. Alana was exhausted by the time she made it into shore. It had been a full and satisfying day of surfing. To top things off, Trevor invited the gang to a beach bonfire. He promised them free food, which drew the guys in right away, and also promised that he and his friends had plenty of flashlights, which helped ease Alana's and Maya's fears about walking down the uninhabited beach trail to their vehicles in the dead of night.

Though the gang had brought a sufficient amount of water to the beach to ease their parched throats, they were running low on snacks. They were relieved when Trevor said he had brought five boxes of pizza and the necessary ingredients for s'mores.

Trevor took turns mingling between his group of friends and the Ventura gang as they sat around a blazing bonfire in the sand. Alana had taken off her wetsuit a half hour ago, but her hair and skin were still a tad wet. She draped her towel around her shoulders and scooted closer to the fire. As she swept her gaze over her friends' smiling faces, she realized Cole was the only one who had a faraway look in his eyes. Something stirred in the pit of her stomach, and she quickly glanced away. She couldn't bear to look Cole in the eye. Every time she did, the butterflies in her stomach became raging hornets.

"Guys," Jake piped up, causing the gang to look in his direction. An uncharacteristic blush graced his cheeks. "Um, Maya and I have an announcement to make."

"Are you sure this is the right time?" Maya hissed, barely audible.

Koa sat back, amused. Blaine stopped chewing his s'more with half of a graham cracker sticking out of his mouth. Cole froze with his skewer in the middle of the bonfire, causing his marshmallow to burst into flames.

"So, I know it's kinda obvious that Maya and I like each other," Jake stammered, "but now we want to make it official." He swallowed. "Maya and I are dating."

Blaine hooted. The gang immediately burst into a round of congratulations.

"We didn't want to make things awkward between all of us," Maya said. "Are you guys sure you're okay with this?"

"If you're happy, then we're happy," Koa reassured her.

Alana was the only one who remained silent, refusing to budge from her seat in the sand. Maya was all smiles until she realized her best friend still hadn't said anything.

"What's wrong?" she asked quietly, sliding over to Alana.

"Nothing," Alana said quickly. "I'm happy for you—I really am."

It was true—after everything Maya had been through, with her parent's divorce and strained relations with her mom, Alana was glad Maya had finally found a healthy relationship.

Maya continued searching her friend's face. "I know something's wrong. Is it about me and Jake?"

Alana shook her head. Maya scooted closer and put an arm around her shoulders. "Then tell me," she urged.

By now, the rest of the gang had noticed Alana's silence. The fire glowed orange-red on their faces as the flames licked the edge of the wood. Trevor's voice rang out from the far side of the bonfire from where he was sitting with his friends.

Cole withdrew his roasting stick and blew the flames off his marshmallow. As he delicately slid it between two graham crackers, he glanced up and met Alana's gaze. The emotions swimming in his eyes made her heart skip a beat. She remembered the last time his eyes had looked that way. They had been sitting in Newport Beach, near the Wedge, and Cole had comforted her after she ran away. What was it he had said? "Friends care about each other, and friends open up to each other. Friends are patient and understanding."

She had more or less told Cole the same thing at Topanga. He had definitely opened up, becoming more sociable, more likeable. He had taken her words to heart. And if Cole could change, so could she.

Alana was scared, but she knew this wasn't another episode like the one she'd experienced at the Wedge. This was a different feeling. Before she could stop herself, Alana stammered, "Um...I have something I need to tell you."

Five expectant faces turned towards her. "A couple days ago, when we were at the Wedge," she continued slowly, "you probably remember how I ran away."

"Alana, you don't have to—" Blaine started, but Maya shushed him.

"It's okay. I need to get this off my chest." Alana sucked in a deep breath and wrapped her towel tighter around her. As her toes dug into the warm sand, she continued, "It wasn't the big waves that freaked me out, or the way the surfers and bodyboarders were suffering the worst wipeouts I'd ever seen, but it was the memories those waves brought to mind that scared me. I just couldn't handle it anymore, so I took off. Looking back, I don't know what came over me, but now I know part of it was because of my past." Alana licked her lips nervously. "More specifically, my parents."

The group fell silent. The only sound was the distant crashing of waves, the crackling of the fire, and the murmuring voices of Trevor and his friends. Alana closed her eyes.

"It's been five years since my parents passed away. I had been twelve at the time, so I still remember what they were like. They were both passionate surfers, and even more passionate Christians, and that kind of rubbed off on Dylan and me. Dylan was such a great surfer that he had his sights set on the World Tour when he was only sixteen. Two years later the accident happened."

She opened her eyes and gazed into the orange-red flames. "That year, one of the biggest swells we had seen in a long time hit Ventura County. I don't know if you remember, but C Street was firing for a week straight. Dylan and my parents surfed the double to triple overhead waves every single day while Tammy and I stayed on the beach. Only a handful of surfers were in the lineup since the waves were so big. But on the day the swell peaked, Dylan had to leave for a competition, so my parents dropped him off at the airport and went surfing soon after.

"I was at home with Tammy. Both of us were still sad that Dylan had left, but we were excited because our parents had promised to take us to the movies that afternoon." Alana let out a shaky breath. "But...they never came back."

"Alana, I'm so sorry—" Koa began.

"It's okay," she interrupted. "You already know the rest of the story: my parents drowned, their bodies were found just south of Ventura Pier, and after they were identified, police officers came knocking at our door. Tammy and I had no idea what was going on, so the officers called Dylan. Since he was eighteen, he was now our legal guardian, and he dropped all of his contests to come home and take care of us." Tears sprang into her eyes. "We moved into our apartment soon after that. Dylan never went surfing again, and he even stopped going to church."

Maya hugged her closer.

"What you don't know," Alana continued, "is that since my parents had always been active in the church, Dylan felt like he couldn't handle the grief whenever he set foot inside the sanctuary. He felt like the accident was his fault since he hadn't been there to save them. Tammy and I were devastated, but we were grateful to have a responsible older brother who went out of his way to care for us. His sponsors helped him out quite a bit financially, and even gave him a few extra boards, but when they realized he had quit surfing for good, the money stopped coming. Dylan found a job a week later and that's where we are now." Alana brushed a few tears away. "Now you know the whole picture."

Whether she didn't want to hear a response, or because she didn't want them to see her break down and cry, Alana suddenly stood up and left. She walked down the beach until she felt like she was a good distance away from the bonfire. Then she sat down, hugged her knees to her chest, and let the tears flow.

Opening up to her friends after harboring that secret for so long was like ripping off a Band-aid. It hurt and it stung. As she cried, her tears mingled with the light traces of salt still brushed across her cheeks. She didn't know someone had followed her until she heard soft footsteps in the sand. She glanced up through a veil of tears to see that it was Koa.

"Hi," he said quietly.

"Hey," Alana sniffled.

Koa draped a comforting arm around her shoulder and brushed some tears from her eyes. "You didn't have to tell us everything, you know."

"I wanted to. I had been keeping that bottled up inside for years." She gazed out at the dark ocean, suddenly feeling cold now that she was away from the warm fire. "Tonight felt like the right time to get it off my chest."

"It was a brave thing to do."

"Thanks."

"No, thank you." Koa smiled. "We were wondering why you ran away at the Wedge and why Dylan never comes to church. Now we know."

Alana glanced up and looked long and hard into his eyes. There was something unreadable in his expression; something she couldn't put a finger on. When she saw surprise flash in his eyes, she realized what had been in front of her this whole time. She had just been too stupid to see it.

"You like me," she blurted.

Shock registered across his face. He was appalled that her sentence was more of a statement than a question. "No—I—what made you think—" he stammered.

"Tell me the truth, Koa."

He glanced down, the arm draped around Alana's shoulders suddenly feeling like lead. "Okay," he confessed after a moment, "I do like you."

"Why didn't you tell me?"

"It's not something I can just say, Alana."

She wiped off her tear-stained cheeks with her towel. "How long?" she asked.

"What?"

"How long have you had a crush on me?"

"I don't know," Koa admitted. "It sort of just...happened."

Alana felt like an idiot. First she took the spotlight away from Maya and Jake, and now she forced it onto Koa.

Koa—someone she had always thought of as a brother, not a boyfriend. She could never see them together in that way. But how to explain it to him...?

"I guess I've always liked you," he continued, "but I didn't want to tell you for the same reasons Jake and Maya kept their relationship a secret. That, and I know you aren't looking for a boyfriend."

Once again, an anxious feeling settled in the pit of her stomach. "Yeah," she said softly. "I'm not."

"Well, then there's your answer. That's why I haven't told you." Koa seemed irritated. He withdrew his arm and shifted restlessly in the sand. "I think I'll head back."

Alana watched as he stood up to leave. "Koa, wait," she begged. "Don't be angry with me."

"I'm not."

"Look, I'm sorry things didn't work out the way you wanted, but now's just not the right time." She offered a faint smile. "Stick around for a few years and see what happens, okay?"

"A few years," Koa repeated. "I might be able to wait that long." There was a teasing tone to his voice, and he quietly wiped the sand off his board shorts before sticking out a hand. "I'm sorry, I was just—"

"Upset," Alana finished for him. "I know." She took his hand and let him help her to her feet.

"Are you heading back?" Koa asked.

She shook her head. "I think I'll stay here for awhile."

He understood, and after one more fleeting glance, headed back to the bonfire alone. Alana stared at the dark mass of shifting waves in front of her and sighed.

Chapter 26

"Now you know the whole picture." Alana's jaw quivered as she ended her story. Cole could see the tears sparkling in her eyes. His heart throbbed in his chest, but he didn't move. He couldn't move. He watched as Alana abruptly stood up and headed out into the twilight, her towel still draped across her hunched shoulders.

"I had no idea," Blaine murmured. "Did any of you...?"

Jake, Maya, and Koa shook their heads. "I feel so bad," Maya said softly. "I shouldn't have let her tell that story."

"It's not your fault," Koa said. He gazed in the direction Alana had gone. "I'm going after her. I need to make sure she's okay."

No one protested, though Cole's insides were screaming at him to do something. He felt like he should be the one running after Alana, not Koa. Cole should be the one to comfort her like he did at the Wedge.

He was locked in mental deliberation for a few minutes. Torn between his head and his heart, he finally set down his uneaten s'more on his towel and stood up.

"Are you going after her too?" Jake asked, surprised.

"No," Cole lied. "I'm going to take a walk. I need to clear my head."

Blaine gave his twin a knowing look but remained silent. Cole squared his shoulders and headed after Koa and Alana. His legs automatically took off into a jog, so he willed himself to slow down and play it cool.

He walked for about a minute before spotting two figures hunched over in the sand. Through the dim glow of the bonfire a good distance away, he could faintly make out Alana's golden hair and Koa's dark skin.

Cole's heartbeat accelerated. Goosebumps peppered his arms from the crisp night air as he slowly approached the duo. Before he could get within earshot, however, he saw them embrace.

Cole froze, his heart thudding in his chest.

They had their arms wrapped around each other, but that wasn't all. From the shape of their silhouettes, Cole knew they were kissing.

His jaw dropped open. He felt crushed by the weight of his hard work, his many sacrifices, and his time spent chasing after Alana—it had all been useless. Alana had been fooling him. She wanted Koa, not Cole. How could he have been so blind?

He whirled around and headed in the direction of the trail. "No!" he shouted, angrily kicking at a piece of debris sitting on the sand. Tears burst into his eyes as his toes throbbed with pain. Of course he had to kick a splintery piece of wood, of all things. "Crap," he muttered. He let out a string of curses, buried beneath a torrent of tears, and took off in a sprint. He fled the beach. Before long, the bonfire disappeared as a red blob behind him, and the dirt trail appeared a few yards ahead.

His eyes gradually grew adjusted to the darkness as he tore down the trail. He nearly stumbled and fell several times, partly due to the fact that it was nighttime and partly due to the tears hindering his vision. When he burst onto the street minutes later, he was a physical and emotional wreck.

His breaths were ragged as he stormed over to the Volkswagen. He unlocked the door and tossed all the gang's belongings out except his own. Once everyone's suitcases and backpacks were piled on the sidewalk, he put the key in the ignition and backed out of the parking spot. He had no music blaring and no one in the vehicle with him, so the drive to Ventura was oddly quiet except for the sounds of the freeway. Cole kept his window rolled down to allow the crisp night air to keep him alert.

It took a little under two hours to reach Ventura County. Most of the time Cole was pushing 85 in a 70 mile per hour zone. He felt nothing but bitterness the entire drive—bitterness and regret. And disappoint, too, that Alana had chosen someone else over him.

He yelled and hit the steering wheel with his fist. "How could she?" he screamed. "After I worked so hard and did everything I could to make her like me!"

He tried, unsuccessfully, to fight back tears as he pulled off the freeway. Once he was stopped at an intersection, he grabbed the nearest article of clothing and wiped his face free of tears. No more crying, he told himself. Get over her. If this is how she treats you, then she's not worth it. He repeated this over and over to himself until the words were firmly engraved in his mind, but the wound in his heart was still open and bleeding. He knew it would be awhile before he fully got over Alana.

He rolled up the window and turned on some music. A Christian radio station was playing, so he angrily pushed a button and let heavy metal flood the speakers instead. When he was only a few miles from his house, he turned down a dimly-lit street. His music was suddenly drowned out by the sound of a thumping bass. The farther he drove, the louder the bass got, and the number of cars that were parked on either side of the street skyrocketed. He finally switched his music off and listened to a techno song blasting from a house a quarter-mile away. As he drove closer, he could make out the outlines of the house and yard better, and realized whose house it was.

Taylor's.

The realization hit him like a slap in the face. The end-of-summer party—it was tonight.

Cole slowed and came to a complete stop in front of the house. The thumping bass pounded in sync with his heart. His fingers twitched as they rested on the steering wheel, while his feet were poised over the clutch and gas, waiting for his brain to decide what to do.

What did he want to do? For the first time that night, Cole realized he didn't even know what he was doing. He definitely wasn't going to drive all the way back to Trestles, but he didn't want to go home to face his father, either.

But here, right in front of him, was a place to crash. It was perfect.

After parking a little ways down the street, Cole threw on a sweatshirt and some jeans. He flung his hood over his head and stepped out of the Volkswagen. He wasn't in the partying mood, but since he needed some food, water, and a place to sleep, he figured tonight wouldn't be that bad.

A raindrop hit him splat in the forehead as he crossed Taylor's lawn. He glanced up and realized the moon was hidden behind storm clouds. He shivered and hurried towards the house. If it was even possible, the music got ten times louder as soon as he stepped through the front door. Teenagers were everywhere, as were red plastic cups. Cole stood awkwardly in the doorway for a moment, glancing over the dance floor and the minibar, thinking back on last year's end-of-summer bash and how he and Taylor had been the life of the party.

Taylor...Cole quickly kept moving, ducking his head beneath the safety of his hood and hurrying up the stairs. Someone pressed a drink into his hand on his way up, and he glanced down at the alcoholic liquid, disgusted.

Then he paused. "Oh, screw it," he muttered, tipping his head back and taking a long draught. The alcohol burned his throat on contact, but he forced it down and quickly tossed the cup away.

At the top of the stairs, there was a long line for the bathroom, so Cole hurriedly edged by a few teenagers to scout out any empty bedrooms. As soon as he found one at the end of the hallway, he closed the door behind him and sat down on the plush mattress. It felt like heaven.

His stomach suddenly growled. He groaned and sat up, knowing he would have to go back downstairs and get some food sooner or later. Making sure his hood was still covering his head, he walked back over to the door and flung it open.

Cole jumped when he realized a tall, skinny blonde was standing directly in front of him. "Whoa!" he exclaimed. "Hey, can you not stand in front of the door next tim—"

"Cole," she said stiffly, placing a hand on her hip. "I thought it was you, but I wasn't sure."

Cole squinted. Through the layers of makeup and thin clothing, he could make out Taylor's accentuated features, including her new freshly dyed blonde hair. "Oh," he said. "It's you."

She rolled her eyes. "I guess it's my turn to ask the question, isn't it? What are you doing here?"

Cole was at a loss for words. He couldn't exactly tell her that the girl of his dreams had just dumped him for someone else, and he had recently driven two hours on the freeway with nowhere else to crash but here. So he said, "Why don't we talk about this somewhere else?"

Taylor glanced at the bathroom line snaking down the hallway. She sighed and headed back downstairs. "Fine. Follow me."

They weaved through the throngs of teenagers until they reached the minibar. It was packed with people, but at least in here it was possible to hold a conversation over the loud music. Cole guessed that was all right, but he would have rather talked to Taylor somewhere where he wouldn't be recognized. He was still a bit peeved that she had actually found him—and also a bit surprised at his new disinterest in the party scene. For some reason it didn't hold as much glitz and glamour as it used to.

Taylor handed him a shot glass and took a seat at the counter. Cole held up a hand. "No, I'm not drinking tonight," he said.

She raised an eyebrow. "It's a party, Cole. Of course you're gonna drink. Why else did you come here?"

He didn't reply. He watched sullenly as she filled his shot glass, then proceeded to fill hers. She drained it in one gulp. "Oh," she said, when Cole remained silent. "I think I know where this is going."

He narrowed his eyes. "You do?"

Taylor smiled sweetly. "I think so."

"Then how long have you been following me?" Cole exclaimed.

She frowned and pointed to his glass. "Drink," she ordered.

Cole glared at her, but after realizing that one shot wouldn't hurt, he tipped his head back and drained the glass. "There," he said coolly. "Now answer my question."

"I followed you to Doheny and back," she replied. "That's it."

Okay, this conversation was making no sense to Cole. How could she have known about Trestles—Alana and Koa—the kiss—unless she had followed him there? He twirled his glass between his fingertips and thought long and hard.

"Need another one?" Taylor asked, giving a little hiccup as she refilled his glass. Part of it spilled onto the table, narrowly missing the sleeve of Cole's sweatshirt.

"How much have you had to drink, Taylor?"

"None of your business."

"Okay, then." Cole shook his head, fingered his shot glass, and took another drink. A slight buzz was taking over, but it felt good. He realized just how much he had missed going to parties—especially good ones like Taylor's.

They took a few more shots until both of them were feeling disoriented and giddy. Though their conversation had moved on to meaningless topics, Taylor's motives were still obvious. Cole was just too wrapped in a fog to care.

"Come 'ere," Taylor said, walking around the counter and putting an arm around his waist. As they headed away from the minibar towards the stairs, he slung an arm around her as well. They stumbled up the stairs and into an empty bedroom, Taylor shutting the door behind them.

She flopped down on the bed. Cole glanced down and realized someone had pressed a cool beer into his hand. "What's this?" he asked.

"I don't know, just drink it." Taylor shrugged and kicked off her heels.

Cole took a long draught and leaned up against the bedpost for support. "Don't you want to know why I'm here?"

She smiled. "I already know."

"N-no, you don't." He frowned and took another drink, but Taylor reached up and took it out of his hand. "Hey!" he exclaimed.

"I think that's good," she said. "You've had too much to drink. Even I know that."

Cole swung at the beer, but Taylor maneuvered it slightly out of his reach. His momentum carried him straight into a wall, where he smacked his forehead and struggled to stay upright. "Ow," he muttered.

"I've been to so many parties with you, Cole," Taylor continued. "I think I know when you reach your limit." She smiled, walked over to the window, and tossed the beer can outside.

Cole stared dumbly at her. "What did you do that for?"

"It's time to concentrate on the real reason you're here."

"No...you don't understand," he slurred, warning bells going off in his head. *What about Alana? What about Alana?* his mind screamed. As Taylor came closer, Cole realized he had to make a decision, and fast. But it took a few seconds longer than usual for his fogged brain to remember why he was even there in the first place.

That settles it, he finally decided. *Alana chose Koa over me, so I'm choosing Taylor over her.*

"I knew you'd come back, Cole," Taylor said, her lips only inches away. "I knew you would."

Chapter 27

Koa glanced over at Alana in the red-orange glow of the firelight. She took her seat next to the bonfire as if nothing had happened. But the anxiety that was still fluttering in Alana's heart was a clear reminder of everything that had occurred that day—from her moment with Cole to reliving her parents' accident to talking with Koa. That was more emotional stress in one day than she wanted to deal with ever again. She was grateful for Maya's presence as she wrapped her arms around Alana's shoulders, holding her close.

Blaine leaned forward, oblivious to their exchange. "Did you guys see Cole?" he asked.

Koa shook his head. "Nope...never saw him."

"That's weird—he came looking for you and Alana just a couple minutes ago. I wonder where he went."

"I thought he went for a walk," Maya said.

"Well, that's what he said he was doing," Blaine muttered.

Maya stared thoughtfully into the fire.

But Cole didn't show for the rest of the evening. Though the gang waited anxiously for him to arrive, he never came.

Trevor and his friends, armed with flashlights, were ready to lead them back up the dirt trail to Christianitos. They were all exhausted from the day's events, especially Alana, but they opted to wait another ten minutes for Cole anyway. When he didn't show, they finally headed back to the road, slightly worried but none too anxious about their missing group member.

So they were shocked when, after making the long trek to Maya's camper, they saw Cole's Volkswagen had disappeared. "Well, there's your answer," Trevor said. "He must have driven some-where."

"But he walked all the way back to his van in the dark?" Jake asked.

No one said anything. It seemed like Blaine was the only one who knew what was going on. The rest of them were in the dark—literally. Only Alana had an inkling as to why Cole left, especially after Blaine mentioned that Cole had gone looking for her and Koa.

She shivered and wrapped her towel tighter around her. Koa, upon seeing her goosebumps, suddenly spoke up. "Why don't we stay here for the night?" he suggested. "Let's wait for Cole to come back."

"Yeah, he wouldn't have just ditched us," Maya added. "We'll just sleep in my camper like we always do. Cole will probably show up sometime tonight."

"And what if he doesn't?" Blaine pointed out.

"We're just trying to be optimistic, man," Jake said. "Why would your brother ditch?"

Blaine didn't reply. Alana's fingers twitched nervously. "I think Koa's idea sounds good," she said quietly. "Let's just get some sleep and hope Cole comes back tonight or tomorrow morning."

Trevor glanced at each of their faces, disquieted by their dampened spirits. His gaze flitted from his friends, who were piling into the back of his truck, over to the spot where Cole's Volkswagen used to be parked. "Um, I could be wrong," he said, "but I think your friend left his stuff behind."

Blaine walked over and lifted up one of the backpacks lying on the sidewalk. "Actually, this is our stuff." He began rifling through the various sleeping bags and suitcases strewn across a ten-foot radius. "This is all our stuff that was in the van." He glanced up at his friends with a worried look. "Cole must have left it here on purpose before he drove away."

Blaine's words hung in the air like a black shadow over their group. All of a sudden, they realized the chances of Cole coming back were very, very slim. And Alana had a feeling it was all her fault.

True to their intuitions, Cole didn't show last night. When the gang woke up to a gray morning in the parking lot, they realized he hadn't come back in the morning either. Alana seemed to be the only one who was relieved. Another night had gone by; another opportunity to sort things out with Cole, and it had been missed. She was content to put off talking to Cole as long as possible—mostly because she had no idea what was going on between them anyway.

As the gang took turns showering and getting dressed in Maya's camper, there was an unspoken plan among them. They had said goodbye to Trevor and his friends late last night before going to sleep. There was nothing keeping them in San Clemente except the surf—and even that was supposed to be less than ideal, as a storm was predicted to roll in that afternoon.

Alana glanced at her Bible, which was partially sticking out of her backpack. This was usually when she did her daily devotions, but now she had no motivation whatsoever to start reading. Despite opening up to the gang, her soul felt hollow and bitter. A deep sense of guilt settled on her shoulders, though she didn't know what to feel guilty about. Cole's disappearance? Obviously, he had left because of her, but that hadn't been her intention, so did that make it her fault?

Yes, she told herself firmly. It still does.

Maya walked over to her friend. "You alright?" she asked. "You seem a little...down, I guess."

"I'm just worried about Cole," Alana replied quietly.

"We all are."

"I guess I should call Dylan and tell him we're coming back to Ventura," Alana sighed, pulling out her phone.

"Yeah...what a bummer. Who would have thought Cole would run off like this?"

Alana nodded and punched in Dylan's number. Before she could hit the send button, Maya sat down next to her and wrapped her hand around Alana's.

They glanced at each other. "I'm sorry," Maya said quietly. "I'm sorry about your parents, about not being honest with you about Jake—"

"Hey." Despite the circumstances, Alana smiled. "Don't think like that. I need to move past what happened to my parents. And as for you and Jake, I'm genuinely happy for you guys. You really are perfect together."

Maya nodded gratefully. "Just...don't worry too much about Cole," she said, squeezing Alana's hand. "Everything will work out."

Alana saw her friend's eyes flicker over her face. She wondered if Maya knew more than she was letting on. But the moment soon passed, and Maya took her usual seat in the camper next to Jake, leaving Alana alone with her thoughts. She cleared her throat, redialed Dylan's number, and held her phone up to her ear.

As the phone rang, Alana couldn't help but eavesdrop on Blaine and Jake as they argued about what to do with the Cole situation.

"Did you call him?" Jake demanded.

"For the tenth time," Blaine replied gruffly. "He's not answering. Either that, or his phone is—"

"Hello?" came Dylan's sleepy voice, jerking Alana's attention away from the guys' argument.

She held her phone tighter against her ear. "Hey, it's me."

"Oh, hey...why are you calling so early?"

"There's been a situation."

Silence. Then: "What kind of a situation? Are you all right? Are you hurt?"

"I'm fine. It's Cole everyone is worried about."

"What do you mean?"

Alana explained Cole's absence and how they were heading back to Ventura. "If you see him," she told her brother, "call me right away. We have no idea why he left, but we think he went home."

"I'll keep an eye out. I have to run some errands downtown later today, so I—" Dylan suddenly paused. "Oh, Tammy heard me talking on the phone, and she wants to say hi."

Alana chuckled softly. "Hey, Tammy."

"Alana!" Her voice rang in Alana's ears. "Dylan told me you were surfing Trestles!"

"I was," her sister said with a smile.

"How were the waves? Were they big?"

"They were overhead and the most perfect waves you could imagine," Alana replied truthfully. "It was amazing."

Tammy listened breathlessly as Alana described her best rides from yesterday. "Wow!" she exclaimed when Alana was finished. "Can Dylan and I come down and surf with you today?"

Alana laughed. "First of all, there's been a situation and we're heading back to Ventura right now. And secondly, the waves are way too big for you."

"Come on, I bet they aren't."

"But they are, Tammy. It wouldn't be fair for Dylan to drive two hours south when the waves are too big for you to surf."

"Alana, I can surf them!"

Blaine and Jake suddenly entered the camper. "We're leaving," Blaine said. "Make sure none of your belongings have been left outside. Are all the boards in here?"

Alana held her free hand over her ear and concentrated on her phone. "Listen, Tammy, I have to go. I'm sorry you can't come down right now, but I'll see you in a couple hours."

"You still don't think I can surf big waves, do you?"

Alana groaned in frustration. "What does this have to do with wanting to surf big waves? You've paddled out in head-high surf and that's plenty big enough for you. Now I've gotta run, okay?"

"Fine." Tammy suddenly ended the call, leaving Alana feeling a bit confused as to why she was so adamant about their argument. If Tammy wanted to surf bigger waves, Alana reasoned, that was fine, but what made her think she could convince Dylan to drive her all the way down to Trestles? A storm was rolling in across the whole of Southern California. There was no way anyone was surfing today.

Alana stuffed her phone into her backpack and curled up on the couch. Maya and Jake were sitting in the two front seats, while Blaine gazed worriedly out the window in the backseat. Koa appeared a few moments later with a Carl's Jr. bag in hand.

"Sorry to keep you guys waiting," he said sheepishly. "I was hungry."

After Koa took his seat and Maya started the engine, they were off. Christianitos Road, and then the ocean, disappeared from view. Alana stuffed her buds into her ears and tried to keep busy by listening to music. Every so often thunder rumbled overhead. The skies seemed to be getting darker every half hour. Maya pulled onto PCH so they could cruise by all the beaches they had already passed. Alana smiled faintly when they zipped by Paradise Cove. The gray-blue water lapped at the pilings of the pier, reminding her of good times with the gang.

Soon, the ocean vanished once again when they angled inland through Palos Verdes. The rugged, rolling hills that rose on either side of the highway looked imminent and threatening in the gloomy weather, so Alana reached into her backpack and pulled out her Bible. The faded leather cover felt smooth against her hands, and she delicately flipped through its pages. She landed on the first chapter of 2 Corinthians, and her eyes automatically fell to a cluster of verses that had been underlined in pen: "Blessed be the God and Father of our Lord Jesus Christ, the Father of mercies and God of all comfort, who comforts us in all our affliction so that we may able to comfort those who are in any affliction."

She smiled thoughtfully. A light smatter of raindrops coated the windows of Maya's camper, but her spirit swelled against the gray skies. *Oh, God*, she prayed, *thank you for being with us throughout this trip. Thank you for protecting us despite injuries and for guiding us along unfamiliar roads. I just ask that wherever Cole is, and whatever he's doing, you would be with him. Amen.*

Though Alana was still drained emotionally, she felt like she had just gotten her second wind. They were an hour and a half away from Ventura County, and Cole could be anywhere by now. Though Dylan hadn't called, Alana had a feeling Cole was somewhere in Ventura—maybe even C Street, knowing his love for the ocean. Alana had been reluctant to see him and talk things over with him, but now there was nothing she wanted more than to see him face to face.

She reached up and touched the lock of hair that was tucked behind her ear. *Please, Lord, let everything work out okay.*

Koa's lip twitched as he watched Alana's sleeping form. He swallowed slowly and forced himself to look away, but he was frozen. The empty bitterness that had descended on him last night was still fresh in his heart. He felt hollow. Betrayed. And yet, in a way, he respected Alana for making her own decision. He was crushed that she had turned him away, but he also felt free now that his feelings were no longer hidden. They had been a burden for the past few months, and it had seemed like the end of the world when Alana looked him in the eyes and blurted, "You like me."

Now, though, it gave him as much of a sense of liberation as it did of regret. He should have known Alana would turn him down.

He should have realized that she wasn't interested in that kind of a relationship.

Koa tried telling himself it would only be a matter of time before everything blew over. Before long, he would be going on a date with some cute girl and laughing at the memory of being so sullen over Alana. "I used to have this major crush on her," he would say, chuckling, "and I thought it was the end of the world when she turned me down."

Only it wasn't the end of the world. With a heavy sigh, Koa forced his gaze away from Alana and shifted in his seat. His movement attracted the attention of Blaine, who was sitting next to him.

"Hey," Blaine said gruffly. "Is your butt sore too?"

Koa laughed dryly. "I don't know how much longer I can sit here."

"Yo, Maya." Blaine stood up, nearly losing his balance as Maya made a sudden lane change. "Can we take a bathroom break soon?"

"We'll be in Ventura in twenty minutes," she replied. "You can hold it."

Blaine made a face and plopped back down in his seat. He sighed and rubbed his eyes, trying to appear relaxed and not at all apprehensive. Koa saw right through his façade.

"Hey, it'll work out," he said quietly. "Cole's a big boy. He can take care of himself."

Blaine rolled his eyes. "Thanks, but I'm not necessarily worried about what happens to Cole. I'm sure he's fine."

"Then what are you worried about?"

"What Cole did, and what he's going to do. I just hope he acts wisely."

Koa's eyebrows scrunched together. "What do you mean?"

Blaine sighed. "When Cole gets riled up about something, he doesn't think straight."

"But you're forgetting something, man. Cole's changed. He's not the same guy he was when he first started this surfari. Remember the day we left for County Line Beach?"

"Oh yeah. Talk about moody."

"He's come a long way. I don't think his actions are going to be as rash as they would have been last month. He's different now."

Blaine nodded and offered a small smile. "I needed to hear that. Thanks, Koa."

Koa just ducked his head and looked away. He had prayed countless times for Cole, for Maya's family situation, and for Alana's burden with her parents—basically, he had prayed for every member of the gang as long as they had been friends. And if there was one thing this surfing safari had taught him, it was to keep praying. Koa's own perspective was limited, but tapping into God's perspective yielded hope and joy.

Koa glanced one more time at Alana's sleeping figure. He felt like his heart had been torn—torn, not ripped in two. He could live with her decision. It was time to move on.

Chapter 28

Cole groaned as a ray of light streamed in through the window. Squinting through the brightness, he groggily sat up and realized he was in bed—more importantly, someone else's bed. He didn't recognize the room at all. Rubbing his eyes, he stared groggily at his surroundings for a few minutes. What was with his pounding headache? It was like he was having a hangover—

Uh oh. The events of last night suddenly came tumbling to the forefront of his mind. As the fog in his brain cleared, he remembered bits of pieces of what had happened, mainly drinking and arguing. He had also let Taylor get the upper hand. Glancing over at her sleeping figure next to him, he realized this had been her plan all along. As soon as she saw him step through the door last night, she had taken advantage of the situation. Cole had just been stupid enough to fall for it.

He quietly untangled himself from the covers and stepped off the bed. His jeans were twisted awkwardly on his hips, and he struggled to straighten them back. His T-shirt, too, was matted and crumpled. Everything after taking shots at the counter was a hazy blur.

He found his sweatshirt and flip-flops scattered around the room. Being careful not to wake Taylor, he slipped on his remaining clothes and prepared to leave. This was the first night he had ever spent with her, and—as he saw her sleeping form concealed underneath the covers—he realized he never wanted to spend another like it.

He froze when Taylor shifted in bed. His mind debated which would be quicker—making a run through the door and down the stairs, or climbing out the window. He didn't have long to make a decision, though, as Taylor raised her head and gazed sleepily around the room.

"Cole?" she asked groggily. "What are you..."

She paused. Her eyes narrowed. He was caught red handed, and there was nothing he could do about it. In any other situation, he might have laughed at the lunacy of it all—Taylor's matted bedhead and smeared makeup, and the look of complete annoy-ance on both their faces due to their hangovers—but this was no laughing matter.

"You have got to be kidding me, Cole Anderson," Taylor growled, sitting up in bed. "You're sneaking out on me! I can't believe you would do this!"

He winced. With every word, her voice grew louder and clearer.

"You come to my house, to my party, and after I find you and share some drinks with you, you treat me like—like—this! I forgave you for what you said to me, Cole. Have you ever thought about that? I should have kicked you out of my house when I saw you sneak in. You never—"

"So why didn't you?" Cole interrupted, partially fed up with her and partially wanting her high-pitched voice to cease for the sake of his pounding head. He crossed his arms over his chest. "Why didn't you kick me out?"

Taylor was caught off guard by the question. "Because...well...I guess I thought you were coming back for me. I thought you liked me." She let out a dry laugh. "I guess I was wrong."

"Look, Tay," Cole sighed, "maybe I used to like you, but there's nothing going on between us anymore. I've moved on. Maybe you should too."

"That doesn't explain why you were here last night, does it?"

Now it was his turn to be caught off guard. "I had a fight with Blaine," he lied. It was the first excuse that came into his head. "I just took off without thinking. I was on my way home to my house, not yours, but I was broke and needed something to eat. I didn't want to have an argument with my dad, so I stopped by your place to get some food. That's when you found me."

Taylor stared at him. "You're lying."

He threw up his hands. "Whatever. That's my story, take it or leave it. At least it's better than getting someone drunk and taking advantage of them."

Color flooded her cheeks. "I did no such thing!"

"Then how do you explain last night?"

A sly smile crept onto Taylor's face. It made him uneasy. "You don't know half of what happened last night," she said vaguely. "You have no idea. You were too drunk to even care."

Cole swallowed. "It was your fault, not mine."

"I bet you don't even remember how—"

"Shut up!" he hollered, his fists clenched at his sides. "You're just bluffing." He flung open the door. "I don't want anything to do with you anymore."

"Fine. If that's what you want, then see if I care!" Her voice rose in pitch when he slammed the door and stormed down the hallway. "See if I care about you and Alana!" she screamed.

Cole stopped in his tracks and whirled around. He kicked open Taylor's door and growled, "Don't ever say that name again. This has nothing to do with Alana. Nothing."

He slammed it closed. As he thundered down the stairs and out the door into the bright sunlight, his heart wasn't the only part of his body that was pounding. The killer headache pelting his brain was a fresh reminder of the idiotic decisions he had made. He should have never let her follow him down the coast. He should have never set foot in her house last night. But most importantly, he should have never gotten involved with Taylor in the first place.

But he knew she wasn't the root of his problems. Taylor was just an annoying fly buzzing around him, something he could swat away and forget about. Yet she had been right—this was about Alana. This had everything to do with Alana. And here Cole was, trying to forget about the girl he had thought so long about and went to lengths to get her attention. This was the girl of his dreams, and he had went and thrown it all away with Taylor!

Cole unlocked his Volkswagen and slid into the driver's seat. "They're all right," he muttered dejectedly. "Everyone who told me I shouldn't date Alana—they were right. She doesn't deserve someone like me."

For the next few minutes, he drove aimlessly around town. He passed his street multiple times, but never worked up the courage to actually go to his house and confront his dad. He felt so torn between bitterness and regret that he finally drove to the one place he knew would calm him down—the beach.

It was bitingly cold as soon as he stepped out of the Volkswagen. A strong breeze was blowing, shaking the palm trees overhead as dark clouds billowed across the sunny sky. Cole knew it would only be a matter of time before they completely covered the sun altogether. A storm was coming, and it was coming quickly.

Where are all the people? he wondered as he walked down the promenade to the beach. Hardly anyone was walking the shops or enjoying the summer day—cold though it was. And today was Sunday, nonetheless. Weren't weekends supposed to be crowded at the beach?

He shivered and sunk lower in his sweatshirt when another gust of wind hit him full force. Oh, right—no one was outside because they had all paid attention to the weather forecast.

Cole continued to grumble to himself as he made the long trek across Ventura Pier, his hands and face freezing. To make things worse, it began sprinkling by the time he reached the end of the pier, and full on raining when he was halfway back to shore. He was hungover, tired, hungry, and felt like the biggest idiot to ever walk the earth—how could the day get any worse? Cole tried to amuse himself by watching the huge waves pounding the pier, choppy and wild from the storm, but even that couldn't get his mind of Alana.

"I need to stop thinking about her," he muttered, pausing halfway down the pier to rest against the railing. He watched wave after wave rear its foamy crest and break in a tremendous crash. Only a few people were walking on the beach, but nobody was out in the water. Nobody was even fishing from the pier.

That's when Cole saw him—a little surfer boy with a tiny short-board underneath his arm. Cole laughed as the boy strapped a leash around his ankle and gazed at the stormy waves. What did that kid think he was doing? He couldn't be crazy enough to paddle out in that mess.

A drenched lock of hair fell in front of Cole's eyes, and he pushed it away to see that the surfer was, in fact, determined to paddle out. Cole swept his gaze down the pier and across the beach, wondering where the boy's parents were, but nobody seemed to be paying him any attention.

An uneasy feeling settled in Cole's stomach. He forgot about his hangover and his pity party. He even forgot about Alana as he squinted through the pouring rain at the surfer struggling to fight through the torrents of whitewash.

"Well, this can't be good," he muttered. He walked down the pier a good distance until he was even with the surfer, wondering how the kid would even get past the impact zone. The waves were so big and the current so strong that it would take a miracle for him to—

Cole gasped. He caught a flash of pink and a head full of blonde hair as the surfer duck-dived under another wave. Wait a second...the kid wasn't a boy. She was a girl—an oddly familiar girl.

Cole's eyes widened when the surfer resurfaced. He realized the flash of pink he had seen was the Roxy logo on her wetsuit. The white-blonde hair and determined expression were so familiar that he cried out in disbelief when he realized who it was.

Tammy. Alana's little sister was paddling out in the storm.

Cole leaned over the railing and cupped his hands around his mouth. "Hey!" he hollered. "Yo, Tammy! Tammy!"

The wind took his words right out of his mouth. The rain began to fall harder, and the waves seemed to rise up even bigger while Cole watched, horrified, as little Tammy struggled to duck dive. Her strokes became weaker as she drifted farther and farther away from the pier, swept out towards the larger waves by the current.

Cole began to grow anxious. "Tammy!" he yelled, but he knew she couldn't hear him. He quickly shuffled out of his flip-flops, tore off his sweatshirt, and ripped his T-shirt over his head. He straddled the railing just as a monstrous set wave broke right in front of Tammy's small figure. Cole saw her board go flying into the air before getting sucked back underwater by the pull of the leash on her ankle. A few seconds later, the shortboard reappeared twenty yards closer to shore.

Tammy's leash had snapped.

Cole cursed and prepared himself to jump. Now that Tammy's source of flotation was gone, he was her only lifeline. He studied the water for a few seconds, waiting to see a flash of blonde hair or a small hand sticking above the surface, but there was nothing—only choppy waves and pounding surf.

Cole breathed a quick prayer, hoping God hadn't abandoned him after all his failures, and jumped. The distance between the pier and the water was even bigger than jumping off Cliff Island in Corona del Mar. Cold seeped through his jeans as soon as he landed underwater, so he launched into freestyle stroke. He struggled to swim in a straight line through the choppy water. Every few seconds he had to suck in a huge gulp air and dive underneath a wave. He had barely swum ten yards before he realized his energy was slowly dwindling.

He stopped swimming for a moment and treaded water. "Tammy!" he hollered, the sea spray and howling wind chilling him to the bone. "Tammy, where are you?"

All he heard was crash after crash of whitewater. He yelled in frustration and forced himself to keep swimming, knowing that the same current that took Tammy was taking him too. After diving under another wave, he resurfaced to see a wetsuit-clad figure struggling in the water a short distance away.

"Tammy!" he cried. He swam even faster, motivated to reach Alana's sister before another wave could strike.

But Cole was too late. It was clear Tammy was struggling to stay afloat in the stormy conditions. Cole accidentally inhaled water and burst into a coughing fit before he could reach her. He barely had time to see a huge wave, the lip curling over and preparing to break, as he reached out to grasp Tammy's hand.

"Hang on!" he hollered as the wave crashed on top of their heads. He felt her tiny fingers squeeze his as they were picked up and thrown to the sandy bottom, spinning underwater like ragdolls. Cole had no sense of direction. The water was indubitably dark all around him. He and Tammy floated upwards for a few seconds before another wave crashed, sending them through the same cycle once again. They were running out of air.

Hang on, Tammy, he thought as panic started to set in. His body could only last so much longer without any oxygen. He felt his lungs start to burn with the need for just one breath, and he wondered if Tammy was even still conscious. And then Cole felt it—her small, strong fingers, clutching his hand, suddenly fell limp. He blindly reached out and tried to grab her arm, but all he felt was water. She was gone.

Chapter 29

Maya's shrill voice jolted Alana awake. She nearly fell off the couch as she sat up and yanked her headphones out of her ears. "What?" she yawned. "What's going on?"

"We're here," Maya repeated.

"Did I seriously fall asleep?" Alana muttered. She glanced anxiously out the window. Sure enough, they were cruising down Harbor Boulevard, with the stormy ocean visible to their left.

"It seems like ages since we were last here," Koa said.

Alana squinted up at the dark clouds overhead. The ground was wet, indicating a recent rain spell, but now only an occasional raindrop fell here and there.

"So what's our plan?" Maya asked the group. "The Anderson house or...?"

"Cole's not at home," Blaine said automatically. "I already checked with Dad. And Cole isn't answering his cell phone. The next best place would be to check the beach."

"Yeah, like he would go surfing in this mess," Jake scoffed.

"I didn't say he was surfing," Blaine corrected. "I said he's probably at the beach. It's his therapy."

Maya flipped on her blinker and pulled into the parking lot. Ventura Pier rose out of the stormy ocean like a sleeping giant.

The beach they had grown up surfing their entire lives was devoid of all life except for a few sweatshirt-clad joggers.

"Well?" Koa asked when they stepped out, shivering, to scan the beach for any sign of Cole. "What should we do next? He's not here."

"I guess we could drive by Surfer's Point; that's the next spot he might—" Maya started, but she was interrupted when Alana gave a sharp cry.

"Oh no—Tammy!" Alana darted across the sand, not caring that the cold pierced her bare feet. "Tammy!" she cried again. The wind carried her voice away, so she pushed herself to run faster. She pumped her arms and legs until she nearly collapsed with exhaustion upon reaching the pier.

Two figures were stumbling out of the water. One was clearly Cole, his jeans soaking wet and his bare chest shivering. The other was Tammy, coughing up water as she collapsed on the sand.

"Tammy!" Alana cried, rushing over and wrapping her sister in a large hug. She brushed Tammy's wet bangs out of her eyes and cradled her against her chest. "Are you okay?"

"I'm fine," Tammy said hoarsely, her small, pale hands returning the embrace. "C-Cole saved me."

Alana hugged her sister's tiny body against her own and glanced over at Cole. He plopped down in the sand, his chest rising and falling rapidly with each breath. "Thank you," Alana said, the words barely forcing their way out of her mouth.

Cole nodded but said nothing. His wheezing breath sounded harsh to Alana's ears, so she turned back to her sister. "Thank God you're all right! What's going on? What were you doing out there?"

"I wanted to surf the big waves," Tammy said quietly, her coughing fit finally over.

"So you paddled out in a storm? Tammy, that's insane. If Cole hadn't been here..." Alana let her sentence trail off as they continued to embrace. "I just don't want to lose you."

"I know," Tammy murmured. "I'm sorry."

"Don't ever think about doing this again," Alana said sternly. "I said you weren't ready for big waves for a reason. And this storm is a whole different ball game."

Tammy nodded somberly.

"Where's Dylan?" Alana asked.

"Not here," Cole wheezed. He sat up, finally able to catch his breath, and added, "He probably doesn't even know she went for a surf."

"He's running errands," Tammy said.

Alana gently let go of her sister and pulled out her phone. "Call him," she ordered, handing Tammy the device. "Tell him exactly what happened and say we'll meet him at the apartment."

Tammy nodded, fully aware of the gravity of the situation, and dialed the number. Meanwhile, Alana turned to Cole and offered him a small smile. "Thanks," she said again. "I don't know what would have happened if you hadn't—"

Cole smiled sadly. "It's fine. You're welcome."

"No, I really mean it," Alana persisted. She held out a hand and helped him to his feet. "You saved Tammy's life. I don't think a simple thank you is enough."

He nodded and glanced away, withdrawing his hand quicker than Alana wanted him to. As the rest of the gang arrived, out of breath from jogging across the sand, Alana turned her attention to her little sister. She took in Tammy's matted, salty hair and cold, pale face. Alana gripped her hand while Tammy explained the situation to Dylan. Alana knew he would drop everything and head back to the apartment as soon as possible.

After the phone call, the sisters told the gang what had happened and how Cole was the hero of the day. Everyone smiled and chatted with relief on the way back to the parking lot. Despite his act of bravery, Cole was the only one who seemed out of place. Alana heard him grumble something about his shirt and shoes left on the pier while he and Blaine talked in hushed voices. Though Alana had every reason to thank God and rejoice for Tammy's safety, part of her still felt as gloomy as the skies overhead. Something was still missing.

With the soft pitter-patter of rain behind him, Cole paused at the entrance to the church. Blaine and Mr. Anderson went on ahead, taking a seat near the middle of the sanctuary. Across from them sat Jake's family, plus Maya. Cole swept his gaze to the other side of the sanctuary and spotted Koa, but no matter how hard he searched, he couldn't seem to find Alana.

With a frown, Cole reluctantly trudged down the aisle and took a seat next to Blaine. "Don't worry," the latter said, "they're probably coming."

"Thanks," Cole muttered. The worship band came on stage a few moments later, and the entire congregation rose as one to sing along. Cole couldn't help but glance over his shoulder every so often, trying to get a glimpse of any latecomers. He sighed in defeat when the worship part of the service was over and Pastor Browne walked onto the stage. The congregation sat down, and Cole slumped in his seat as the sermon began.

"Hey, listen," Blaine said quietly. "If she doesn't show up tonight, just give her a call tomorrow. It'll work out—trust me."

Cole nodded stiffly. He knew what Alana was like—if she wasn't on time, she probably wasn't coming at all. But Blaine's words turned a few gears in his head. He smiled faintly as he remembered the day in Venice Beach when he had first taken his brother's advice. Blaine's instructions had almost worked perfectly.

Pastor Browne's voice suddenly rang out through the church. "For the next few weeks we're going to take a break from our normal study of the book of John and focus on what the Bible says about our attitudes—more specifically, the outward actions that others see. We call them 'works' or 'bearing fruit.' Once we let Jesus take control of our lives, our attitudes should take a drastic change. When nonbelievers see how we talk and act, they should see a reflection of our Lord."

Cole's mouth suddenly felt extremely dry. That was what he had been trying to do for so long—change. He was fed up with being selfish and immature. But change, even with Alana as a motivating force, was too difficult. Cole had slipped into his old habits in a heartbeat. He had come crawling back to Taylor, to her party, like he used to in the past. He had made a resolution to never talk to her again. But how long would his self-control hold out this time?

Cole realized it was pointless. No matter how hard he tried, he would never measure up. He could never change into the person Blaine wanted him to be—the person Alana would look up to. Cole's efforts were fruitless.

"God's Word is clear," the pastor declared. "We can't get to heaven based on anything we do, no matter how good or godly we think we are. The truth is, we are saved by God's grace and

God's grace alone. Salvation is his work. Nothing we have done or will ever do can measure up to his standard of righteousness. But by accepting God's free gift of grace—essentially, by humbling ourselves and admitting that we can't do it alone—Jesus Christ gives us his righteousness.

"See, this is where our works come into play. Before salvation, everything we do is done in sin. But after salvation, our primary motivation is to glorify God. When our heart's desire is him and him alone, we are transformed. Our attitudes change drastically, and we choose to glorify God through our works. That is why the apostle Paul wrote, 'For the grace of God has appeared, bringing salvation for all people, training us to renounce ungodliness and worldly passions, and to live self-controlled, upright, godly lives in the present age.' Jesus Christ died for us in order to provide access to God's free grace. He wants to purify us and make us zealous for good works."

Cole's mind was opened. He had seen what his friends experienced because of this Jesus, and now he wanted to find out more. It was starting to make sense. It was all starting to make sense.

"Maybe God is calling you tonight," Pastor Browne said. "Maybe he is tugging on your heart to change for him. If you feel that he has grabbed your attention and you know you want to surrender your life to him, pray this prayer with me."

Cole suddenly knew what he had to do. He thought he had changed his attitude for Alana, but in reality, he wanted to change because he was tired of himself. He couldn't do it alone. He had to turn to God.

"Father in heaven," Pastor Browne began, "I come to you tonight to ask forgiveness for my sins. I admit that I fall short of your glory. I am sorry for all the things I have thought, said, or done that go against your commandments. Please forgive me. I surrender my life to you. I believe that your son, Jesus, died on the cross to forgive me of my sins, and I want to live for him starting right now. Please come into my heart and wash me free from sin. Help me to walk in your ways from this moment on. In Jesus' everlasting name, amen."

Pastor Browne murmured a few words about the worship band coming back onstage, but Cole wasn't listening anymore. He was fully concentrated on what he had just done—what he had just prayed. He had focused on the pastor's words with his whole heart, asking God to forgive him for his many mistakes, knowing that only he could bring about a radical change in his life—a complete and perfect change. Only then would Cole's efforts truly matter.

Despite this, he felt no different. He was still Cole Anderson. He was still anxious to see Alana and weary from the day's events. The only difference was that he had a renewed sense of hope. He now had someone to cling to; someone to depend on. He felt a deep, saturating peace.

As the band finished their final song, Pastor Browne's voice echoed through the microphone. "May you go in peace," he declared. "May the Word of God be a lamp for your feet and a light for your path. Trust in the Lord and let him direct your steps, turning neither to the right nor the left. And always remember, if anyone is in Christ, he is a new creation! The old has gone, the new has come!"

Cole felt a thrill of excitement rush through his body. For the first time in his life, he believed in every word the pastor said—and he believed it with his whole heart. He struggled to keep his face impassive as the congregation began filtering out of the sanctuary. He faintly heard Blaine and Mr. Anderson talking behind him, but he was still too bewildered to make sense of anything. Only one sentence continued pulsing through his mind: The old has gone, the new has come!

Suddenly, Cole's eyes alighted near the exit when he saw a familiar blonde-haired girl and her older brother. So they had come. He pushed through the crowd in an effort to reach the door quicker. As soon as he was back outside in the chilly night air, a few raindrops still falling on the wet pavement, he swept his gaze over the parking lot.

"Dylan!" he called when he spotted the duo getting into their car. "Dylan, wait up!"

The oldest Walker sibling seemed to be just as surprised to see Cole as Cole was to see him. "Hey, man. What can I do for you?" he asked.

Cole's face fell when he jogged over to their car. It was just Dylan and Tammy. "Alana didn't come with you?" he asked hesitantly.

"No, she stayed at home. She's drained."

"Oh. Well, it's good to see you back at church," he said lamely.

"Yeah, I know it's been awhile." Dylan offered a small smile. "I guess after Tammy's accident I realized how important it was to connect with the body of believers again. I need this fellowship, this encouragement...you know? The accident was a definite wake-up call for me. I need to start investing in the lives of other people."

Cole nodded, but Dylan's next words cut him off from replying. "Cole, I haven't gotten the chance to properly thank you yet. You saved my little sister's life." His gaze flickered towards the backseat of the car where Tammy was sitting, reaching forward to fiddle with the radio.

"I just happened to be in the right spot at the right time." Cole shrugged.

"True, but you don't really believe that, do you?" Dylan smiled mysteriously. "There's no such thing as coincidences with God. He makes all things work out for the good of those who love him, who are called according to his purpose."

Called according to his purpose. Cole suddenly remembered why he was so eager to talk to Dylan. "Um, I became a Christian tonight," he blurted.

"What? You did?" To Cole's surprise, Dylan immediately engulfed him in a large hug. "That's fantastic!"

"Yeah," Cole said awkwardly. "I'm a little late in coming, though."

"Better late than never. I'm happy for you, man." Dylan gave Cole's shoulder a friendly punch.

"That's not all I wanted to say," Cole added quickly. Dylan raised an eyebrow and motioned for him to continue. "I know I've been a major jerk in the past. You probably hear that from Alana every now and then."

Dylan cocked his head to one side. Both guys knew they only spoken on occasion, maybe just a few times a week whenever Alana's presence happened to bring them together. "Listen, Cole," Dylan said kindly. "I can't thank you enough for saving Tammy. Whatever you need, I'm here for you."

"Well..." Cole's face turned red at the thought of what he was about to say. "Actually, I do need something. I've been wanting this for a long time. But I know it's only right to come to you first."

Dylan looked slightly puzzled. "What is it?"

Cole sucked in a deep breath. "It's about Alana."

Epilogue

B laine trudged downstairs in sweatpants and a loose T-shirt, stifling a massive yawn with the back of his hand. He turned into the kitchen and grabbed a glass from the cupboard. After filling it up in the sink, he took a long draught and settled back against the counter.

"Hey," Cole said wearily, rounding the corner.

Blaine raised an eyebrow. "Hey yourself." He eyed his twin and realized just how exhausted Cole looked. His droopy eyes and hunched shoulders gave off the appearance of a weary traveler. "You okay?"

"Just tired." Cole offered a small smile and grabbed his own glass from the cupboard. "You know, Dad hasn't lectured me yet."

Blaine shrugged. "I think he overlooked the fact that you ran away after you saved Tammy's life."

"Yeah. I'm still expecting a long talk, though."

Blaine moved aside to let Cole fill up his glass in the sink. "Hey, if you don't mind me asking, where did you go last night?"

"You aren't wondering why I ditched you?"

"I already know why you left us."

Cole stared at him. "Yeah, I guess the reason for my disappearance was pretty obvious." A flicker of emotions crossed his face, but Blaine sensed his brother was hiding something.

"Look, you don't have to tell me if you don't want to, but the gang has been wondering where you went," Blaine said. "There's no hard feelings, believe me—not after you rescued Tammy. But everyone is curious."

Cole twirled his glass around in his palm. He still hadn't taken a sip. "You can tell them I was driving," he said after a lengthy silence. "I was driving and didn't pay attention to where I was going. I ended up sleeping in my van and waking up the next morning in Ventura. Then I happened to be walking along the pier when I saw Tammy."

Blaine knew he was lying. He was as sure of it as he was of the fact that Cole had ditched them because of Alana. Though Blaine didn't know all of the details, he figured something had to have happened between Cole and Alana that made his brother run off. They had been distant ever since their visit to Salt Creek.

Cole obviously sensed his twin's hesitation. "Take it or leave it," he said curtly. "That's my explanation."

"You don't have to do this," Blaine said quietly. "You can tell me. I won't tell the others if you don't want me to."

Cole shook his head. "I can't. There are some things that I just can't tell anybody, okay?"

Blaine wondered if his brother had done something that he was too ashamed to talk about. The two had a staring match for a few seconds. Finally, Blaine sighed and drained the rest of his glass, realizing that this was one conversation where Cole wouldn't give in. Blaine placed his now-empty glass in the sink. "Alright," he said. "I'll take it. You should really get some sleep, though."

"Actually, I've hardly slept all night." Cole ran his finger around the rim of his glass. "I became a Christian today."

If Blaine still had any water in his mouth, he would have spit it out right then and there. "You what?"

Cole rolled his eyes. "Is that everyone's answer when I say that? Sheesh."

Blaine grabbed his shoulders. "Dude! That is awesome!"

Cole shoved his twin away, trying to hide back a smile. "Calm down, it's not like I'm getting married."

"No, this is even better! You just became a part of the family of Christ."

"Yeah, well..." He sighed. "I don't know why it took me so long, but tonight at church, it finally clicked. I realized what I had to do."

Blaine nodded.

"You know," Cole said, "I didn't understand what you were saying at first when you gave me advice about Alana. I thought you wanted me to change my attitude all by myself. But that was hard—way too hard."

Blaine smiled. "We can't rely on ourselves."

"I learned that the hard way. The only true, lasting change comes through Christ." Cole let out a deep breath. "You know, I'd never thought I'd say that."

"And I never thought I'd ever hear you say that," Blaine added. They shared a laugh.

"So how are things with Alana?" Blaine asked in a quieter tone.

"I don't know. I guess I'll find out soon enough."

"Hey, look on the bright side. You saved her little sister's life. That's got to be some big brownie points," Blaine said with a smile. "Plus you just became a Christian. How awesome is that?"

Cole nodded and attempted to stifle a yawn. "Thanks, man. I think I'm gonna head upstairs and get some sleep before I collapse."

"Oh, you're not getting off the hook quite yet," Blaine chuckled. He swung an arm over Cole's shoulders and marched him up the stairs. "We have some big news to share with Dad. He's been praying for you for a long time."

Cole blushed. He thought back to a few weeks ago, when he first left the house on the surfing safari. He had come a long way since then, and he was ashamed of some of the things he had said and done in the past.

But all that was over now. He was changed for the better — and it felt great.

"You know," Blaine added, "Dad decided he isn't going to charge you for that board you airbrushed a few weeks ago."

Cole paused, racking his brains for a memory. Then he realized what his brother was talking about. He glanced at Blaine, but he had already moved on to a different subject, ushering him up the stairs to their father's room.

The surfboard...

Did Cole really deserve this unexpected grace? His father had charged him quite a sum for his waste of a design. But maybe there was something he could still do with it. Maybe, instead of being worthless, the board was actually more precious than Cole had imagined.

Cole sucked in a deep breath and knocked twice on the Rosalind's huge wooden front door. The sound seemed to echo throughout the house. He swallowed nervously and shoved his hands into his pockets, anxiously fingering the small note he clutched between his fingers. When nobody answered the door right away, he rolled his lips into his mouth and rocked back and forth on his feet. I can do this. I can do this.

Suddenly, the sound of a lock being turned reached his ears. He snapped back to attention and watched as the door opened a crack. "What do you want?" a tired voice asked.

Cole could only assume the tall, potbellied man was Taylor's father. He had a day's growth of stubble on his chin, and his eyes held every sign of weariness. "Mr. Rosalind, sir," Cole said in a firm voice. "Is Taylor home?"

The man sighed. "Listen, kid, it's ten in the morning."

Cole frowned. He should have realized that ten was too early for the Rosalinds.

"But Taylor is grounded anyway," Mr. Rosalind added.

"Oh."

Mr. Rosalind cocked his head to one side, as if wondering why Cole didn't sound too disappointed. "Yeah, she threw a party while my wife and I were away. We got back early and couldn't believe what she had done." He spat the word "party" between his thin lips as if it were a dirty four-letter word.

"I'm sorry about that, sir."

"You weren't one of the kids at her party, were you?" he demanded.

"No, sir!" Cole said automatically. "I mean...yes. I was, but then I left. Parties aren't really my thing." Not anymore, they aren't. The memories of that night stung Cole's heart. He regretted it with his whole being.

"Well, come back another time," Mr. Rosalind said gruffly, about to shut the door. He obviously distrusted Cole.

"Wait!" Cole placed a hand on the door, preventing it from closing all the way. "Can I at least give her a message?"

The man narrowed his eyes. "Fine," he sighed after a few moments' deliberation. "But make it quick."

Cole glanced behind his large figure and saw a few plastic cups littered on the floor. The furniture had been rearranged haphazardly, and the white carpet was stained in multiple places, most likely from alcohol. He swallowed. "Just tell her I never want to see her again," he said, his voice coming out surprisingly confident.

Mr. Rosalind seemed amused. "Now that I can do."

"Oh, and give her this, too. Please," he added, handing Taylor's father the note.

Mr. Rosalind nodded. After glancing at the folded-up piece of paper between his fingertips, he gave Cole a weary look and closed the door. Cole let out a sigh of relief and turned away, his steps significantly lighter as he headed back towards his Volkswagen.

He was proud of himself for doing what he did. He had confronted the enemy and won—sort of. In a way, he was glad that he hadn't been able to speak to Taylor face-to-face. She was a thing of the past now. He was relieved that he never had to speak to her again.

Jerking open the door of his van, Cole slid into the driver's seat and started the engine. Now there was only one more thing he needed to do.

"Alana?" Dylan called. "Hey, there's someone here to see you."

"I'll be right down." Alana tossed her Surfing magazine aside and rolled off her bed. As she passed her bedroom window, she caught a glimpse of the choppy ocean and stormy skies. It had rained on and off all last night and that morning. After Dylan had a long talk with Tammy, both of them had gone to Sunday night church without her. She had been exhausted from the days' events and couldn't find the strength to join them. At the same time, she had been astonished when Dylan declared he was going to church. It was the first time he'd been in over five years.

"Alana!" Dylan called again.

"Who is it?" she asked as she jogged downstairs. She froze when she saw Cole standing in the living room, wringing his hands nervously. "Oh...Cole!" Alana glanced at her brother questioningly, but he glided out of the room without another word. She turned her attention back to Cole. "Well...hey."

"Hey." He shuffled his feet nervously. "Um, I have some important news that I wanted to tell you."

"Yeah?"

He took a deep breath. "I had a long talk with my Dad last night—and Blaine, too—after going to church with them."

Alana waited patiently.

"While I was there, I realized just how much of a jerk I had been in the past—and not just to you and the gang. I was a horrible brother, and a horrible son. I tried to change over the course of the trip, I felt like something was still missing. When I realized I was never going to get what I wanted, I gave up."

"What are you talking about?"

For the first time since he had arrived, Cole glanced up and held Alana's gaze. "I think you know."

Alana felt her breath catch.

"I talked with your brother last night after the church service—after I became a Christian."

"Wait, what?" Alana stepped closer to him, scanning his face. "You're a believer?"

He nodded, smiling.

"Cole, that's amazing! Thank God. We've been praying for you."

He was at a loss for words. It seemed like everyone had been praying for him. In the past, he would have laughed it off. But now, after finally coming to grips with what it really meant to be a Christian, he was touched.

"Thanks, Alana. But...that's not all I wanted to tell you."

She cocked her head to one side. "What's wrong?"

"Nothing's wrong."

"Don't be embarrassed. You just gave your heart to God—that's the best thing you could ever do."

"It's not that." He took another deep breath. "I...uh...I guess I should just come out and say it." He gulped. "I've had this major crush on you."

She blushed.

"It started out as something small," Cole rambled, "but then, as the surfari went on, it just kept getting bigger and bigger. I realized it wasn't some high school crush that would go away in a few months. I love how you act with other people. I love how fun you are and how talented you are at surfing. And, honestly, I love how much you love God." He paused to gauge her reaction. "I know you don't feel the same way about me, but I needed to tell you. I couldn't keep it to myself any longer." He reluctantly took a step back. "I just hope I haven't made a mistake."

"No," Alana reassured him. "You're fine."

When she didn't say anything else, Cole sighed. "Well...I guess that's everything." He laughed awkwardly. "I hope things with you and Koa work out."

She frowned. "With me and Koa? What are you talking about?"

Both wore mirrored looks of confusion. "I thought you and Koa were—you know—together," Cole said slowly.

"Well, we're good friends, if that's what you mean."

"So you aren't in a relationship? As a couple?" It was hard to miss the excitement in Cole's tone.

Alana laughed. "No, we're not."

"Oh. Wait—so you didn't kiss him when we were at Trestles?"

"I what?" Alana laughed at the absurdity of his question. She knew it would be wrong to tell Cole about Koa's crush on her, but was it possible he had suspected Koa's true feelings anyway? "No," she said, "there's nothing going on between Koa and I."

Cole sighed with relief. "I saw you two at Trestles," he admitted, "and I thought...well...you know."

Alana suddenly realized what he was saying. She covered her face in her hands, laughing. "Oh, Cole! Koa and I were just talking. There wasn't anything else going on."

He blushed slightly.

"But I need to know something," Alana said, turning the tide of the conversation. "And please tell me the truth—are you and Taylor done?"

"I've been done with her ever since this surf trip started," Cole said. "And that's the truth. Taylor and I never had anything, and we never will."

Alana nodded. "I'm glad. She was never a good influence on you."

"Well, you won't have to worry about that. I'm over her." Cole quickly reached out and grasped Alana's hand. "Hey, do you remember our conversation from Ruby's?"

"The night you were starving and ate two cheeseburgers?" She laughed. "Of course."

"Thank you for giving me a second chance that night. I know I didn't deserve it, but you came through for me."

"Cole, I would do anything to patch up a relationship."

"Yeah, well, do you think you could give me another second chance—this time as a Christian?"

She smiled and squeezed his hand. "That's not a job for me to do. Christ already gave you a second chance when you became a believer. And he'll keep on giving you second chances for the rest of your life."

"I can't believe I've been missing out on this for seventeen years." Cole shook his head. "Why did it take me so long to realize everything I needed was right in front of me?"

"God got ahold of you," Alana said simply. "Just like he got ahold of me..." She swallowed. "All the times I encouraged you to open up to our friends, I was being a hypocrite. I was holding myself back. I was—"

Cole grabbed her other hand. "It's okay. You did a brave thing by telling us what had happened with your parents. I can't imagine what that must have been like."

She nodded. "It was one of the hardest things I've ever done. But I just had to do it, you know?"

"Oh, I know." Cole shifted from one foot to the other. "Look, Alana, I know you don't necessarily feel the same way about me, so..."

Alana glanced down at their intertwined hands. "What if," she said softly, "what if I told you that I might feel the same way?"

His eyes widened. "What—"

She felt a rush of adrenaline. It was the only way to explain what she felt every time they touched, every time they talked. She had grown to care about him in a way that was undeniably deeper than friendship.

"What are you saying?" he asked quietly.

"I'm saying that I think I like you too."

Cole smiled. Alana smiled. They squeezed hands before pulling apart.

"Oh, wait," he said suddenly. "I almost forgot."

Alana watched, a little surprised and a little curious, as Cole jogged over to the front door and disappeared outside. He reappeared with a pristine white shortboard in hand, its bright blue fins gleaming.

Alana's jaw dropped open. "Did you shape this?"

"My dad did. But I airbrushed it."

She gasped when he turned the shortboard around so she could see the front. In bold, striking colors, he had designed a surfer girl watching breaking waves. The lines and colors were obviously inspired by an artist's hand.

"It's beautiful," Alana breathed, reaching out to trail her hand down its smooth rail.

"It's yours," Cole said.

"What?" She nearly dropped the surfboard when he passed it to her. "Are you serious?"

"No, I'm joking." Cole rolled his eyes, though he was still smiling. "Of course I'm serious! That's why you're the surfer girl airbrushed on the front."

Alana turned the board over in her hands, taking in the amazing artwork for a good minute. "I can't wait to try it out," she gushed.

"Want to go for a surf tomorrow morning?"

"What about the storm?"

"It's supposed to die down this afternoon. Tomorrow should be fun."

"Then I'd love to." She grinned and carefully set down her shortboard. "Thanks so much, Cole—for saving Tammy yesterday and now for this awesome surfboard."

"Aw, it was nothing."

Alana gave him a brief hug. "Thanks," she whispered. "You gave Tammy a second chance."

He rested his hands on her shoulders. "Only because you gave me one."

"Only because God gave both of us one."

Cole pulled away from her and headed to the door. "I'll see you tomorrow morning for our surf session."

"Bright and early!" Alana moved to the doorway and watched as Cole headed back to his Volkswagen. He flashed her another smile and waved before pulling away from the curb. She waited until his surf van disappeared completely from view before closing the door.

"Thank you, Lord," she breathed, grinning from ear to ear. Her new shortboard was lying only a few feet away, its bright surface shining. She couldn't wait to take it out for a test ride tomorrow. She pictured herself bobbing up and down in the lineup at C Street, duck diving under the waves, and sharing rides with her best friends.

That was the life. For Alana and the gang, surfing was more than just a sport. To them, it was a way of life. It was the sand behind their ears and the saltwater on their skin. It was the feeling of trailing their hands across the surface of the water, feeling the cool sea spray and the powerful surge of the ocean.

To them, being able to stand up on a piece of fiberglass and glide across the water wasn't just surfing. It was riding a wave. It was to enjoy that beautiful, inexpressible feeling and rush of adrenaline that accompanied every ride and every drop.

In a way, Alana thought, life was a lot like surfing. There were good waves and bad; there were amazing moments and wipeouts. But life wasn't as unpredictable as the ocean. Alana knew God was in control, and there was a bright future ahead of her.